Anxiety was setting in. If January 10th arrived and there still was no one to take over my night duties at Trafford, then the whole county was in trouble. In the meantime, I was running myself ragged, working Hogue's family practice by day and the graveyard shift in the E.R. at night. The extra money was most welcome, but there was no place to spend it. At Grady's two ratty indoor theaters, "Gone With the Wind" and "Jaws" were still playing, just as they had been last summer when I arrived. The only civilized recreations were hunting, fishing, church-going and sex. I hated hunting, Shelly hated fishing and we both hated church-going. My ridiculous work schedule was threatening to make a chore out of our only hobby.

Also by Neil Shulman, M.D.:

FINALLY, I'M A DOCTOR

DOC HOLLYWOOD

Neil Shulman, M.D.

Formerly titled: WHAT? DEAD. . . AGAIN?

FAWCETT GOLD MEDAL · NEW YORK

I'd like to dedicate this book to the many people who have made a major impact on my life in medicine:

Jim Alley	Gail McCray
Tom Arnold	Jo Anne Morrow
Jack Birge	Sandra Owen
Brent Blumenstein	Jerry Payne
Cecile Cate	Larry Pett
Margarett Chiappini	Frank Polk
Jim Crutcher	Brian Remington
Gary Cutter	Pat Rentrop
Tom Gibson	Arthur Richardson
Shirley Green	Ivor Royston
Dallie Hall	Irene Sanders
Cat Hampton	Sandy Schuman
Garland Herndon, Jr.	Sonnie Shulman
Connie Hiaasen	Stanley Shulman
Jim Hotz	Josephine Stovall
Marie Hunter	Maureen Sweeney
Willis Hurst	Elbert Tuttle
Ron Jenkins	Ken Walker
Gary Kahn	Graham Ward
Henry Kahn	Joe Wilber
Terri Langston	Jerry Wilson
Kathy Liedtke	Gary Wollam
Joyce McClintock	Bob Woodward

And all the others

PREFACE

During the summer of my third year of medical school, I traveled across the United States looking for an ideal hospital to do my internship. I slept in hospital emergency rooms to save money. While completing my training, I spent a few years moonlighting in different Southern rural emergency rooms. My cross-country travel and emergency work experiences provide a basis for this novel. The characters are fictitious; however, the episodes are based on fact. Any resemblance between characters in the book and real folks is purely coincidental.

I am indebted to my good friend
Carl Hiaasen
whose efforts made this book possible.

Special thanks to
Caroline Harkleroad and Lyn Shehane.

*THE GAS STATION ATTENDANT WAS A FRECKLE-*faced kid, maybe seventeen, who wore a red baseball cap on his head and a well-worn copy of *Penthouse* under one arm. He peered into the car and grunted, "How much you need?"

"Fill it up."

The kid set the magazine on top of the pump and opened the gas tank.

"Where can I get some coffee?"

He nodded toward the office. "Got a machine in there. Ten cents."

It smelled like liquid car wax but I drank it all and climbed back into the car. I handed the kid seven dollars. He grabbed his magazine and sat down on the stoop by the office.

"Wake up!" I shouted to the five zombies in the car with me. "My turn to sleep."

Leon was sitting next to me. He grinned and brushed his dirt-brown hair out of his eyes. He didn't want to drive. "Too tired," he shrugged.

"Corey?"

No answer.

"Diane?"

Panting sounds from the back. Corey and Diane.

"Brian, then. Wake up, man. I can't drive one more mile."

"Not me, Doc," Brian protested from somewhere in the dark upholstery. "Too many Quaaludes, man."

"Zorro?"

Sniggers from Leon. More panting.

1

"Zorro and Corey and Diane?"

"You guessed it, Doc."

U.S. 80 tumbled by. I felt like I was working one of those road-racing machines in an arcade, except that no lights or bells went off when I strayed off the road. Behind me were Bakersfield, San Francisco, Albuquerque, Dallas, and Christ, I forget the rest. I wanted to get back home. I was tired of self-service gas stations, speed traps, dead jackrabbits on the center lane, truckers, CB freaks, toll-booth attendants with stares like dull ice, numb at their jobs.

It seemed like a good idea, once. Not a great idea, but not a bad one. Having finished an unremarkable internship at Jackson Memorial in Miami, I decided to take off for a few months to go job-hunting. Scout out other hospitals and see what was what. Competition for residencies being what it is, it would have been stupid to count on an offer from Jackson or anywhere else, not without a personal interview.

The routine was hardly original. The first place a new doctor will visit in a strange town is the hospital emergency room. If he needs a place to stay, they'll generally let him crash on one of the cots. In the morning, he'll chat with the administrator or department heads about jobs, salaries, patient loads, that bitch of a dogleg 17th hole at the local country club. If it's a small hospital hungry for doctors, they'll drag out the cutest nurses, take him to dinner at the Ramada, show him where they're building some real smart town houses, and beg him to stay and set up a practice. If it's a big hospital, they'll send him to the cafeteria for lunch, ask him a lot of psychological questions to make sure he's not psychotic, make him wait two hours to meet the top guy, and then tell him the job situation is real tight. "Sorry, but your chances aren't great."

It gets old.

I was glad to be going home. Highway 80 would take me all the way east through Montgomery, Alabama. Then up to Atlanta, and from there, I would follow the seaboard back to Washington, D.C., where my folks were waiting to hear My Plans. "Have you made any plans?" my father would write. His letters always came on the first Tuesday of the month. "What are your plans, Otis?" my mother would ask. Her calls would come on the first Wednesday of the month. She figured it gave me a whole day to think on my father's letter and have something concrete to tell her bridge club on Thursday.

For the moment, I said to myself, practicing, my plans were to relax. To forget about medicine for a couple of weeks and poison my mind with vice. Lots of old, dear friends waited in Washington. One of them had been married and divorced twice while I was in med school. She wrote to tell me she was on her third analyst, but that this one was very "in tune with her."

As I thought about this, my car snuck off the road again. I picked up my five passengers in a moment of lunacy outside of Dallas: Leon, Corey, Diane, Brian and Zorro, crazies on their way back to Atlanta from a Willie Nelson concert. They sang and clapped with great gusto, but none of them had any gas money, and they all had managed, at one time or another, to misplace their driver's licenses. When I told them I was falling asleep at the wheel, they sang louder.

When Brian discovered my stethoscope in the glovebox, he reasoned out that I was a doctor. Instantly, the whole crew started badgering me for pills. "Please, Dr. Stone, you gotta have some Quaaludes, right?" And then the girl, Diane, told me that a friend of hers was in trouble, yeah, that kind of trouble, and Diane was wondering if I would help her out. "She's only fourteen, see, so it's kind of a bad scene at home with her old man, see, and she's got some money, but she can't find anyone who'll do it, y'know, 'cause she's only fourteen."

"Bad scene? I'll tell you what's a bad scene . . . never mind. Sorry about your friend. Nope, sorry, no pills. Nothing but a stethoscope. What? I look too young to be a doctor? Thanks."

The conversation deteriorated from there until Corey decided he wanted to tell a joke. "Okay, Otis. What do you call a guy who finishes last in his class at med school?"

Flipping by me on my right was an Alabama state line marker. My left eye was closed asleep, and my right eye was going fast.

"Come on, Doc," Corey whined. "What do you call a guy who finishes dead last in his class at med school?"

"Doctor," I answered automatically.

Corey pouted. "You heard it before."

"I don't get it," Diane said.

I pulled off the road to rest for a minute. No question in my mind but that these people were winners. Even so, the trip might have been labeled a success if it weren't for the last lap. As I spread the road map across my lap, I was unaware of the implications of those few short moments when I charted my course across the state of Alabama. There, two hours away, was a red circle of ink on the map. Inside it, inside the earthy brown underbelly of Alabama, was a little town called Grady. I folded up the map, pointed the car east on Highway 80 again, and put my foot to the floor.

TWO THINGS MAKE GRADY, ALABAMA, A REGULAR stopping place for eastbound motorists on Highway 80. One is the laborious detour around the unfinished David Eisenhower Bridge, just west of town. The other is a two-minute stoplight at the intersection of 80 and Gresham Boulevard. Were it not for these two landmarks most drivers would clip through Grady at about 80 miles an hour, and probably notice little more than the big new Zayre department store.

Turley Dekle had built the store three years earlier while he was mayor. Turley is dead now, and I won't spend much time on him except to say that the way Turley died is the way many die in Grady County.

He was 51 then, a year or so before I arrived. Turley was out one Friday night with two good old boys, Charlie Skinner and his brother, Ben, drinking for four hours solid at a drive-in movie west of the city on Highway 80. According to the ambulance driver Shelly Farmer (who seems to know these things), the movie was either "Linda Lovelace for President" or "True Grit." Whichever it was, Turley and the Skinners sat through it twice.

At two in the morning they peeled off for town, Turley at the wheel of his '72 Chrysler Newport (the first and last ever seen in Grady County) with the red-faced Skinners passed out in back. They headed east at 85 miles per hour over a ragged two-lane stretch of the highway until they came to the David Eisenhower Bridge.

A little history on the Eisenhower structure: it is not really a bridge. Not yet. On the night Turley missed the detour the bridge was only half finished. Turley finished the rest.

He tore past the striped wooden barricades and up the ramp, right off the end at 85 miles per hour and right straight down into the slow, mud-gray Alabama River. The State Police said he never even hit the brakes. The Skinners floated up two days later, but Turley, being rather stout, stuck in the car and they squeezed him out after they hauled up the wreck four days afterward.

I first ran afoul of the Eisenhower Bridge when I entered Grady County with Leon, Corey and company. I'd been driving for more than nine hours and, with three joints going simultaneously in the back seat, had inevitably ingested a shitload of cannabis residue. So when the Eisenhower Bridge popped up out of the early morning fog, it looked like a huge, gray ribbon to the heavens. I spotted the detour—a gravel-and-lime grade that sneaks off to the driver's right over the old original wooden bridge—about two seconds late. I hit the brakes with both feet and we spun out dizzily off the highway into a boggy clump of trees.

Although none of us was injured (Leon slept peacefully through the incident), the rear axle on the Charger was cracked. I phoned a service station and no sooner had I hung up the receiver than a red-and-white wrecker showed up, its yellow emergency lights flashing wildly in celebration. With ease it dragged my crippled car out of the swamp.

The driver, an unshaven black-haired mechanic, looked friendly enough so I asked him, "When are they going to finish the big bridge?"

He was greatly amused. "Ain't never gonna finish it, I don't believe. No sir. Can't have no bridge named after that fellow Nixon's son-in-law, now can we? Folks might think we approved of Watergate and all that."

I was touched by the sudden attack of morality suffered by the town of Grady. During the next few days, I was to learn that such attacks were rare, and never fatal.

The driver, whose name was Melvin Dryden, towed us into Grady and dropped me off at Trafford Memorial Hospital. "We'll take care of this axle tomorrow," he promised with another toothy grin.

"What about the kids?"

Melvin sized up the five drowsy longhairs. "They welcome to sleep right where they are. I'm gonna leave the car at my station till daybreak and I don't think nobody'll mess with 'em."

"Fine. How much do I owe you for the tow?"

"I'll work up the tab tomorrow after I look at that axle," he said, portentously. This smiling man with the grease-black hair had me in his power: not only could he decide when, but also how much it would cost me to get out of Grady.

Trafford Memorial is a low, brown, one-story brick building that sits in the very pit of Alabama River Valley. It was built in 1936, three years after Squire Trafford died and willed a full one-fourth of his handsome pecan fortune to a new hospital that would carry his name.

It was constructed right on Highway 80, which was then known as Grady Road. The decision to build on that particular site was a prophetic one by the planners: in later years most of Trafford's profitable business would be derived directly from the highway. It is no accident that the visitors' entrance and outpatient clinic is on the south end of the long building and the emergency entrance is on the north, facing the hazardous two-lane road.

I pushed my way through the heavy wooden double doors and came face-to-face with a stubby woman with thin gray hair and raw-looking hands who was licking envelopes at the admissions desk. Her eyes were equally gray and raw-looking.

"Hello."

"Yes?"

"My name is Dr. Stone. I wonder if I might catch a few hours sleep here until morning. My car broke down by the bridge."

The hatchet-faced nurse turned her head sideways and looked at me out of one gray eye. "Go away, before I call the cops."

7

I extracted my identification cards and she scrutinized each piece, chuckling cruelly at the photograph on my driver's license. "So you're a doctor. Still don't mean you can barge in here and sleep for free."

"I'd appreciate the courtesy."

"If you're a doctor why can't you afford a room up at the Rodeway?"

"Hey, I'm just starting. Give me a couple of years and I'll buy the damn Rodeway."

Her jaws set. "My brother Frank sure wouldn't appreciate that, mister. He's worked hard with the place."

I apologized instantly and set about to convince her my case was desperate. "I've got to make it back to Washington on thirty-seven bucks. Please let me catch some sleep here."

"On one condition," she finally agreed. "Can you lick envelopes?"

Nothing in my past medical history, including several exotic childhood diseases, had debilitated my tongue so I answered, "As far as I know."

Her red hands grabbed a stack. "These are the July patient invoices. They go out today at ten a.m. That leaves you four hours to sleep and two hours of licking."

"Wonderful," I sighed.

"When you're through with these, bring them down to my office. My name is Margaret Holt and I'm the nursing supervisor."

"And you're working at four in the morning? That's real dedication."

"No, that's stupidity," said Mrs. Holt, and flashed me a look that said exactly what I could do with my flattery. "Not my stupidity, either. I normally don't come to work until noon, but the night nurse got laid up. She's back there now." She pointed down the one and only corridor to some unspecified room. "In labor."

"You don't have an obstetrical staff?"

"Staff, hell. She's the patient!"

I fell asleep on an oiled cot in the doctors' quarters. Snoring next to me was another young man who was in every way my opposite: tall, broad-chested, sporting a full head of blond, straight hair. I took him for an orderly. A loud orderly.

He awoke at five, a mere hour after my eyelids had slammed shut. "Gawdamn," he growled and extended his ape-like arms. "Five already? Jeeeesus."

I opened one eye. "Keep it down, please," I said bravely, obviously too tired to realize how badly I was outmatched.

Nurse Holt woke me at 8 a.m. sharp by setting a box of two hundred envelopes on my bed. On my legs. She handed me a cup of coffee and reminded me the bills must go out by ten. She said the administrator wanted to see me. For some reason.

Of course, but the time I finished licking my fiftieth envelope, I had sustained three painful paper cuts on the surfaces of my tongue and lips. When the orderly returned, I saw my chance for a break, so I started a conversation.

"What's your name?"

Buster Hogue, he told me. "And Buster is not a nickname, either. It's my Christian name, so no jokes."

"I'm Dr. Stone."

"I know," Buster said indifferently. "My old man's a doctor."

"How about you? Orderly?"

"Sometimes." He doubled over and slapped himself on the leg. "Been waiting to use that one."

"Very good," I congratulated him. "Your dad works around here?"

"Might say that. He's only the best doctor in Grady County, maybe even in southern Alabama. I'm surprised you never heard of him."

I dabbed a bloody spot on my lip with a handkerchief.

"Well, I'm from Florida so I don't know too many doctors around here. What's your father's specialty?"

Buster was obviously confused. "What you mean?"

"Pediatrics? Gynecology? Orthopedics? What field does he specialize in?"

Buster brightened. "All of 'em. He does a little bit of

9

everything. He'll be here soon and I'll introduce you. You probably have a lot in common."

I looked at him kindly, the way I approach orphans and elderly widows. "How old are you, Buster?"

"Twenty-three."

"And you're gonna be a doctor?"

"Damn straight. Soon as I get into college."

"You mean med school," I corrected.

"No, college. They kicked my ass out of the state university when I lost my football scholarship. That was four years ago and ever since then I've been trying to get in every damn college in the state. I got accepted at two others but the same thing happened."

"Grades?"

His big face clouded. "Yeah, Daddy don't have the time to sit down and help me with the books. But I'll make it, Daddy promised I would."

Terrific, I thought, contemplating the inestimable damage a pair of hands as large and unskilled as Buster's could do to some innocent and unsuspecting victim of appendicitis.

"How old are you?" Buster asked.

"Twenty-nine."

"Least I ain't too old yet. I still got time."

Buster and I licked the last one hundred envelopes and I delivered them neatly to Nurse Holt's office. Then I made my way to the south end of the hospital for my ten o'clock interview with the administrator, Marshall Needham.

His office was very big, furnished smartly in walnut, but very cold. Needham seemed to have a chronic perspiration problem because he was sopping wet in the 65-degree chill of his office. Maybe he jogged to work and forgot to shower, I guessed. He had a small, pale face with reddish cheeks and a long slender nose that made him look like a rodent. He smoked nervously and fingered the buttons of his brown suit.

"Have a seat, Dr. Stone."

"No, thanks." I handed him the resume.

"I heard about Mrs. Holt making you lick all those envelopes and I'm very sorry," Needham said. "She has been reprimanded. It won't happen again."

"No trouble," I said. "Just a few little cuts on my tongue."

Needham winced. "Blood?"

"A little."

"Damnation! That's no way to treat a guest." He glanced over my resume, closed the plastic cover and set it on the desk. "We'd like you to come to work for us, Dr. Stone."

Just like that—no bickering, no swordplay, no politics. So I folded my hands and played dumb. "Don't you want some references?"

"I've checked them all out. Your background is very impressive. Magna cum laude from Emory and then a year at Bellevue. Excellent!"

My heart sank. "No, it was Stanford. And I took my internship at Jackson Memorial in Miami."

He breezed on. "Oh yes, Jackson Memorial. Know a radiologist in Jackson. Good place to learn, Mississippi is."

"Miami."

"Oh, yeah, fine hospital," Needham stammered. "The point is we'd love for you to settle down here in Grady, open a practice and admit your patients here at Trafford. True, this isn't Miami, but we've still got fifteen thousand folks out there that need a good, well-staffed hospital. And we pay pretty well for these parts."

The mercenary in me grabbed the bait. "How well?"

"Fifteen an hour to start. Of course, you'll get a raise when some of our federal monies come through. We got big plans for Trafford." Needham lit another cigarette and stood up to readjust the wall thermostat. "Hot as hell in here, isn't it?"

"What kind of plans?"

"Well, the federal money totals about $50,000. But the Hutchinson money is where we're sitting pretty—two million buckeroos for a brand new wing."

I whistled. This is not my style, but I had a vague feeling Needham expected it. "When is that due?"

11

Needham fidgeted. "We got a slight problem with that. See, Benbow Hutchinson isn't dead yet." He laughed nervously. "In fact, he's one of our most loyal patients. Comes in a couple times a week for oxygen and stimulants. Doctors say he's got a real bad heart."

"How bad?"

"Real bad," Needham reported gravely. "Any day now, Dr. Stone. Benbow is eighty-seven and a man just doesn't live much longer than that, not with a bad heart."

"When did he promise the money?"

"He put it in his will ten years ago, eleven this September."

We talked some more and as we did, Needham's desperation evidenced itself. He needed a doctor to work the emergency room. The last one quit to open a private clinic in Mobile. On weekends and at night the E.R. was virtually unstaffed, save for a nurse or Buster Hogue. Any doctor would do; it was the old story of trying to lure medical talent from the cities to the boondocks.

"I'll get back to you as soon as I return to Washington," I lied, rising to leave.

"I think you would like it here in Grady," Needham said.

When I returned to the doctors' quarters in the south end, Buster Hogue had a message for me. Melvin Dryden had called to say the car was ready. Melvin's service station was next door to the big Zayre at the intersection of Gresham and Highway 80 (and if you timed it just right you could get a fill-up and a tire check while the light was red). I walked there from the hospital; it took twenty minutes.

Melvin was still working under the Charger when I arrived. "I thought it was ready," I complained.

"Just tinkering." Melvin stood up and gulped down the copper-colored remainder of a Coke. "Here's your bill."

I took one painful look and shoved it back in his face.

"What is this for? I can't afford $230!" Smooth as moonshine Melvin itemized each expense. Through clenched teeth, I agreed to pay.

"I haven't got the cash. Will you take a check?"

12

"I don't believe so," Melvin said apologetically. "Can't take out-of-state checks."

"Credit cards?"

"Nope."

"You're kidding, of course."

" 'Fraid not," Melvin said, failing to sense how fast he was losing my friendship. "Folks come hightailing through here all the time with stolen credit cards. I lost damn near $600 last year on worthless charge plates."

"I gotta get out of here. I need to make Montgomery by three. Where am I going to get $230 in cash?"

Melvin shrugged. "I'll keep an eye on your car till you do." I haggled with him, offering cufflinks, a self-winding watch and even some medical instruments as collateral. He refused everything. The pay phone rang in the grimy office and Melvin handed it to me.

"My nephew tells me you've got a problem," Marshall Needham chortled. "Melvin says you can't pay your bill."

I bit my lip. "I'll get the money."

"Well, I've got a proposition," Needham said. "Spend two nights in the E.R. at Trafford. We'll pay you fifteen an hour, then you can pay Melvin and be on your way. Who knows, you might even like it."

"I doubt that." I scowled at Melvin, who had opened another Coke. "Two nights," I told the administrator, "and that's all."

If he could have, Needham surely would have tried to slap my shoulder with his sweaty, paw-like hand. "That's all," he said cheerily. "Who knows, we might have ourselves a new doctor in town."

"I wouldn't bet on it." I hung up and turned on Melvin. "You knew about this, didn't you?"

His eyes widened innocently. "Don't jump on me, man. I just want my money."

"You'll get it." I moved toward the door, then remembered. "Where are those kids?"

"Oh, they wandered off early this morning. Took some sleeping bags. Asked me where the nearest park was, so I

13

pointed 'em toward to Boy Scout campgrounds down Gresham.''

I schemed to slip out of town without them.

"We'll take good care of your car," Melvin said. "You want the tires rotated or anything?"

"No!" I snapped. "I'll see you in two days."

Melvin nodded vacantly. "That's all, huh?"

"That's all."

That was six months ago.

IF THERE WAS A LESSON TO BE GLEANED FROM Grady during the first days there, it was this: assume everyone is a blood relative of everyone else. It makes it so much easier to accept the most unlikely persons having important kin in high places, low places, and anyplace where a favor might come in handy.

Marshall Needham was a good example. He had used his nephew mechanic to prearrange the automobile extortion plot which now trapped me in Grady. Melvin had my car; Needham had me. And despite Needham's rat-like appearance, he was more astute than most rodents. Not more respectable, just more astute.

No sooner had I left Melvin's filling station than I began to gloat. Needham could not force me to work in the Trafford E.R. because I had no license to practice medicine in Alabama. And no sooner did I bound into the administrator's office with my announcement than the weasel slapped me on the shoulders and said warmly, "Relax, Stone. I got you a temporary license from the state board of medical examiners. Just one phone call and bingo! Course, having my wife's brother over in Montgomery didn't hurt. He works for the health department, did I tell you?"

So there was no way out. I resigned myself to a Friday evening of rural medicine sideshows and, using a credit card, went out and bought a book to read for the occasion.

The emergency room at Trafford Memorial is approximately the size of a modest one-bedroom apartment. Unfur-

15

nished. Chilly. The waiting room is L-shaped and seats five people, three on an old pink sofa and two on folding chairs set out in the corridor.

Coming through the heavy, creaky double doors into the E.R., one is first likely to encounter Mrs. Holt at the nurse's station on the left. The waiting room is opposite Mrs. Holt (if Mrs. Holt is in a particularly bellicose mood, most of the waiting is done outdoors or in the main lobby at the south end). The examination room, the operating room, the cardiac care room and the recovery room are found through a door on the left-hand side of the corridor; they are in fact one and the same room.

It is here the grim theater of emergency medicine is performed. Except for the single operating table under a single, ancient surgical lamp, the room has all the atmosphere of a bus station men's room. The walls are a sickly lima-bean green, and the floor is a lively gray-flecked linoleum. The medicines are stashed in an unlocked cabinet and a wall unit harbors the overflow from central supply: bedpans, linens, gowns, hypos, catheters, tongue depressors, cotton balls and reams of clerical forms.

After sizing up the place, I resolved not to get involved with it, just to get the wild nightmare over with. If later in my career a question should arise about Trafford Memorial, I would deny ever stopping here.

The first night started badly when I complained about a sign taped to the custard-colored wall of the corridor. It read: "The Doctor on duty today will not accept Medicaid in payment for his services."

"It seems to me that sort of defeats the purpose of Medicaid," I remarked to a shy nurse. "And what kind of joke is that?" I pointed at another sign, this one hanging from the roof near the E.R. entrance. It read: "This is an emergency room, not an outpatient clinic. Emergencies are very serious medical problems for which treatment cannot wait. For example: gunshot sounds, poisoning, broken limbs, deep cuts and painful head injuries. The staff here will treat emergen-

16

cies only! In plain language, an emergency is something terrible that has just arisen.'' It was signed by ''The Doctor.''

"Those are the rules,'' the nurse explained meekly.

"Whose?''

"Dr. Hogue's orders. He had his reasons.''

"You mean Buster's father. But, how are poor people going to afford medical care without Medicaid? And what is he trying to do with that sign, scare people out of the emergency room?''

"I don't know,'' the nurse muttered, scuttling away.

In retrospect, I should have shut up, written the whole thing off as one of the town physician's parochial mannerisms to which Grady Countians had become accustomed. This hospital was no place for liberal pontifications.

On slow nights in August, nurses talk to each other. And if the mood is right, they even talk to their supervisors. Mrs. Holt loved to talk to her charges. Check that: she loved to talk, period. As it happened, and I'm not sure how it really did, I frightened the timid little floor nurse into talking to Mrs. Holt for the first time in eighteen months. Mrs. Holt was delighted and she charged right out of the ladies' room to pursue the matter.

"I heard you been raising hell about Carl Hogue's signs.'' She had crept up on me as I skimmed the latest Theodore White treatise, which was somniforously similar to his others.

"I think the signs are unprofessional. They don't say much for Hogue's dedication to the patients.''

Mrs. Holt bristled. "And who the hell are you? You don't even know Dr. Hogue. He's the best in south Alabama.''

"I can recognize sarcasm. The people who come here don't need to be told in Alice-and-Jerry language what an emergency is. Is it necessary to insult them?''

"Maybe they don't know they're being insulted.'' Mrs. Holt screwed her face into a smug smile and put her bony hands in her uniform pockets. "If you worked here for one crummy year instead of two nights, not only would you agree

17

with Dr. Hogue's rules, you'd be offering to repaint those signs when the letters faded."

"Bullshit," I mumbled.

Ten minutes later I was deep into Teddy White's delicate and ethereal explanation of the Watergate scandals and beginning to yearn for yet another interruption, perhaps the frightened nurse to sit and apologize for finking on me. I was not hoping for Marshall Needham to call.

"How's it going?" he asked cheerily. "Nothing? Well, be patient. That's what we pay you for."

His tone shifted to serious, but politely diplomatic. "Dr. Stone, now I don't mean to be critical, but we've got to watch ourselves around here. It has come to my attention"—and he began to sound like a memorandum—"that you've been criticizing our emergency room policies about Medicaid and outpatient illnesses."

"I understood the policies were Dr. Hogue's."

Needham cleared his throat and I imagined him to be patting a damp handkerchief over his perpetually sweaty forehead.

"Yes, yes, they are Dr. Hogue's wishes so we adopted them. He's the best doctor in south Alabama and we're very lucky to have him here at Trafford."

"What do the other doctors think?" I asked.

"Uh?"

"You do have other doctors here at Trafford, don't you? I mean, the hospital is supposed to be serving a county of fifteen thousand. There must be other doctors."

"Sure. Five, in fact. Well, actually four since Dr. Ward left to open the clinic down in Mobile. And we've got a couple of specialists who work out of Montgomery. They come around now and then. As for the other doctors in Grady, they appreciate Carl and they agree with those rules."

"Figures," I said coldly.

Long pause. A rustling of tissue. "Well. Okay. But please don't complain so much around the hospital. We wouldn't want any patients to hear you talk about Dr. Hogue. You're only going to be here two days—unless, of course, you decide to settle in Grady—but Hogue is going to be here another twenty years, God willing.''

"God willing." Apparently my behavior had ruined Needham's evening. I caved in and told the administrator, "You win: no more outbursts. I'll just work my two nights and get the hell out."

"We're in no hurry to have you go." Needham's tone was lukewarm. "And I knew you'd understand about the signs. I have just one more tiny item."

"Yes?"

"Could you please refrain from using, eh, poolroom words around the nurses."

"You mean 'bullshit'?"

"I think that fits the category."

"Sure, no problem. Sorry it slipped out."

"Thank you, Dr. Stone. Have a good night."

Do not make it any worse, I told myself. Just do your sixteen hours, get the car and clear out.

The remainder of the evening was spent watching television and removing a fish hook from Clay Dilborn's finger. Clay was the brother of Dan Dilborn, one of the two emergency medical technicians who manned the Grady County ambulance. Clay had been catfishing over on the Alabama River when the mishap occurred; three of us spent a full two hours in efforts to effect a painless minor surgery.

The other emergency medical technician was Shelly Farmer—bright, buxom, and bubbly, the only woman ambulance driver in the state. She studied case law between emergencies and was planning to enter the Vanderbilt Law School as a freshman next spring. I feigned watching television and concentrated on Shelly, who was curled up in the waiting room on the moldy pink couch. Her infrequent glances in my direction carried unmistakable disinterest.

At midnight, six hours after I'd gone on duty and five hours after I'd forsaken Teddy White, a call came through. Shelly peeled out of her cozy couch and hopped into the ambulance on the driver's side. Dan shelved his *Mad* magazine and scrambled into the rear compartment. They whined

19

out of the parking lot, Shelly hunched over the wheel like a bootlegger making for Georgia.

At the nurse's station I asked Mrs. Holt, "Have you got any kind of telemetry?"

"Heart monitoring, you mean? No, but we got radio contact with the ambulance."

"Does Hogue do surgery?" I anticipated the arrival of an accident victim in need of reassembly.

"Some. The fancy stuff is done by some Montgomery surgeons."

I went for the phone. "What's Hogue's number?"

Mrs. Holt wrested the receiver from my hand. "You can't call Dr. Hogue. Not yet. Wait till we see what they got. Then we call, provided it's a real emergency."

"Not this bit with the rules again."

"What are you, some kind of anarchist?"

The radio cackled and screeched. "Shelly, can you hear me?" I said into the microphone. "What have you got?"

She gave her location in Gresham Park, a modest subdivision four miles northwest of the hospital. "I've got a . . . with abdominal . . . sudden onset. . . ."

"Please repeat."

"I said I've . . . boy . . . tenderness in the lower. . . ."

I slammed my fist dramatically against the radio; this served only to worsen the static and shear a pink slice of raw skin from my knuckles. "This radio is terrible!"

Mrs. Holt shrugged. "Sometimes it works pretty good. One of Mr. Needham's cousins, a trucker, donated it to the hospital last year."

Fifteen minutes later the ambulance screamed up to the E.R. and Shelly and Dan carried the stretcher into the dingy corridor. The patient, a towheaded fourteen-year-old boy named John Oaks, complained through tears of severe pain in his abdomen.

"Go wake up Billie," Mrs. Holt advised Buster, who was laughing uproariously at the Bob Hope monologue on the Carson show. "Buster, you hear me? We need a blood work-up."

20

John Oaks wailed and clutched at himself. He damn near jumped off the stretcher when I inspected his abdomen. "Could be appendicitis," I ventured. "But he hasn't got any fever."

The blood test revealed a slightly elevated white cell count. Figuring the boy's doctor might want to know, I told Nurse Holt to call Hogue at home. Besides being a "visiting physician" with a temporary license of dubious validity, I felt unqualified (and unwilling) to perform an appendectomy in Alabama or anywhere else.

Mrs. Holt wasn't much help. Displaying a rare trace of timidity, she said, "You call Dr. Hogue yourself. He'd rather hear about the patient from another doctor."

She gave me the number and I called from a telephone at the nurses' station. It rang seven times before a groggy, cantankerous male voice snarled hello.

"Dr. Hogue? I'm Dr. Stone down here in the emergency room and one of your patients is here with possible appendicitis."

"You must mean the Trafford E.R. 'cause that's the only one I work out of," he said, "but I sure don't know any Dr. Stone."

"I'm new here, and temporary."

"Who's the patient?"

I told him and described the symptoms. Hogue sounded unconcerned. "Probably John just gorged himself on dinner to get a bellyache like that."

"He's got a lot of pain in the right lower quadrant," I replied cooly. "I think you ought to take a look at him."

Twenty minutes later a Cadillac slid into a parking space outside the emergency entrance and Carl Hogue stormed in. He was big, nearly as tall as Buster, but his hair had thinned and grayed over sixty-nine years; his broad chest had sunk somewhat loosely into a jelly-roll midsection. He had a big beak-shaped nose, a square strong chin and luminous green eyes (which were not red and foggy). His face was leather-brown—golf will do that for you.

Even in a ridiculous white T-shirt and wrinkled gray slacks

21

Hogue looked imposing. I would come to find him a proud, hardworking, stubborn and annoying man who cherished his reputation as the Medical Czar of Grady County. At sixty-nine, he was one of the few remaining doctors in Grady who had not died or retired or was seriously considering one of those alternatives. It was a memorable vision, the first time I saw him, as he churned into the E.R. with a steaming cup of coffee in one hand and his black medical bag gripped in the other.

"You're Stone," he said when he rambled by me. His sureness was such that, even had I not been Stone, I would have answered in the affirmative.

Hogue roosted over the stretcher. "How's your pappy, John?"

The Oaks boy grinned dumbly. "Okay."

"How about you?"

"Better. Not too bad, I guess."

"Dr. Stone says you have some bad pain."

"I heard you might have to operate."

"We'll see," Hogue said, and began palpating the right lower abdominal quadrant. When I had touched the boy in the same region only thirty minutes earlier, he had screamed demonically about certain impending death; now he merely watched Hogue curiously. I wondered if the doctor's mere touch had soothed the pain. "That doesn't hurt?"

"Not really."

In my own defense, I interjected the information about the boy's high white cell count. Hogue shook his head impatiently and scanned the chart. "You got me out of bed for nothing. I think John here's got mesenteric adenitis. The nodes feel a bit inflamed but that'll go away."

"But you can't be certain?"

Hogue's jade-sharp eyes bored into my pitifully puppy-like brown ones. "Oaks is my patient. The family has been coming to me since before you were born, much less into med school. Take my word for it and relax. Go back to your book."

From the acidity in his reaction, I discerned Carl Hogue

was not accustomed to argument or debate, and possibly totally unfamiliar with the concept of mistake. "Can we keep him here for a few hours?" I bargained.

"If you want," he shrugged, "but I'm going back to bed. And next time, Stone, try to remember this is an emergency room." And with that he was out of the doors—coffee cup, medical bag and all—into his car, which, incidentally, had been left with motor running during the pit stop.

"Do I have to stay?" John whined.

I scowled at the whimpering adolescent. "An hour ago you were doubled up, begging for painkillers. Now you make like the boy who cried wolf and I look like an ass—amateur. What's the story, kid? Did Melvin pay you to get me in trouble?" John's eyes widened. "It don't hurt anymore, honest. That's the truth." If the boy was a conspirator, he had been well trained for his mission. He was convincing. So convincing that two hours later he doubled up again and vomited.

Hogue was summoned, this time by a reluctant Mrs. Holt, and he arrived more cranky than before. Only this time he turned off the Cadillac's ignition: he could hear John Oaks screaming all the way out in the parking lot.

"Want me to assist?" I volunteered gleefully, trying hard not to gloat. But Hogue just took one searing look at me and ordered Mrs. Holt and another duty nurse to prep for an appendectomy.

"We need some experienced medical staff for this," Hogue replied with a touch of gravity usually reserved for open-heart surgery.

After the operation I caught Hogue sneaking out toward his car. "Wait!" I hollered down the corridor. "Dr. Hogue, wait! What was the pathology on Oaks?" I wanted to find out whether the operation had indeed found a near-perforated appendix, or merely the puffy lymph glands Hogue had earlier diagnosed.

When he heard my voice Hogue's shoulders drew together sharply and he wheeled around to deliver his standard curt dismissal. "Were you talking to me?"

23

"How was the operation?"

"That, Stone, is my business because John Oaks is my patient. Your business—and I don't know how you managed to get into it—is the emergency room. I suggest you mind it."

He spun around and stalked toward the exit. "Just as I thought," I said, plenty loud enough. "Appendicitis!"

Hogue snorted something under his breath as he walked away, something which sounded distinctly like the word "Asshole." It was not, I found later, a remark totally out of character.

THE BOY SCOUT CAMPGROUNDS COVERED THREE
acres off Gresham Boulevard, two miles from Trafford Memorial. The early morning walk was pleasant, the sun was still low in the sky and a fine cool mist rose from the damp valley floor. Had it been sleeting I would have walked anyway. Anything to get away from the hospital.

I covered the distance in twenty minutes, not being in any particular hurry to rendezvous with my travel companions. They stood out like an oil slick in a tropical lagoon. Three sleeping bags lay under an old mossy oak, surrounded by a dozen empty beer cans and a soggy box of Ritz crackers. The foliage was scarred by a sizeable charbroiled blemish, the remains of a campfire. High in the oak tree a squirrel chirped his disapproval and munched on a discarded marshmallow.

Aside from the vocal rodent there were no signs of life, but three disproportionate lumps told me something inhabited the sleeping bags. I braved a greeting.

"Leon? Anybody home?"

One of the bundles groaned and Diane stuck her head out. "Hey, Doc. What time is it? When we gonna get out of here?"

"First thing tomorrow morning. Where are the others?" I expected a sheepish story about getting caught smoking dope in a Boy Scout camp. Instead, to my delight, I learned the caravan had shrunk.

"Leon and Corey are still asleep," Diane said, "but Brian

25

and Zorro split last night. They got a ride with a trucker on his way up to Indiana. Brian had never seen South Bend before and Zorro really couldn't remember whether he had or not. So off they went. Took half our stash, too."

I offered my condolences and tried valiantly to mask my high spirits. "Just the four of us, huh? Well, I'd like to get started early tomorrow, about nine. I'll be on duty until two in the morning if you need to reach me."

Diane dragged herself out of the musty cocoon and zipped up the front of her jeans. "How about a beer? I think we got one or two cans left over."

"No thanks. Don't forget to clean up this mess before you go. One thing we don't need is you three getting busted for littering and vagrancy."

As I strolled back towards Gresham Boulevard I heard a foggy shout from the campsite. Leon and Corey had stumbled out of their sleeping bags and each gave a wave before cracking open two cans of unsavory warm beer. I wished heartily for another saintly trucker to lure them all away with the promise of romance and high adventure on the interstate.

At Melvin Dryden's service station I found the wiry mechanic rotating my tires and I exploded, threatening him with a proctoscopic lube job. "No charge," he said defensively. "Left front was getting bald so I stuck it in the trunk. Can't stand to see bald tires just set there. I won't charge you nuthin', honest."

"I'll be here with the money tomorrow morning."

Melvin wiped his hands on his hips. "That's what Uncle Marshall said. Said to make sure you car is A-one ready to go."

"And?"

"Oh, it is. I don't believe you'll have a bit of trouble. Not a bit. Runs like a rabbit."

I put my face close to his and said, "I hope you're right, Melvin, because if this car doesn't work tomorrow morning I will personally come back here and rotate your glands. No charge."

Frightened, Melvin was eager to appease and readily acceded when I asked to borrow the office phone. I called my parents in Washington, collect, and explained the situation at Trafford Memorial Hospital. My mother was properly sympathetic; having never ventured south of Roanoke Beach, she envisioned Alabama as a brutal bayou infested with pickup trucks, Baptists and Ferlin Husky records. My father, who was once stationed in Huntsville, decided two days in Grady was worth a whole year of med school and praised the adventure as a "healthy challenge for any new doctor."

"Did I get any mail?"

"Let me think," my mother pondered. "The Book of the Month Club says you owe them $12.50 for *The Joy of Sex*. . . ."

"I didn't buy *The Joy of Sex*."

My father cleared his throat. "I'll take care of that one, Otis."

". . . and some letters from Jackson Memorial," my mother added, "and something from a hospital out West."

"Which hospital? Did it come by registered mail?"

"I don't remember, son," my mother said lamely. "I'll go find it . . . if I can just remember where I put that stuff."

"This is collect," my father reminded her sternly. "Be quick about it."

Three minutes and $2.30 later the receiver banged against the desk in our family's study and my breathless mother tore open the envelope from the San Jose City Hospital in California. She read the letter from the Chief of Medicine. I giggled ecstatically.

"I can't believe it. A residency? It thought that guy hated my guts. He kept bitching about my hair and my casual attitude."

"Evidently you impressed him in other ways," my father observed with no small edge of paternal pride. "Are you going to accept?"

"Yes. Yes, I am. It was by far the best hospital I've seen on the whole trip and its residency training program is very highly regarded out West. It's just the kind of place I was

27

looking for," I kidded. "Thirty-five hundred miles from Miami Beach."

"When will you be home?"

"Two days at the most," I assured him. "Could you write them today on my behalf and let Dr. Halberstam know I'm interested?"

My mother whimpered an indiscernible reply but my father agreed to answer the hospital post haste. "I'll be leaving tomorrow morning," I said. "Pray the Charger behaves. Some scatterbrained. . . ." I spotted Melvin lurking near the Coke machine. "Yeah, some sharp mechanics they got around here, Dad. Not like Washington where they steal you blind."

I danced back to Trafford, imagining myself on the beach at Carmel, or dining along San Francisco Bay, or watching the A's win the Series. Scraping the pasty Alabama clay off my shoes, I congratulated myself that the odyssey had paid off after all. I pictured myself regaling the San Jose staff with the tale of my arduous two nights in the Grady County emergency room. "Yeah, I spent a month in Alabama one weekend," I'll jape.

When I went on duty that night I forced myself to be civil as I greeted Nurse Holt. "You look lovely tonight," I teased. "Bet you got yourself a hot date."

At my jolliness her sharp eyes narrowed. "Hiram ain't been dead a year and I don't intend to degrade his memory by stomping around this town where everyone can see me. What's gotten into you, Dr. Stone? Maybe you finally made up your mind to like it here?"

"Not a chance." I fiddled with the knobs on the old black-and-white television. "Don't tell me Cronkite is still on vacation. It's been three weeks. Maybe he and Johnny Carson took a cruise together."

Mrs. Holt frowned. "We usually watch 'Let's Make a Deal,' " she informed me. "That's on Channel 14."

I was in such fine spirits, I changed stations instantly and even laughed at the Racine housewife dressed up like a pineapple.

"Heard you're on your way out West," Mrs. Holt remarked as she pretended to scribble on some charts.

"That's right," I chirped. "Going to California with a banjo on my knee."

"That's not how the song goes!"

Shelly Farmer and I played "Go Fish" for an hour and discussed our respective blueprints for future happiness, professional fulfillment and financial security. The way Shelly planned it, she would practice law and save her money until she was thirty-seven, then marry and bear her two children— one boy and one girl—before age 40.

"I'd like to be a storefront lawyer in Atlanta or Nashville or some other big city. You know, a free clinic type of arrangement," she explained. "Of course, I couldn't save much that way because I wouldn't make much. So I'll probably stick to corporate law for the first ten years just to build up a bank account. How about you?"

"Actually I haven't given it much thought. I suppose I'll give California a chance. After my residency I might stay at San Jose and specialize. Maybe in surgery, I don't know."

"What about your wife?"

"I'm not married," I said quickly. "Not even engaged."

She cocked her head and brushed the blond bangs out of her eyes. For a moment she reminded me of a young Doris Day but I swept the saccharine image from my mind. "Sure, I can see you aren't wearing a wedding band. Of course, that's an old trick: just slip it off the finger whenever a pretty girl comes along."

"I'll have to remember that," I jibed. "But I'm not married. Take my word for it. Better yet, don't take my word for it. Here's my black book. Call any one of these girls and ask—no, not her. She married a Green Beret. . . ."

Shelly was skeptical to the point of psychosis. "I dated a fellow about a year ago when I first started to work here. He was an older man. Good looking, intelligent, witty, affectionate. Swore up and down he was divorced. I believed him until one day his wife threw a brick through the windshield of the ambulance."

29

I sighed, "I am not married, Shelly. I'll take a polygraph test if you like. I wouldn't lie to you."

"Oh, sure. I've heard that line before."

Mercifully, a porky farmer named Hollis Rhodes interrupted the debate by waddling into the E.R. with a noble face that seemed to have the word "pain" carved into it. "I feel poorly," he said softly. "My arms and legs are real sore." I looked him over and found his joints swollen and tender. "It hurts to walk, sir. I can't really afford to be laid up. I got to walk and right now it hurts just too damn bad."

"Who's your doctor? Hogue?"

"No, sir. Dr. Lee Bob Parker," Rhodes said.

Mrs. Holt tugged at my jacket and pulled me off out of Hollis' earshot. "Just treat him and send him on his way," she whispered. "Please don't raise a fuss about this, Dr. Stone."

"This man has got a simple case of the gout," I protested. "A third-year med student could treat him. Who is this Parker, one of Hogue's proteges?"

"Hush!" She glanced over at Hollis who was rubbing his ankles and making low moaning sounds like a calf. "Parker is an older fellow, in his fifties. Been around a long time. He makes some mistakes so Dr. Hogue sometimes must, ah, take care of Parker's patients. It's not too often this sort of thing happens."

Disgustedly, I turned my back on Mrs. Holt. "Hollis," I said, "I'm gonna give you some medicine right now and you'll feel better soon. Mrs. Holt will give you some colchicine pills. I want you to take one every hour until the hurt goes away. Stay off your feet and drink plenty of fluids, but no whisky, okay?"

He squinted at the pharmaceutical label on the bottle of tablets. "Dr. Parker says to put hot compresses on my joints. Didn't say nuthin' about pills. I don't like pills, Doctor."

Through clenched teeth: "Try it, Hollis. You don't want to be laid up for the peanut harvest now, do you?"

He inched out the doors and I cornered Mrs. Holt in the nurses' quarters. Apologetically she explained to me the reason for Lee Bob Parker's survival: "There are so few doctors in Grady County. You've got to understand: Carl Hogue cannot treat all fifteen thousand people. If we get rid of Lee Bob Parker that leaves three doctors for the whole blessed county. And you yourself know what our chances are of finding a replacement out here in the sticks."

"I sympathize, but think of all the people hobbling around Grady with swollen joints!"

Mrs. Holt was insistent. "Parker's done some good work. Did a fine gallstone operation on Ruby Carter two years ago and even Dr. Hogue admitted it."

"So Hogue knows about Parker?"

"Of course Hogue knows." Mrs. Holt threw up her hands and in doing so nearly smacked me in the nose. "Doctors don't go around accusing each other of incompetence. The folks in Grady would think it a disgrace. In this county doctors are like ministers—revered, respected, but not questioned. There is no such thing as a bad doctor."

"What do you tell them when he kills somebody?"

"Don't ever say that," Margaret Holt said jaggedly. "It's never happened yet and with the grace of God it won't."

When I asked Shelly Farmer about Lee Bob Parker she rolled her flower-blue eyes and made a schoolgirl's face. "Ugh! It's not my place to say, but as an EMT, I promise you I trust myself before I trust Lee Bob Parker with a patient. I don't care if it's laceration of the shin. Of course, talking like that's hearsay around here. Lee Bob's a hometown product, Otis, and Grady trusts him. Not as much as they trust Carl Hogue, but Hogue is an institution, like Schweitzer. But don't say anything bad about Parker in Grady County."

"Don't worry. Come tomorrow morning I'll be on my way out of this place as fast as my poor car will go. If Hogue knows about Parker and refuses to do anything, then I know damn well there's nothing I can do."

Shelly shrugged and opened a book of Alabama case law. I went back to quarters to watch television with Buster. At ten, a skinny, hysterical woman barreled into the E.R., clutching her left wrist in her right hand and screaming she was going to die. "A black widow bit me!" she announced breathlessly. "I haven't got long, now. Please do something. Operate!"

I examined her wrist and found a small red irritation approximately one half the size of a sunflower seed. There was no swelling, no discoloration and no localized pain. "It itches like hell so I know the poison's in there," she said.

"How do you know it was a black widow?" I asked.

"See for yourself." She opened a ratty brown handbag and carefully withdrew a crumpled satchel of folded tissue paper. Inside was the badly mangled corpse of a common harmless house spider.

"Ah, a case of mistaken identity. You have executed an innocent spider," I pronounced. "Your wounds are not fatal."

"You're blind? That's a black widow spider, dammit. I am going to die. Where is Dr. Hogue?"

"If you get him out of bed now, he'll come down here and bite you himself," I said. "The spider that bit you was harmless. We'll put some antiseptic on the wound and you can go home."

Her reaction, after finally realizing she was going to survive, mirrored both relief and disappointment. Her minister arrived in a sweat and she asked me to explain her frantic phone calls; she even urged me to show the old man the body of the perpetrator so he wouldn't think she had fabricated the story. The clergyman was polite, asked her if she needed any counseling and then departed. The woman was bitter. "It'll be all over town. Just what I need. Lorie Cameron thought she was bit by a black widow spider." She left without saying thanks.

At midnight Shelly and I got a Coke and toasted my last two hours in Trafford Memorial. Thirty minutes later a call came in from the filling station on Highway 80 west of town. A motorist reported a bad auto wreck near the bridge. "A couple in the car in front of me. They flipped it over six or seven times."

32

Shelly and Dan Dilborn hopped into the ambulance. "Figured I wouldn't get through two days without one of these," I griped. Buster paced nervously. "I hope it's not a bad one," he said.

"Well, I'm calling your father."

Mrs. Holt gasped. "He'll be furious! Please wait."

Carl Hogue was irritated. "I'll be glad when you're gone so I can get some sleep," he said. I impressed upon him the distinct possibility of serious injuries in the car accident; he promised to be on hand when the ambulance returned.

I struggled with the two-way radio and managed to reach Shelly at the scene. "Signal Four, Signal Four," she repeated.

"Shit," Buster whined. "It is a bad one."

Nurse Holt, Buster and I were startled when the double doors burst open. "Hollis Rhodes, what are you doing back here?" I exclaimed. "It's only been four hours."

I rubbed my eyes, but the mirage wouldn't evaporate. Next to Hollis was a two-hundred pound hog at the end of a leash. "I feel so good, Dr. Stone, I just had to come back and thank you. And since I don't have much in the way of cash money, I brought the hog here."

The animal grunted and shifted uncomfortably, its cleaved feet scraping on the tile. "Thank you, Hollis, but I really can't accept this. . . ."

"Please, Dr. Stone!" He handed me the leash. "I don't want to be accountable to nobody."

"The hospital pays me, Hollis. I don't take private fees."

"Then give the pig to Trafford." He grinned and slapped the fat animal on its rump. "There's a heap of pork chops right there."

When Carl Hogue breezed in he didn't give the pig a second look. Mrs. Holt led the animal to an unoccupied examining room while Hogue and I sat down over coffee. We made small talk and the subject of Lee Bob Parker never came up. I had no wish to start another duel when I was so close to a peaceful escape. Besides, auto victims are favorites of no doctor and I am no exception. Give me old-fashioned

33

pneumonia any day. The mood as we waited for Shelly was positive. We set down our coffee cups when the ambulance blared into the parking lot. Tires screeching, Shelly backed the bright wagon up to the E.R. and Buster slid wooden doorstops under the big double doors.

Dan Dilborn jumped out and called for Buster to help with the stretchers. I took one glance at the first victim and saw the whole damn game plan for an expedient departure from Grady County fall apart. At one a.m. Marshall Needham was pronounced dead on arrival at Trafford Memorial Hospital.

"I SUPPOSE WE BETTER GET DOWN TO BUSINESS,"
Dan Satterwhite said. "This is a terrible time for all of us
but Marshall would have wanted us to move ahead. You know
how he was sort of compulsive."

In the weak light the conference room was a pale yellow
and from where I sat in the rear I could hardly see Satterwhite's bovine face. Then again, it was four in the morning
and at that hour I could see little of anything. Buster sat to
one side of me, fidgety and morose. Carl Hogue sat to the
other, sipping coffee and thinking of plans to be made. Mrs.
Holt sobbed unabashedly, stopping only to praise Marshall
Needham as "a good Christian man whose heart was in the
right place."

Literally she was incorrect, for after the accident nothing
of Marshall Needham's was in its right place. Hogue con-
soled the stunned members of the hospital board by telling
them Needham had died instantly. No one took issue because
no one wishes to be told, "Well, maybe not instantly. But
certainly within ten or fifteen minutes after the wreck." No,
instant death is much preferred by all concerned.

"As you know, we can't run a hospital without an administrator," Satterwhite prefaced the meeting, "We board
members are too busy to worry day and night about how
much gauze was ordered and why the cost went up ten percent in two months. That's what Marshall was good at."

The other eight board members nodded. Among their dis-
tinguished ranks was a farmer, a pharmacist, a grocer, an

attorney, an insurance salesman, a wholesale produce dealer, a used-car dealer, a geography teacher and a restaurant owner. Though they actively sought positions on Trafford's hospital board, they were happy it rarely met monthly as scheduled. Many had not seen each other in six months and the incessant murmuring of whispered amenities threatened the decorum of urgency that Dan Satterwhite, the conscientious pharmacist, wished to maintain.

"We need an acting administrator," Satterwhite said gravely. "Someone who can replace Marshall until the county commission nominates a successor."

Harry Defoe, a practical sort of fellow whose pecans and peanuts always earned plaudits in regional agricultural circles, suggested the board postpone any action. "Can't Marie Ford take care of the paperwork until next week when the commission meets? She's been with Marsh ten years. I'm sure she knows how to run the office without him, no disrespect intended."

Satterwhite shifted uneasily. "I don't think so, Harry. Marie was the other passenger in Marshall's car when it rolled over tonight. She died, too."

Harry nodded numbly and reached into his hunting jacket for a cigar. Satterwhite rambled on for an hour, mulling and maligning a variety of candidates, each of whom was rejected unequivocally for obvious reasons: alcoholism, ineptitude, poor manners in church, irregular attendance at the Kiwanis meetings, a daughter of questionable reputation.

Satterwhite flared, "Can't we find one person in this damn county to run the hospital? Don't tell me I'm going to have to take the job."

Nurse Holt choked. "Oh no, you don't! You haven't seen the inside of this place since you were elected board chairman a year ago. If you take over, the morale around here won't be worth pig dung."

Dan swallowed and said meekly, "That's not entirely correct, Mrs. Holt. I've visited Trafford since I was elected."

"Sure," the head nurse sneered, "that time you thought

36

the wart on your hand was cancerous and you ran into the E.R. half-hysterical.''

"It still counts as a visit," Satterwhite said.

"What about the blood test?" Mrs. Holt asked. Dan reddened.

Harry Defoe cleared his throat noisily. "Let's choose a staff member, a senior staff member who has been here long enough to know how this place really works." He scanned the white jackets clustered in the back of the conference room.

"Carl, how about you?" Dan piped up.

Hogue declined immodestly. "I'm sure I could handle the job, but my practice is simply too time-consuming. As you know, my patients must always come first." The board nodded approvingly. A discussion of the three physicians ended with Hogue's qualifications. "Even in a temporary capacity it's highly unorthodox for a doctor to serve as a hospital's administrator," Hogue concluded.

Dan sighed. "Nix on the doctors. How about other staff?"

Hogue raised his meaty brown hand. "I think I've got just the fellow. He's been here longer than almost everybody else and knows Trafford Memorial up and down."

The board members looked gratefully at Hogue. "Who?"

The doctor pointed to the corner. "Billie Simmons! He's been here seventeen years. He is reliable, knowledgeable and he gets along with the whole staff. He's a dear, close friend of mine and I will vouch for him!"

"The lab technician?" I bleated. "You want the lab technician to run the hospital?"

"And why not?" Hogue retorted.

"Are you related to Billie Simmons?" I demanded.

Billie stammered and his brown spaniel eyes grew fearful. "Thanks anyway, D-Doctor, but I d-don't think I can handle the job. I d-don't even think I want to try."

I triumphed, "See? Billie's got enough sense to turn down a job he's not equipped for. There must be a dozen others

37

more qualified to administrate a three million-dollar budget.''

Hogue scowled. "Where? In Montgomery? We need someone now."

"But Billie is a lab technician." I turned to the quiet, polite little man and explained, "Don't get me wrong. You're dynamite doing urine samples but have you ever applied for a Hill-Burton grant?"

"A what?"

"Or drawn up a budget?"

He shook his head.

"Or lobbied at the state capital for more hospital funds?"

Hogue raised his hand. "Don't let Dr. Stone scare you off, Billie. I'll be here to help. Why, Marshall Needham didn't know a dern thing about this job when he took over twelve years ago, but look how well he was doing until tonight. You'll get plenty of on-the-job training. Anytime you need advice, just come to me."

Billie wore the look of a soldier ordered first over the hill. "What about your private practice? When will you find time?"

"Never too busy to help in a crisis," Hogue boomed amicably.

I put my face in my hands and groaned out loud. Plain and simple, Carl Hogue was going to run the hospital, and was not going to be stopped. In my fatigue, moral questions reared like a cobra, a cobra wearing a stethoscope: could I walk out of here at daybreak leaving the fate of fifteen thousand people, fifty inpatients and three million dollars in the hands of a stuffy egomaniac who couldn't diagnose a simple case of appendicitis? A cobra spit in my eye while the board voted without dissent to appoint Hogue's lackey Billie Simmons, a timid 38-year-old lab technician with no ambition, administrative experience, or ambition for administrative experience, as the acting administrator of Trafford Memorial Hospital.

Harry Defoe summarized, "We've got that out of the way.

38

Now all that's left is the funeral for poor Marsh and Marie. Does anyone know when?''

No one knew for sure. Dan Satterwhite guessed three days, based on the usual length of time required by the Billings Funeral Home to repair accident victims.

I raised my hand. ''As most of you know, my name is Dr. Otis Stone. Mr. Needham hired me for two days only and tonight is my last night. At the risk of sounding crass, I'd like to find out whom I can consult about my paycheck so I can be on my way.''

Dan waved at Billie. ''There's your man. Fire away, Mr. Administrator.''

Billie's eyes widened. He looked helplessly to Hogue.

''Shame to see you go,'' Hogue rambled. ''Too bad you couldn't give this place a few months at least. But, we know you're a busy young fellow and Billie will be happy to get your check. Let's see, two nights at fifteen bucks an hour. Comes out to . . . $240.00.''

Billie was off the hook. ''Maybe Mrs. Holt can show me where the payroll checks are kept.''

Margaret Holt answered through a Kleenex tissue. ''Marshall took them home tonight to sign them.''

Shelly Farmer informed the board that an object thought to be Needham's alligator briefcase was found in the smoldering remains of the administrator's car, burned beyond salvage.

''Does that mean we don't get paid for tonight's meeting?'' wondered Dan Satterwhite.

''It means the whole damn staff doesn't get paid until we can order new checks,'' Mrs. Holt said bitterly.

''What about me?''

Harry Defoe was not helpful. ''It wouldn't matter, Dr. Stone. Trafford regulations specify that employees other than full-time staff must be paid by a special voucher signed by the administrator. Full-time staff are paid by computer checks validated with a facsimile signature.''

''Sure you aren't a banker, Harry?'' Hogue grumbled. ''What are you trying to say, anyway?''

"I'm trying to say Dr. Stone cannot be paid by this hospital until we have a bona fide, elected full-time administrator to succeed Marshall Needham. That's all," said the farmer.

"When can I get my money?" I asked, bracing for the bad news.

Satterwhite said, "The county commission meets a week from Tuesday. At that time, candidates for Marshall's job will be nominated. On the following Wednesday, ten days from today, this board will meet again to vote on the commission's nominations."

"I can't wait that long," I cried. "I've got a family emergency back in Washington and I've promised to be home in two days."

Harry Defoe and the other board members were properly sympathetic, as was Carl Hogue, who wanted me gone as soon as possible. "I'll tell you what," he said generously. "I'll pay you the $240 myself and the hospital can reimburse me later."

But before the suggestion could be approved, judicious Harry Defoe had raised yet another hospital regulation prohibiting such a sloppy transaction. Carl Hogue cursed under his breath and for once our sentiments enmeshed perfectly, both of us desiring my immediate departure from Grady. Margaret Holt wailed, "How can either of you talk about money at a time like this? Ha, you call yourselves Christians. Give Dr. Stone his paycheck and good riddance."

It's nice to be loved. I briefly considered imparting to Mrs. Holt the earth-shaking scoop that I had not now or ever called myself a Christian, but I thought better of it. "The money is going to Melvin Dryden anyway," I said. "Couldn't you just forward my paycheck to his garage?"

"Good idea," Harry brightened.

Satterwhite was not so enthusiastic. "I'm sorry, Dr. Stone, but that still won't help you."

I trembled. "How do you mean?"

"When Melvin heard about his uncle's death . . . well, he's very, very upset. He went off to be by himself."

40

"And?"

"He closed down the garage for a week."

"What?"

"I saw the wreath on the gas pump."

"My car is locked in there!"

"Yep, saw that too. Green Dodge, isn't it?"

Satterwhite managed a feeble apology. "We'll compensate you for your time, of course." The other board members looked startled. "What I mean," Dan fumbled, "is that if you want to keep working in the emergency room for the next ten days or so, we'll be glad to have you. Why, then you'd have a nice little nest egg to take home."

Disconsolate, I dragged myself out of the conference room as Harry Defoe and Benjamin Turlington, the grocer, bid on the 200-pound hog donated to the hospital by Hollis Rhodes earlier that evening. Harry won, left a personal check for thirty dollars at the cashier's window and took the pig home on its leash.

I sagged down the ramp outside the E.R. Shelly Farmer sat next to me. "If Marshall Needham were still alive, I'd kill him for doing this to me," I remarked. I talked at length of my obsession for leaving the county, my black fear that Carl Hogue would transform Trafford into a personal monument, my outrage that a milquetoast lab technician should be selected as the acting administrator. She listened dispassionately and took my hand.

"What do you care?" she said finally. "You're leaving."

"Am I? When? How? I'm beginning to think there's a conspiracy to keep me here, to make me suffer the comedy of rural medicine so I'll yearn for some big city med center."

"Jesus, Otis, you act like this place is the last stop on the way to hell. It wouldn't be that bad, you know. Think about all that money earmarked for the hospital. Two million dollars."

I could not stifle a sardonic laugh.

"Bénbow Hutchinson will not live forever," Shelly said.

"He's off to a pretty good start. Besides, that money won't change Carl Hogue or Lee Bob Parker or the hospital board."

"For once I agree with you, if you'll let me be the cynic just once. We do need changes. We need young doctors to make those changes. New blood, if you'll pardon the expression."

"And what exactly is your interest?" I asked her. "You are going off to be a corporate lawyer next spring. Don't lecture me about running away because that's just what you're doing. Remember, I'm a foreigner in these parts. I've got no obligation here. But you, you're home-grown and that makes you accountable."

She lowered her eyes. "Guilty as charged."

Abjectly I launched into a cruel discourse about Trafford, the furniture in ruins, the X-ray equipment straight from Army surplus, the unprofessionalism of Lee Bob Parker, the god-like aloofness of Carl Hogue, the overcrowding, the faulty television, no paper towels in the men's room—in short anything I could think of. It was very dramatic, but largely an exercise in self-pity.

"You finished?" Shelly asked with a knowing smile (I never am quite sure what it is they are knowing).

"Let me tell you something," she said. "This may be a ratty little hospital but the people here still deserve better. How are they ever going to find it without more young, qualified physicians?"

"Whoa. I've had my degree only one year and you're coming on like I'm Albert Schweitzer. Let's wait awhile for the Nobel Prize."

Shelly leaned close. "I'll tell you a secret. When Hollis Rhodes brought in his pig I heard him raving to Mrs. Holt about you. He called you 'The Miracle Man' just because you cured his gout. To Hollis, that was five years of pain gone. There are hundreds of Hollis Rhodes out there, Otis. Some have never been to any doctor."

I shuddered. "And some have had the misfortune of seeing Lee Bob Parker."

Shs shrugged. "They trust him, like I say. It's the old story. How do you teach Faulkner to a person who's spent his whole life reading Mickey Spillane?"

42

"Uh?"

"You get my drift. Here's another tip: Hogue heard about Hollis' gout and the way you fixed him up. Needless to say, he was unimpressed. But he's no idiot, Otis. He's scared. You're eating into his constituency. You're a threat and that's why he wanted you gone. Consider it a compliment from the 'best doctor in southern Alabama.' "

I winced. "Do you believe that?"

"He's very good. No matter what you think." She smiled and tugged at my arm. "What are you going to do?"

"Break into Melvin's garage and get my car."

"Good luck."

The sun was rising and it cast an orange blanket of warm light over the damp green and brown hills of Grady County. I yawned mightily and asked Shelly what she thought I should do.

"Stay. Please. At least till you get your car back legally."

"Where?"

"There's a vacancy at the HEW apartments where I live. It's about two miles from here. You can ride to work with me since we both work the werewolf shift."

Insanity was closing in; Shelly's proposition sounded inviting. Certainly it was a cozy improvement over ten days on a cot in the hospital. Still, my disappointment over the latest delay was clouding any thought of a future in Grady County: I wanted fervently to go.

"What was that family emergency you were talking about at the board meeting? Or is that too personal?" Shelly inquired.

"A dear friend of mine, a very dear friend, is suffocating," I said wryly. "His survival depends absolutely on my getting out of here."

"Cute," said Shelly, unamused. "What are you going to do now?"

I stood up and stretched. "Make a phone call."

"Tell your wife I said hello," she said, retreating to her lawbooks.

I staggered down to a pay phone at the shopping center

43

and phoned my parents in Washington, where it was eight-thirty and too early to talk of disasters.

"This is the Miracle Man," I told my father, explaining the bizarre catastrophe that was miring me in Grady for another week. "What would you say if I were to take a cab to Montgomery and catch a flight back to Washington."

Groggily, "What for? Your mother and I are leaving for St. Petersburg tomorrow."

I had forgotten the biannual Stone family pilgrimage to Florida's Gulf Coast mecca for the aged. "Could you pick me up along the way?" I begged. "I could use a change of scenery."

"Sure, if you don't mind sharing a motel room with Fred Goldman."

Freddy Goldman was my mother's brother—or so he claimed; I have yet to see legal evidence of this—and the most witless, obnoxious man I've ever encountered. Fred is at once boring and revolting, insulting and vacuous. He was the only calamity, besides another date with Harold Solomon's sister, that I rated worse than ten days in southern Alabama. I grappled with my options, then backed down.

"Thatta boy," my father encouraged. "This is likely to be the challenge of your lifetime, Otis. I'm proud of you. Why, ten days at this Trapper Hospital is probably worth three years of medical school. Think of these next few days as an education."

"Well, the campus architecture is 1940 Moonshine, very distinct," I said.

"Don't be sarcastic, son," he scolded.

"See you in two weeks," I said drily. "Have a good time in Sun City."

"Fine. And don't worry about your mother. I'll explain everything," said my father with a nervous laugh. "Otherwise, she'll probably think you were burned up at a White Citizen's rally."

THE NEXT DAY LEON, COREY AND DIANE DEPARTED.
Out of patience, out of dope and out of favor with the local constabulary, they caught a ride back West with an unemployed Knoxville couple heading out to California.

I envied them. I watched the old station wagon roll away from the shopping center and actually found myself fighting a very real urge to hop on the rear bumper. It sped up when it reached Highway 80 and Leon stuck his head out a window and raised his right arm in a clenched fist salute.

"Alone in Alabama. It could be the title of a Sam Peckinpah movie." That had been Leon's final observation before pressing his cherished glass hash pipe into my hands and saying, "I want you to have this, Doc." He fought back tears, doubtlessly for his prized pipe and not for having to bid goodbye to his chauffeur. I thanked him for the gesture, even though I suspected his intentions were less than altruistic: possession of narcotics paraphernalia would be just one more ugly charge to run from.

After they drove off, I made a furtive trip to the Boy Scout campgrounds to check for damages. The only legacy was a mountain of Budweiser cans. I disposed of them and returned to my modest, musty one-bedroom efficiency in the HEW apartments where Shelly Farmer lived. I was on the third floor and had a clear view of every clothes line on the project. I shared the flat with a pair of cockroaches and we got along famously; they kept to themselves and rarely went out. The only real problem was adjusting to life in a private apartment

45

after four weeks of automobile living and emergency rooms. Life in Grady Gardens, as the project was cleverly named, was noisier than any emergency room. Children acted out various war crimes with each other on the stairways; wives and husbands screamed invectives over dinner; teenagers drag-raced through the parking lot. At least the inhabitants of the commune were animated; back at the hospital, the staff was still recovering from Marshall Needham's death.

I was not exempt, even though I had only known the man for two days. "I don't really know what I'm mourning for," I complained to Shelly.

"Just look aggrieved," she advised.

Two thousand weeping Grady Countians turned out for the graveside ceremony. Melvin Dryden was not among them.

"He's on a hunting trip," Dan Satterwhite confided. "Whenever he gets real upset he just packs up his truck and heads for the woods. He'll be back when he's over it."

"When will that be? He's got my car locked up in that garage." Dan shrugged. "Grief is a difficult thing to measure. I 'spect Melvin will be back as soon as he finds peace with himself, or an eight-point buck deer—whichever comes first."

Reverend Jimmy Bullock, a red-faced ox of a man, forgave Melvin almost immediately. "Some men find a deeper faith with nature than they do in church," Jimmy told the solemn mourners. "Of course, Melvin is a Baptist, but sometimes even that don't help."

Margaret Holt was taking Needham's death very hard, as was the entire 35-member staff of Trafford Memorial. "When are we gonna get paid?" was an oft-heard lament. The new checks were slow in coming; the stamp company was taking interminably long to produce Billie Simmons' facsimile signature, almost as long as it usually took Billie to produce the real thing.

The morbidity of the place made me seek refuge and companionship with Shelly, or so I told her; it was as good an excuse as any. We shared many meals in her second-story apartment, and in return for her generosity I promised her a seven-course dinner at the most lavish restaurant in Montgomery. "I don't like cafeterias," she protested. I was heartened when she finally accepted my bachelorhood.

On Wednesday, three days after Needham's accident and one week before the board was to select a new hospital administrator, San Jose City Hospital phoned Trafford to talk with their new resident. I spoke to Earl Halberstam, the chief of medicine.

"How soon do you need me?"

"It's very iffy right now," he said. "We're waiting for one of our residents to leave. He's more or less postponed his departure. Can you be here in January?"

"Six months? I was ready to start next week."

Even over the phone, I could sense Halberstam's embarrassment. He cleared his throat. "Dr. Stone, you know how long these immigration things can take. They drag on and drag on."

"Immigration?"

"Maybe I'd better explain. The doctor you're replacing is Juan Jiminez, from Sao Paulo, Brazil. For two years now, the government has been trying to deport him. I don't know why, but it has something to do with a cousin getting arrested up in San Francisco. Anyway, we hired him about six months ago because he's a good doctor."

"And now you think he'll be deported?"

"No!" Halberstam quickly replied. "Absolutely not. Some Latin American civil rights group has hired a top-notch lawyer and he's got the government so tangled up in its own red tape, it'll never get loose."

"So where do I come in?"

"When Jiminez leaves, you take his place."

I figured I must have missed something.

Halberstam said, "See, Jiminez wants to leave, but they won't give him a visa. He has a girl back in Brazil and he wants to open a practice there."

"Let me get this straight: he wants to leave but he doesn't want to be deported?"

"Right. And the government won't give him a visa be-

47

cause he's been fighting deportation so hard. The bureaucrats said it will be six months before he can get visa clearance.''

''But you're sure I've got the job.''

''Absolutely,'' Halberstam roared. ''Be here in January. Eh, I bet you're anxious to get back to the big city and practice real medicine.''

''Oh sure. But, what am I going to do for the next six months?''

Halberstam laughed. ''Sounds to me like you're doing it.''

Carl Hogue overheard the conversation about Dr. Jiminez, ''Those idiots in Washington,'' he said angrily, gesturing in the general direction of the capital. ''They can't do anything right. Look how they messed up Medicaid!''

''What's the answer?'' I asked in my best Voice of the Pupil.

''They don't pay me to find the answers. That's what politicians are paid for,'' Hogue snapped. ''They pay me to heal.''

''Who pays you?''

Hogue frowned. ''They pay me. They. You know, the people. Don't be such a wiseass.''

At eight p.m. Shelly and I were watching a medical show on television; the plot was intriguing. A brilliant surgeon (is there any other kind?) with a family of four finally admitted his transexuality and asked the big urban medical center to perform the necessary operations.

''What would happen if he worked at Trafford?'' I asked Shelly.

''Oh, we'd send him to Birmingham. Any time we have anything we can't handle we just refer it to Birmingham.''

Just as the fictional (and properly offended) hospital board was meeting to consider the controversial request, Mrs. Holt bounded into the quarters. ''Dr. Stone, we've got a couple gunshot wounds out here. Better hurry.''

Shelly straightened up. ''Gunshot wounds? How did I miss them? Did they call an ambulance? My boss will be furious.''

The two victims lay on stretchers on opposite sides of the

48

main corridor. One was a teenaged boy who obviously was in great pain; he had a rapid heart rate and his blood pressure was falling. His parents fretted over him and held his hands as he cried out. I ordered some painkiller and started IV fluids. "Call your father," I barked at Buster. Borrowing a line from prime-time. I added, "Tell him this is stat."

The other victim was an older man in his sixties who lay on his stomach, hands tucked under his chin, and breathed heavily. "Where you been, Doc?" he grunted. His wife looked up from her *Reader's Digest* and smiled pleasantly.

"What happened to you?' I asked. "You didn't get in a shoot-out with that boy over there?"

The teenager's parents flashed me an indignant glance.

"Naw," laughed the old man. "Just a friendly little poker game, that's all. Drew three aces to a pair and raked in thirty dollars."

"You got shot for thirty bucks?"

"Well, maybe slightly more than thirty. Ha, Howard Bankhead threw in the keys to his brand new John Deere! Ha!"

I ordered X-rays of both the boy and the poker player, and told Mrs. Holt to prep for surgery. Buster reported that his father (contacted by phone) was not at all happy. "He was in the middle of a television show, but he said he'd be on his way."

I asked the old man, Demus Williams, if he wished to press charges. "Against Howard? Lord! No, Doctor. Howard's a good boy. He just lost his temper, that's all. Ain't the first time a man's lost his temper, now is it?"

Lucy and Dale Benton, the parents of the teenaged victim cornered me. "Jake has been hit real bad," Dale said, his face drawn and gray. "He's lost a lot of blood. Do you think he's going to be all right?"

"What kind of gun was used?"

"A .22 rifle. It happened during target practice behind the church."

"At night?"

"Every Wednesday. Jake was the best shot in his whole

49

Youth Group. But tonight the lights went out and one of the kids squeezed one off by mistake. Caught Jake right in the leg.''

Carl Hogue arrived in time to view the X-rays of both victims. "This one is very serious," he announced over Jake Benton's. He examined the boy, palpating the groin to find the arterial pulsations. "The bullet has hit the femoral artery so we'll have to operate. Damn shame. Kid might lose part of that leg."

I pointed to the skeletal image of Demus Williams. Hogue shook his head. "This is a puzzler. He said he was shot once? I can count seven separate slugs." He pointed on the X-ray to various white blemishes, apparently the iron relics of past poker games. "Go find the entry wound," he ordered. "Use a paper clip on the outside to mark it. That way we'll be able to see it on the new X-rays."

While Jake Benton was prepped for surgery by the duty nurses, Hogue and I scrubbed together. As we suited up he made it abundantly clear my tasks would be minimal. "Not that you're incompetent," he stressed, "it's just that you are inexperienced and new and . . ."

"You don't want Trafford liable for any of my screw-ups."

He tied his cap on. "If you want to put it like that."

Only his marble-hard iridescent green eyes were visible after his face was masked in surgical blue, so it was difficult identifying Hogue's expression. I narrowed it down to either scorn or condescension. I feigned resentment, but secretly was overjoyed not to be burdened by the responsibility. I appreciated Hogue's discretion even more after we got Jake Benton on the operating table when the decision to amputate was made. For the first time since we met, I admired Hogue's judgment and composure. "Stone," he said, "we're going to have to take it off above the knee."

It was not posed as a question, but still he waited after saying it. I nodded agreement. "It looks like the bullet has severed the femoral artery."

His work was flawless. I expected clumsiness and I witnessed fluidity. He tied the stump neatly, only forty-five minutes after the operation had begun.

Next in line was Demus Williams. We could hear the old gambler's voice rise as Buster wheeled him in. "I don't want no gawd-damned anesthetic. I wanna be wide awake. You hear me?"

The second set of X-rays showed the bullet was not in deep, situated about six inches below the old man's right shoulder blade. Hogue decided on a local anesthesia, but Demus caught the drift of our talk and protested louder. "I don't want none! I can take the pain, Doc. I'm strong as Muhammed Ali! Don't give me no painkillers."

Hogue signalled for the xylocaine so I diverted Demus with idle talk. "How many times you been shot?" I asked him.

"Why, this is the only time," he huffed. "Lord, this young fella must think I'm some kind of criminal. Demus is a law 'biding citizen. I ain't never been shot before."

"I don't know how to tell you, Demus, but I think someone else must have shot you, too," Hogue said. "Because here I am looking at a .38-caliber slug in your shoulder blade and not two inches away is another one. How do you figure that?"

Demus tightened his eyes in concentration. "Hmmm! I suppose I was shot and just nobody ever told me about it. Like I said, I'm real strong. I probably just didn't feel it, Doc."

As they wheeled out the crusty old cardplayer, I asked Hogue if he'd ever seen him before. "Nope," he answered coldly. "That's Lee Bob Parker's patient." He started stripping off his blues. "Don't know how that bastard could overlook six gunshot wounds."

Hogue went home without another word. Demus Williams was discharged two hours later after cursory observation, but Jake Benton was sent to Intensive Care. Intensive Care actually was nothing more than a regular hospital room with an outdated cardiac unit, an oxygen tent in mothballs, rare venetian blinds that closed completely and twice the daily rate of other rooms—all this presumably made it the best seat in the house, and thus, Intensive Care.

The stuffiness of the operating room forced me to seek fresh air outside the E.R. Shelly followed and sat down on the rear bumper of the ambulance. "I can't get over it," she repeated. "Two gunshot victims and neither one takes an ambulance to the hospital. See what happens when the economy slackens?"

Suddenly we were aware of a muffled, rhythmic noise emanating from the ambulance. "Shelly," I asked hesitantly. "You, you didn't forget anybody in there, did you?"

I stood up and walked around to the side of the wagon, but the noise was blocked by curtains drawn tight over the narrow horizontal windows. The noise continued, unabated. I said in a half-whisper, "What in the hell is going on in there?"

Shelly rose off the bumper and started back indoors, "Come on, Otis. I don't really think you want to know."

I held up my hand for silence. Back and forth, rolling and squeaking and moaning. Then a human noise I decided was either a grunt of discomfort or a small squeal of delight.

"Scandalous," I said. "What could that be?"

"Take a wild guess," Shelly said impatiently.

"I know! The Catholic Women's League is playing bingo in there. Oh, I bet the D.A.R. kicked them out of the lodge tonight."

I put my ear to the van and whistled. "Maybe it's a roller derby for midgets." Shelly yanked me away. "It's Buster," she admitted. "It's Buster and the new clerk from the drug store."

How original. I scolded myself for having given up on Buster as an incurable simpleton. Some day that young man might make a million bucks, I thought admiringly, writing the lascivious memoirs of his exploits as a hospital orderly.

Shelly and I quietly backed away. "Don't you mind?" I inquired. "I mean, you're the one that has to drive that thing."

She was surprisingly sympathetic to Buster's plight. "He's

got to work from six p.m. to two a.m. When his buddies are in the back seat, Buster's here at the hospital cleaning bedpans. The poor guy earns his . . . sport. Sure, it's kinky, but so what? Buster digs it."

"Apparently he's not the only one."

We were interrupted when Margaret Holt bolted through the double doors. "You got a call, Shelly. Probably heart attack."

"Get Dan. He's asleep in the waiting room." Her eyes were aglow. "Finally some excitement. The boss really gets rankled if we go a whole night without one client, eh, patient."

"Business is business," I shrugged. "Now, what about Buster?"

Shelly snapped her fingers. "I almost forgot." She banged on the side of the ambulance. "Buster, wrap it up in there. We got a call. Hurry up, you've got about fifteen seconds."

From inside came moans and curses punctuated by the dull crack of knees and elbows against steel. Finally, the rear gate doors opened ever-so-slowly. Ever chivalrous, Buster climbed down first so he could hold the girl's hand while she struggled out of the ambulance. "A true knight," I complimented. He smiled weakly, straightened his pants and walked back into the emergency room.

"See what I mean?" Shelly whispered. "Doesn't he look desperately lonely?"

Dan Dilborn clumped out of the E.R. and hoisted himself into the cabin. Shelly hopped into the driver's seat and gunned the hungry engine.

"Wait! Let me give you the address," Mrs. Holt shouted over the din. I detected a macabre cheeriness, a sense of suppressed morbid gladness in Margaret Holt's crow-like helpfulness.

"Four-thirty Melon Drive," Mrs. Holt said. Her eyes met Shelly's and Shelly let the ambulance idle.

In a schoolgirl's angelic voice, the pretty driver repeated, "Forty-four Melon Drive."

Mrs. Holt nodded and seemed to stifle a giggle. With obvious difficulty, she managed to regain her Marine sergeant's timbre. "Hurry up!" she commanded the ambulance crew.

"This could be it," Shelly said, shifting into first gear. "Let's go, Danny boy!" The tires cried briefly and the ambulance sliced through the fog. Its red roof lights winked down the highway.

I turned to Mrs. Holt for an explanation. "Why all the good cheer? What's so funny about a heart attack?"

Dreamily, the veteran nurse listened to the fading siren. At the sound of my voice she snapped back to form. "Nothing! Of course, heart attacks are terrible. Leading killer of men over forty-five."

I agreed. "I could have sworn you and Shelly were sharing some kind of happy secret a minute ago."

"Not at all. Heart attacks are very sad, that's all," she said. "Especially when they hit the old-timers like Benbow Hutchinson."

SOME DOCTORS SEEM TO HAVE A SIXTH SENSE
about death. They seem instinctively to know, by a glance or
a sniff or a touch of the hand, when a patient becomes a
former patient. They seem to know when life-saving mea-
sures will waste money and emotions.

I do not pretend to have this ability, instinct, or whatever
sensitivity it might be called. But when I saw Benbow Hutchinson that night I was certain he was dead. His face was a
dismal bluish hue, his eyes were half-open and his jaw
dropped like a tired hound dog's. Dressed in wrinkled pajamas, he lay limp on the stretcher save for one gray-knuckled
hand which gripped a copy of the *National Enquirer*.

Shelly stood over him. "He's dead," she decided.

I checked Benbow's pupils—which were equal and reac-
tive to light—and listened for his breathing, which was shal-
low and labored but nonetheless encouraging in that it was,
after all, a small sign of life. I astounded myself by saying,
"He's still with us."

Shelly shook her head. "You're always such a pessimist,"
she muttered. "Now, all of a sudden, you think you can bring
back the dead."

"I don't think he's dead. I can't get a pulse or a blood
pressure, but I swear he's breathing." I leaned close to his
chest and in an instant realized Benbow was indeed "with
us." It became obvious when he wheezed into my ear, "Get
my nitro."

No one had bothered to clue me in. Benbow suffered from

angina pectoris, and his attack was probably not the full-fledged myocardial infarction—heart attack—that Mrs. Holt had indicated in her alert. Benbow had heart disease, to be sure, and one day it would undoubtedly be the death of him. But not tonight. We put him on Digoxin and started intravenous medications. Within minutes, his breathing deepened. Even Shelly admitted he was alive. She and Margaret crept off, whispering about something.

"Thanks, Doctor," Benbow said weakly. "I thought this was it. The minute the pain hit me I thought it was all over."

I held his hand. "Why didn't you take some nitro at home?"

He smiled wanly from the stretcher. "My housekeeper saw me grab at my chest. She's new, you know, not used to these things. Naturally she was scared. Called the hospital and told 'em I was dying." He paused to inhale laboriously.

"Anyway, she threw a blanket over me and before I knew it she was telling me to shut up and rest. I tried to tell her where the medicine was but she wouldn't listen. Then the ambulance came and I must have passed out."

"I want you to stay here overnight so we can keep an eye on you."

Benbow smiled in gratification. "That would be nice. I've always liked this place." His eyes roamed fondly, as if revisiting a favorite childhood haunt.

"You take it easy now," I cautioned. "No more excitement for the night. We'll get you checked in and tucked away."

"The regular room will be fine," Benbow said matter-of-factly.

"What?"

"Forty-seven is my regular room. The one with the lovely view of Gresham Pond. Some days I can even see the bass hitting out there."

I checked the charts and found an expectant mother camped in Benbow's precious room. He was crestfallen at the news. "That's my favorite room, dadgummit," he whined, eyeing me uncertainly. "You must be new around here. Have you heard about my will?"

"A little," I acknowledged.

"Heard about all the money I'm going to give this fine old place when I die?"

"It sounds very generous."

Benbow sighed. "It's the least I can do. Trafford means a lot to me. I brought my Daddy here the day he died. That's what he wanted. He knew the Squire real well. They was like brothers."

"Trafford?"

"Himself. He was quite an old boy. I met him once or twice."

Mrs. Holt interrupted. "Benbow, you know better than to talk Dr. Stone's ear off. You've got to get some rest. We're going to give you more medicine and put you to bed."

Benbow would not be swayed. "How can I sleep when I'm not in forty-seven?" he fussed. "I could rest a whole lot better looking out at Gresham's Pond." When a man is eighty-seven and suffering from heart disease, a discussion of such magnitude qualifies as a heated argument. But, as Benbow's impatience bubbled into anger, his face never reddened, but remained the greenish-blue husk it had been during the attack. I would later find out this was Benbow's natural skin coloration.

"How about if we check you into room forty-five," Mrs. Holt bargained. "It's got a very pleasant view."

"It's too drafty. I hate drafts. Might catch pneumonia." The head nurse finally caved in. "Well, maybe Mrs. Welch won't mind moving down the hall," she said, trotting off to make the necessary arrangements. Whether Mrs. Welch minded or not would not be a factor, I suspected. Benbow was the closest thing to a VIP of whom Grady could boast and room forty-seven apparently was the Presidential Suite.

I checked Benbow one more time, found his blood pressure normal and pulse regular. He reported happily that the pain had disappeared, and dozed contentedly until Mrs. Holt came for him. Then he awakened, and objected testily when she tried to confiscate his *National Enquirer*.

Shelly watched as Margaret wheeled the old man down the corridor. "One of these days it'll be the real thing."

"And I bet you and Margaret will be delighted. Am I invited to the big celebration?"

"Otis! Don't be cruel. I like Benbow. Why, he's a grand old fellow. But, just think what two million dollars can do for this hospital! A new cardiac unit and a new X-ray machine . . . and a new surgical light in the operating room."

"I thought it was all going for a new wing."

Shelly shrugged. "That's what Needham always said. Marshall's the only one who actually saw the will. Except for Benbow's attorney."

"Then how do you know the old man's got it?"

She stared at me, stupefied, "Got what?"

"The money. The two million dollars."

"Of course he's got it!" she snapped. "The Hutchinsons own a whole bunch of steel mills up in the northern part of the state. Benbow's father was a millionaire, and Benbow was his only child. I'm sure the legacy was passed on."

I laughed. "From what I understand, his medical bills could chew up that fortune real fast. I heard he's in the hospital every month."

Shelly smiled, "Benbow doesn't have to worry about medical bills. It doesn't cost him a penny for treatment here at Trafford Memorial. The county picks up the whole tab."

"What?"

Shelly explained, to my disbelief, Benbow's nifty medical deal. Ten years earlier, when the news of the old man's intended largess traveled the Grady political circuits, several of Benbow's friends got together and "suggested" to the county commission that Benbow, because of his generosity, be exempt from paying any medical bills incurred at Trafford and not covered by insurance. He was felt to merit Carte Blanche treatment, or so the commissioners agreed, because all that beautiful steel money was earmarked for the hospital coffers. At the time the deal was cemented, Benbow was already seventy-seven and regularly ill; no one seriously expected him to live past eighty.

"I've never heard of such a thing," I told Shelly. "It sounds like Benbow has already taken a good measure of his donation out in trade. It sounds like he intends to use the money as a sort of C.O.D. payment for all the hospital bills he'll probably run up while he's still alive."

"He's made good use of the place," she admitted. "That's why some of the folks in Grady are getting impatient. They want to see some of that money." She paused long enough to inject a note of innocence. "Of course, we would never let him expire. I mean, we've got to try our best to save his life."

"Then why did it take you thirty minutes to make a four-block ambulance run to Benbow's estate?"

Shelly was unnerved by my persistent suspicions. She mumbled something about "heavy traffic" and retreated to the ever-present lawbooks. I spent the remainder of the evening thumbing through an old *McCall's* and watching Johnny Carson.

When our shift ended, Shelly left for the housing project without me. I bummed a ride with Margaret Holt, who bored me with the story of her brother's latest endeavor at the Rodeway Inn—a Parisian girlie revue—and then had the gall to charge me two bucks for "mileage."

The hospital sulked for an entire week. Collectively and individually, the staff was glum and ill-tempered, even when payday finally arrived. It seemed the only antidote to the grief of Marshall Needham's death was Benbow Hutchinson's death, which was once again safely out of the realm of immediate possibility. Thanks to medical science. Carl Hogue tried to cheer up his legion. "His condition is worsening," he assured them. "It's only a matter of time." The day of Benbow's release had been joyous for the old man's guilt-ridden housekeeper, but lugubrious for the Trafford rank-and-file. Dreams of a new two-million-dollar addition seemed to blur even more when I handed several hefty bottles of nitro to Benbow: a few third-level employees refused to speak to me after that.

The county commission met the following Tuesday. It drew up a list of three nominations for the hospital administrator post. One name belonged to William E. Anderson, a middle-aged fellow with a dozen years in the administrative end of hospital management. He flew in from Mobile to size up Trafford. "Rustic, isn't it?" he said tightly. "But I like it." He inquired about the budget, the salary, the staff, the bed capacity and the proximity of the nearest country club. After one hour with Dan Satterwhite, Anderson decided to accept the position; it took the board a mere fifteen minutes to approve his selection.

The other two names on the list of nominees were Billie Simmons and, incredibly, Margaret Holt. Margaret was distraught when she learned of the board's final choice. "I fixed all of them a barbecued chicken dinner last Sunday," she cried. "I can't believe I didn't get a single vote."

"Maybe the drumsticks were tough," I suggested in a helpful tone.

Billie Simmons was not so content to let Anderson's selection pass without public comment. "Aren't we even going to vote on the other nominees?" he demanded at the meeting. In his previous existence as a humble lab technician, Billie Simmons would never have braved so much as a sneeze at such a high-level conclave. But as acting administrator his ego had swollen. In fact, Billie had acquired something of a loyal following within the hospital. Unfortunately for him, this loyal following was markedly absent from the board meeting. Billie's question was politely ignored as the bureaucrats moved on to consider the "new business" side of the agenda.

Melvin Dryden still had not returned from his hunting trip, and I was beginning to worry that his body might never be recovered. One night I actually tried to jimmy the heavy sliding door, just to visit my car, but I failed to budge it and broke my pocket comb in the process.

"You're stuck here for a while. Make the best of it," Shelly counseled. "You're getting three meals a day, a decent salary and a little female companionship. What more could you ask for?"

"A great salary and constant female companionship."

"Come on," she said. "I'm beginning to like you. You're very . . . interesting. Smart."

"Really?" I grimaced. "And all this time I was considering having myself committed to a home for the retarded."

It was about this time, two weeks after my arrival in Grady, that I began receiving mysterious mail from Miami, Washington and elsewhere. Carl Hogue opened the first letter "by accident" and conveyed his sympathy. "Life must be difficult with relatives like yours," he said.

It was a short, tear-stained note from my well-meaning but misguided mother, vacationing in St. Petersburg. Enclosed was a postcard picture of a red tide epidemic in Tampa Bay.

"I am having trouble on Tuesdays," she began cryptically. "Tuesdays, as you know, are bridge days here at the club. And bridge days mean a lot of chatting with Mrs. Hughes, Mrs. Heilman and Rose Menninger. They have been dying to know about your career which, up to this most recent episode, seemed to impress them.

"I told them you were in Alabama and, of course, they thought I was joking. Rose cackled, 'Alabama? Gee, I hope they taught Otis how to speak Alabamian while he was at Stanford.' But I defended you, son, and explained to the ladies how you were staying only because they needed some help reorganizing the hospital management. Isn't that right?

"At any rate, don't worry about me. You're the one in trouble. I can handle Rose Menninger and even Irv the butcher. Irv was slicing some knockwurst the other day and he made some wisecrack about 'rednecks' or 'redlegs' or something. Well, I set him straight in a hurry! No son of mine will be maligned behind his back. You remember the tough time we had when Benjie went into the shoe business?

"Otis, when are you leaving Alabama? Give me a clue why you have decided to stay, if you have. Give me some ammunition for Tuesdays. I am not so strong as I used to be.''

The next day I got a letter from my sister Elizabeth, a psychiatrist in Santa Monica. She lives with a fellow who once played linebacker for the Los Angeles Rams, owns three Siamese cats, smokes dope with some of her patients, and in her opinions about politics generally preaches to the left of Abbie Hoffman. I like her tremendously, but I hardly recognized the letter:

"Mother is very upset, as you know. I cannot say I really blame her, Otis. She was ill-prepared for this latest adventure of yours, such as it is. You and I have always been able to talk freely—remember after my first date with Peter Baines? I came into your bedroom and told you about his appendectomy scar and you nearly got sick.

"So tell me, Otis, is there a reason for staying in Alabama? A deep reason? Perhaps you are striking back at Mom and Dad. I realized they were strict with you, but don't you think this kind of counterreaction is a little too stringent? Did they do something to make you angry? Remember the time they made you go to summer camp in the Poconos and you came down with poison oak? Could the incident be in some way related?

"I like to think this is just a phase, like the psychosocial moratorium Erikson discusses. However, Otis, you understand my concern: Erikson was speaking to the point of adolescent traumas; at your age, a similar application would be stretching his theory. Don't you agree?

"But I know you must follow your conscience. I, too, am in a personal dilemma. How do I tell Mom and Dad about Brad? Mom opposes premarital cohabitation and Dad is a Redskins fan!

"Please do what you think is right, but hurry home before Mother has a nervous breakdown."

Two days later came a brown-paper package from my brother Benjamin, a shoe salesman in Newark. "Enclosed are the latest in Elton John platforms. If memory serves me, you are about five-ten in stockings. With these shoes you should stand at least six-two, and that's man enough for any farm girl or Southern belle you chance to meet down there in Wallace Country.

"Oh well, anything is better than Newark. I have taken to carrying a switchblade. Not for protection, but so I can split open my pockets when I see the muggers coming. It saves time, and they seem to appreciate the gesture.

"Mom and Dad tell me you're staying in Grady indefinitely. Something about your car being imprisoned by a deranged auto mechanic. I think you should be advised: Mother is praying for you at the temple and Dad is considering buying you another car so you can affect an escape. Dad sent a postcard from St. Pete and I got it yesterday. He won $57 at the dog track, and you'll be glad to know Freddy Goldman has been released from the hospital. Apparently those man o'wars can inflict a nasty burn. Especially in the groin."

IN THE APARTMENT WAS A SMALL COUNTER I USED for a table, bar, desk and ironing board. It was topped with aging formica and, except for a few magazines I smuggled in from the outside world, the counter was kept bare. Because of its many utilitarian functions it became the bedrock of the apartment. On rare pensive occasions, I would perch an old tan barstool, plant both elbows on the counter, sip half-heartedly on a can of Red, White and Blue beer, and meditate. The letters gave me something to think about.

For in addition to the aforementioned hints from my family, I received one day a somewhat disturbing, disjointed note from an old girlfriend in Coral Gables. We had dated during my internship at Jackson Memorial where she was a student nurse. From the outset our relationship had not been the stuff of which great soap operas are woven: I was lackadaisical, nonchalant to the point of forgetfulness and suffering from a condition she termed "overunderstanding;" she was more frisky, arduous, flirtatious and romantic. Besides the hospital, we had little in common except for my cat, whose name escapes me now but whose behavior I will never forget.

The cat was a tortoise-shell and turtle-brain. It slept only on street corners and after wild nightmares (involving, I suppose, great packs of starving dogs) would end up sprawled in the busy intersections of metropolitan Miami. For all its eccentricity, it was a durable old cat; it was hit three times, caused two other collisions and lived to meow about it.

Marie Duggan, the student nurse, ran over my cat one

morning on her way to the hospital. I will never as long as I live forget the sight of this gorgeous blonde in her white uniform crying outside my apartment, cradling in her lovely tan arms one stunned (but fully intact) feline. In fact the cat was slightly bruised and missing a patch of hair off its back, but otherwise it was in perfect condition and only the thespian in its animal soul prevented it from bounding out of Marie's warm arms and heading straight for the kitty litter.

"I'm so sorry," Marie sobbed. "I think I just killed your cat. I saw him in the highway but I figured he was already dead. Just as my car passed, he jumped up and ran into the side of it."

I assured her the cat would survive. "He's a pathological insomniac," I explained. "Highway noises are the only sounds that put him to sleep . . . oh, that's a bad choice of words."

Marie dabbed at her face. "I hope he'll be okay."

I flashed the cat a dirty look; it stared back with smug green-eyed innocence.

"I'm a mess," said Marie. "Can I freshen up here before I go to work?"

I assented without hesitation; at that early hour my motives were undoubtedly more chivalrous than lecherous and, fortunately, were never questioned. "Oh, you're a doll," Marie said.

And that is how we met. Later, when my internship ended and I readied for my hospital-visiting odyssey, Marie's perfume lingered on the collar of my medical jacket. She pressed for a commitment and when I balked she came up with her own: a twelve-dollar friendship ring and a classic "I'll wait for you" routine. In return, I promised her a steady correspondence about life in Middle America.

I wrote only once: it was a postcard from Topeka and it featured the fall harvest of wheat, "golden fields of grain to fuel a growing nation." I scribbled a brief note on the back: "Think of me with your next bowl of bran flakes. Love Otis."

My peripatetic schedule prevented Marie from wiring directly, so she kept in regular touch with my parents. Every week my father earnestly would attempt to appraise her of my whereabouts, only to be thwarted by my mother. My mother, who carried an almost religious aversion to nurses because of the "nonvirginal" esteem which they are so often held (or fondled or caressed), would lie about my trip. "He's in Vancouver," she told Marie one time. Two days later: "He's in Tacoma and heading south."

While the Stone family hibernated in St. Petersburg, Marie had somehow managed to get a call through to my father, who diligently reported my "grave situation" in Grady, Alabama. Marie's urgent letter arrived in a pink envelope with cherry-colored trim and a light aroma that brought back lurid memories of a moonlit Miami.

"Otis, I have tried to forget you, since I sometimes worry you have forgotten me. I tried to track you but everywhere I checked—Tacoma, Vancouver, Council Bluffs—no one heard of you. Have you been traveling under a presumed name?" (English courses have never been the bulwark of student nursing curricula.)

"I am concerned about our future," Marie continued. My eyes drifted off the letter, away from her handwriting, to begin examining the flecks of gold in the formica countertop. The word "future" had obviously triggered an emotional barrier. Ever since my arrival in Grady, pondering any aspect of the "future" had become an exercise in masochism.

"I have missed you terribly. I am trying to stay busy here at the hospital but the work does not solve my most immediate problem—seven straight Saturday nights without a date." At this juncture there was by virtue of an ellipse, a dramatic pause. I tried to let the last sentence sink in. It refused.

"I'm sorry if I sound upset. I am upset. You graduate from one of the top med schools in the country, intern at one of the top hospitals in the southeast, and then get marooned in some stinky southern town because your car is stuck in the shop! You expect me to believe that? When my parents asked about you the other night, I told them you were at Bellevue in New York. I said you'd be home as soon as they didn't need your help anymore. See what I've become? You're making a liar out of me. Please come home soon so we'll be together again."

"P.S. Your cat ran away and I'm just sick about it, honey. Maybe he's gone to look for you. I read a story like that in *National Enquirer* last month."

The letter is quoted in portion. There were other incidental minutiae: an anecdote about a prostate patient, concern over drug thefts in the hospital and further assurances she would be "faithful" during my absence.

I folded the letter and returned it neatly to its envelope. I set it on the counter squarely in front of me. I vowed to write her back with some hilarious stories about rural medicine. Maybe that would satisfy her until we could talk again. As for her faithfulness, the issue never crossed my mind. To my complete frustration, I failed to compose any sort of note diplomatically giving her the go-ahead to shed the manacles of our love. It was a job for Kissinger, or Abigail Van Buren, not I.

Shelly stopped by with some lettuce from the Winn Dixie. "It's green! I hardly recognize it," I marveled, holding the leafy sprout in one hand like a big softball. "This time I won't let it get so ripe."

"Try putting it in the refrigerator," Shelly said.

I pushed Marie Duggan's letter across the counter at her. "From brown lettuce to broken hearts: here, read this." The more I thought about Grady, the more indefensible became my staying another minute, but because I was so new at introspection, I wanted Shelly's reaction to the letter.

"She thinks you're letting her down," she said after reading the last paragraph. "She's saying, 'What's a nice doctor like you doing in a place like this?' " Shelly paused for my momentous reply. Hearing none, she badgered, "So what's the answer?"

"Easy. I'm waiting for Melvin Dryden to give me my car."

Shelly rolled her eyes. "That's bullshit and you know it.

67

You could have left two weeks ago and come back later for your precious car."

She was right. The love for my automobile was platonic at best and my hatred—or professed hatred—of Grady County was virulent. I had railed with great passion about the professional depravity at Trafford Memorial and made my desire to escape a well-known fact. So why hadn't I hopped a bus?

"You're not fooling me," Shelly declared. "You're getting to like it around here, aren't you?"

"You're crazy!" I snapped. "True, I am finding it almost bearable, and two weeks ago I would have said that impossible. But being bearable and enjoyable are two different things."

She shrugged.

Aloud I categorized the good aspects of working at Trafford. Money was the first: I was making far more than I could spend in the city of Grady. Experience was second. Shelly was the third: her company was always warm and we enjoyed being together. As a preoccupation I was second only to her lawbooks. In times of intimacy she liked to characterize our relationship as "aloof coziness" highlighted by "stimulating social intercourse."

We had one thing in common: a future which did not include Grady. Hers was the Vanderbilt law school; mine was San Jose City Hospital and a residency in internal medicine. I suppose what nagged at both of us was: What will happen here?

"If everyone felt like you did, there wouldn't be a decent rural hospital anywhere," Shelly remarked one night.

"Is there?"

"You complain about Dr. Parker and in the next breath you can't wait for San Jose and the bright lights of a decent operating room. That's hypocritical. At least Lee Bob Parker is here, giving these people some medical attention."

"That's a very generous description of his work," I sallied. "But you've got a point. Too bad all the old country doctors are dying off."

We had more discussions—some arguments, some harangues, some monologues—before eventually I decided to hell with Washington. In effect, thanks to Dr. Juan Jiminez and his deportation troubles, I had six months to kill so I figured I might as well do what I could for Trafford Memorial. Shelly was overjoyed, my mother was traumatized, my father was philosophical and the apartment cockroaches were distraught. Our symbiotic relationship had deteriorated badly: after a week of peaceful coexistence I had taken to mashing them as a means of easing the afternoon boredom.

William E. Anderson, the new administrator, was pleased at the news. "Marshall Needham would have been very happy to hear you say that, Dr. Stone."

"Oh? I didn't know you and Needham knew each other."

Anderson shifted. "Well, I feel like I know him. I mean, just sitting in his desk tells me something of the man. I know he appreciated your talent and would want a man like you on the staff here at Trafford."

"And Dr. Hogue?" I tested.

Anderson began to doodle abruptly with a felt-tip pen. "Well, I'm sure Dr. Hogue will be most happy to hear of your decision, but why don't you let me tell him? I'll be seeing him anyway this afternoon."

It had taken Anderson less than one week to inherit Marshall Needham's nervous sweat.

"Okay, you tell him." I feigned disappointment. "It's just that I know what his reaction will be. I'd love to see that look on his face."

Anderson smiled weakly. "Oh, yes. I can assure you Dr. Hogue will be absolutely surprised. It's not every day he gets a new partner."

Now it was my turn to sweat. "Partner?" I was suddenly beset by dark visions of sharing Hogue's antebellum brick office. In all my thoroughness when weighing the pros and cons of staying at Trafford, I had not considered it. In my magnanimous haste, I had failed to confront the most obvious question: Where would I practice medicine? I tried the most obvious alternative. "Can't I just work in the Emergency Room? As I told you, I'm leaving in January. No sense in changing Dr. Hogue's shingle for six short months.''

"Good point," Anderson mulled. "Of course, we don't have a staff position for a full-time emergency room physician. And I can't say I've ever seen a hospital this size that's had one. I'll have to check with the board about this.''

I appealed to the politician in him; administrators are usually frustrated campaigners. "Look at it like this: you're on the vanguard of a new trend in rural medicine: immediate emergency care. Instead of waiting for Hogue or Parker to show up in the E.R., you'll have a permanent doctor on duty there for eight hours a day. No more sending patients off to Montgomery or Birmingham when Hogue is out of town.''

Anderson brightened. "Hey, that's not a bad idea. I can go to the board with a proposal for a brand new position here at Trafford. We can call it 'emergency room physician.' I bet they'd go for it and I bet Dr. Hogue would, too. He is getting older, relatively speaking of course . . .''

"Of course.''

". . . and it isn't easy hopping out of bed every night when the hospital calls with a sore throat or a fender-bender. Yep, I think we've hit on something here. If it works here it could spread to other hospitals all over the state.''

It was impossible to anticipate the bureaucratic excitement with which Anderson accepted the suggestion. I shared his enthusiasm, for a permanent niche in the emergency room would save me from the retractable clutches of Carl Hogue, whom I knew would resist with embarrassing bluntness any partnerships with a young upstart like myself. As for me, I preferred the E.R. any day.

"I'm glad we had this talk," Anderson said gratefully. "This could be the perfect solution. All it takes is another slot in the budget. What are you making now?''

"Fifteen an hour.''

"Plumbers get more than that," he observed, jotting figures on a legal pad. "No sir, the board can't bitch about that. But . . . what do we do when you leave?''

"What else? Find another doctor!'' I answered impatiently. "Six months from today I will be in San Jose City Hospital. You've got my official notice on that."

Anderson lowered his voice. "Otis, the board doesn't like to spend money. You know that. I think they'll be amenable to this new E.R. job if we can guarantee a qualified physician to fill it. Can you help me out in this area? Maybe some of your friends from med school. . . ."

I shook my head vigorously. "You don't understand, Mr. Anderson. This place, no offense, is not exactly the dream residence of every doctor. My friends have sent my name into Ripley's Believe It or Not: 'Otis Stone, who graduated from Stanford Medical School second in his class, turned down several high-paying jobs in metropolitan hospitals to work in an emergency room in Grady, Alabama.' They think I'm a freak."

"So there's my problem," Anderson said glumly. "Who wants this job?"

"Maybe a local boy."

"Ha! From what I understand, the closest thing to a new doctor coming out of Grady is Buster Hogue, and it's a safe bet the closest he'll get to an M.D. degree is when he dusts the one hanging in his father's office. Otis, I need your help. I can stall that board. See if you can find someone who'd be willing to take over your job in six months."

"Oh, sure," I lied. "I'll get right on it tomorrow." Anderson exhaled happily. "Great! Now, just one more thing before you go. Did you examine Mr. Hutchinson before he was released the other day?"

"Of course I did."

"How does he look?"

"Terrible."

Anderson's features sharpened. "Oh?"

"He always looks terrible. If you're wondering about his health, it's pretty good for an eighty-year-old man with heart disease."

Anderson nodded and said nothing.

The next night was cause for celebration. Melvin Dryden

71

made a spectacular homecoming, escorted by Shelly Farmer in the ambulance. I was the first to greet him in the E.R.

"What happened to you?" I asked.

Bearded, smelly and obviously in great pain, Melvin still managed a spirited smile. "Shot my toe off," he said through his teeth. "I was camping about forty miles out of Selma when it happened."

"An accident?"

Melvin squinted at me. "Well, I damn sure didn't do it on purpose, Doc. I was dozing off one night when I felt this animal scuttlin' around my sleeping bag. I opened one eye and I could see it was a rat, damn near as big as a house cat. Well, I hate rats and I guess I panicked."

"So you grabbed the gun and shot at him."

Melvin nodded wearily. "Guess I was lucky. I do believe I could have lost my whole damn foot with that twenty-gauge."

"I'm sorry about your toe," I recited with professionalized regret.

"Aw, it's nuthin'. I got eight left." Melvin lay his head back down. "Say, I forgot all about your car. I'll get it for you first thing in the morning, Doc."

"No hurry," I replied, struggling to cut the remains of his hunting boot off his right foot.

Arriving back at the apartment after work, I sat down at the bare white counter and squashed a hefty cockroach in his tracks. I sent the corpse out to sea via the toilet and sat down again, this time to write Marie Duggan a letter. "I'm making good money and spending very little," I wrote. "I'm sorry if my being here has caused you some embarrassment at home. I do want to leave this place, really I do. But where else can I go? My sentence expires in six months, and then it's on to San Jose. Until then I will write—if you want me to. Don't worry about me. This place is not the jungle of ignorance you believe it to be. As for your faithful waiting, what can I say? I'd feel better if you started to date other men and I really wouldn't mind it if you indulged in a noncommital embrace now and then."

I reread it and ripped it up. Too apologetic, I decided. Marie would love it. She'd probably make a decoupage out of it and put it on her dresser. I started another letter. "Marie, Sorry to hear about my cat. He hasn't found his way up to Alabama yet and I don't think he will. He has no sense of direction, beyond knowing that his food dish is due east of the cat box. If you really want to find him I suggest you check the East-West Expressway. He's probably fast asleep at the 125th Street intersection. Love, Otis."

ONE NIGHT IN LATE AUGUST, SHELLY AND I TOOK A
break from the stuffy boredom in the E.R. It had been
an evening absolutely devoid of surprises: my contribution
was two tetanus shots, and Shelly's was two hundred pages
of tort law.

We went outside to ponder such weighty issues as the future of the New Orleans Saints football team. Shelly forecast
another last-place finish and I concurred. From the shadows,
twenty yards away where the ambulance was berthed, I discerned a muffled clamor.

"Ah, the call of the wild," I crooned. "Buster? Is that
you, son?"

Shelly scolded my thoughtless intrusion. "Let him be,
Otis. He's not hurting anybody."

"Give him time. In such cramped quarters a person could
really get bruised up."

"So what? He's got every first-aid gimmick known to man
at his fingertips. Bandages, splints, sutures, local anesthetic,
even oxygen. There's no better place than an ambulance for
high-risk sex."

"And how would you know?"

Shelly suppressed a smile. "None of your business."

I hate coy replies and I hated this one. I place coyness in
the same distasteful category as smugness and conceit. My
aversion to these tactics is one of the few chauvinistic traits
to which I will openly admit; however in this particular in-

stance, not wishing to kill a conversation with such tantalizing ramifications, I just played along.

"Oh?" I flashed an affected look of amazement at Shelly. "So you have experienced the joys of emergency fornication!"

"I said it was none of your business."

"I bet you've never tried it in a golf cart." I challenged.

Before she could answer, the headlights of an approaching car blinded us. A tan Mercedes hummed to a stop next to the grunting rescue wagon and a tall, sallow fellow, about one hundred pounds underweight, emerged with a black bag.

"Unless I miss my guess, that's either Lee Bob Parker or a CIA bagman," I reasoned.

"Right on the first guess," Shelly said. "It must be a real emergency to get him out of bed at this hour."

"It's only ten o'clock."

"I was being sarcastic," Shelly said. "I've called his place at six in the evening and his wife tells me he's in bed for the night. It's his stock excuse."

In one month at Trafford I had never laid eyes on Dr. Parker until now. As he walked toward the E.R. doors, he surveyed Shelly and me uneasily. I stood up and introduced myself.

"Yes. Carl told me about you," Parker said gravely. He shook my hand; his grip was weak and moist. "You're from Stanford, right?"

"That's right."

"You must know Dr. Stillwell. Best liver man in California."

I considered lying, but fearing it might just be a ruse, I decided to stick to the truth. "I'm sorry, I've never heard of Stillwell."

Parker was disappointed, his one link with Stanford having been nullified. "Earl might be retired now, anyway. He's a real old-timer."

"Yes, that's probably it."

Parker nodded in Shelly's direction but his fishy eyes never met hers. "How you doing, Miss Farmer?"

75

"Pretty good."

"Gettin' all ready for law school, are you? I almost went to law school myself, you know. Did I ever tell you about why I didn't? 'Bout how pappy wanted a doctor in the family so all of momma's bills would be taken care of. . . ."

"You told me about that."

"Oh." Parker nervously pulled up his sleeve and glanced at his wristwatch. "If you'll excuse me, I've got to go in and take a peek at Mrs. Rhames. Things don't look so good for her tonight. I don't think she's got much longer."

Harriet Rhames had lung cancer, a diagnosis not even Lee Bob Parker could screw up.

"Nice meeting you, Dr. Parker," I said.

When he was safely out of earshot, Shelly questioned me about Mrs. Rhames.

"What can I say? She's dying, all right. Her lungs look like the La Brea tar pits."

"But I've seen her walking in the halls, smoking a cigarette."

"Yeah. She smokes a pack a day," I said.

Shelly's eyes widened in horror. "And you let her?"

"Hey, take it easy. I'm not her doctor." I motioned down the hall after Parker. "Talk to the Phantom of the Hospital. Apparently he thinks she's so far gone that there's no harm in letting her smoke and no good to be gained from making her stop."

"Well, it doesn't sound too damn professional to me."

"Maybe not," I conceded, "but she's going to die anyway. It's too late for the Surgeon General."

We walked inside just as the telephone rang at Mrs. Holt's station. Shelly perked up instantly. Months of driving the county's only functional ambulance (the 1967 Pontiac hearse didn't count) had tuned her reflexes. A phone call, the screech of a tire, the pop-pop-pop of gunfire in the wee morning hours—the senses must be trained to react to all clues. Each ambulance run meant twenty-five dollars for the company; anything more than five per night translated into a bonus for

Shelly and Dan Dilborn, her partner and fellow emergency medical technician.

Mrs. Holt scribbled an address as she talked into the receiver. "Looks like Number One for the evening," said Shelly, rubbing her hands together. "I was beginning to worry we'd be shut out for the second time this week."

"Cheer up," I said sardonically.

"Grady Gardens," Mrs. Holt bellowed to Shelly. "Lady fell down the stairs and broke her leg."

From my own observations of domestic behavior at the housing project, I was willing to wager the victim did not fall down the stairs, but rather was "encouraged" downward by a male sparring partner. Several older tenants blamed such regular violence on the absence of useable shuffleboard courts.

No sooner had Mrs. Holt prescribed the destination than Shelly grabbed Dan Dilborn and bolted for the ambulance. Mrs. Holt extended the slip of paper with the name and address of the victim and, like a well-drilled halfback, Shelly snatched it on her way out the doors. I whistled in admiration as the ambulance wailed out of the parking lot. I turned to a nurse and asked her to go wake Billie Simmons for X-ray duty. Then it hit me: Buster Hogue!

I scrambled outside and screamed for Shelly to stop. "Come back! Buster's in the back of the wagon!" But it was too late. The ambulance hung a right turn onto Highway 80 and the tailgate doors swung open. Buster Hogue and his pretty redheaded date bounced crazily off the rescue truck and into the highway. Miraculously, the overloaded stretcher made a safe, four-point landing on the pavement and skidded harmlessly into some roadside shrubbery. Buster was on top and he rose slowly, checking his bones. His companion was crying hysterically, but appeared basically uninjured. I ran up the road to where they stood, trembling with adrenalized fright and more than a little humiliation.

"Hey! Are you okay?"

Buster flushed and looked away. "We're okay." His girlfriend covered her face and sobbed.

"Her too?" I offered my handkerchief to the disheveled damsel, who declined it ungraciously.

Buster inspected the girl and made feeble, and equally ill-received attempts, at consolation. "She's just shaken up. That's all. We'll be fine."

"You were lucky," I observed indiscreetly.

Buster glared. "No kidding? Why don't you teach that maniac girlfriend of yours how to drive?"

"It's not a motel room-on-wheels, it's an ambulance. Shelly was just doing her job. What's your excuse?"

The girl stopped crying and began to smooth out the wrinkles in her slacks. "I want to go home," she muttered. "Please, Buster, take me home."

I tried one more time. "You're sure you don't have any bruises or anything?"

"None you can look at!" she insinuated angrily.

Buster blundered to my defense. "It's okay, Judy. He's a doctor."

"What about you?" she blurted at the frightened young man. "You told me you were a doctor, too. You are, aren't you?"

Buster looked to me for help. "Sure I am," he stammered. "I'm, uh, a pediatrician. That's what I am, a pediatrician. I specialize in foot care. Dr. Stone here, he specializes in bruises."

"Contusions," I corrected him.

"Yeah, those too."

"It was nice meeting you, Judy," I said before returning to the emergency room to await the ambulance. No doubt by this time, Shelly, Dan and the patient had noticed the conspicuous absence of a stretcher. I visualized the two attendants hoisting some overweight matron into the wagon with a blanket.

As it turned out, the woman with the fractured tibia was husky Louise Rhodes, a cousin to the man who gave me the huge hog during my first week at Trafford. Where Hollis was sanguine and cooperative, Louise was obstreperous and combative. She and her boyfriend Thomas Dixon apparently

78

had scuffled at the top of the stairs before Thomas got the upper hand and tossed Louise down two flights—no easy task. As a matter of policy, we called the Grady police to investigate; as expected, Louise refused to press charges.

"But this is the third time this year," complained the young patrolman. "First time it was a brain concussion. Then he stuck a fork through your fingers. Louise, when are you going to learn?"

"Quit talking about Thomas like he was some kind of axe-murderer or pervert, unless you want to be sued for slander," she threatened. "We was just playin' is all. Thomas gets a little rough sometimes."

Stupidly, I promised the well-meaning lawman I would chat with Thomas Dixon about his chronic inability to make peace with the Girl of His Dreams. I should have left it to Ann Landers. I spied Dixon in the waiting room, six-four and two hundred and fifty steely-eyed pounds. He chewed on his fingernails and pored over the advertisements in the back of the latest *Argosy*. I approached him carefully.

"How is she?" he asked impassively.

"Fine, considering. She's got a fractured tibia. I've taken the X-rays and we'll be setting it very soon."

"Good," Thomas said, and turned back to his magazine.

"Would you like to see her?"

Thomas looked at his watch. "I don't think so. I've got to get up early tomorrow. Better be on my way."

Later the cop asked, "Did you talk with him?"

"Yes, I talked to him."

"Did he say what the matter was?"

"No."

The cop was disappointed. "I'll be damned. You know, Doctor, I'd rather work a robbery any day. These goddamned domestic things get so messy. Hell, you practically need a psychiatrist to figure it out."

"I think we've done all we can," I ventured. "The rest is up to Louise and Thomas."

The patrolman laughed sourly. "They're gonna kill each other, you know. Thomas is strong, sure, but that Louise can handle a paring knife as good as anyone in the county. Next time old Thomas tries to throw her down the stairs, he's liable to look down and find his muffler missing."

I pretended to be listening to the cop's social commentary, but in fact was watching Buster Hogue steal into the E.R. with a crooked, battered stretcher in tow. Knowing his guard was down, I confronted him immediately.

"It is illegal to misrepresent yourself as a physician, or didn't you know about that?" I said accusingly. "Why'd you tell that girl you were an M.D?"

"Because she'd never go out with an orderly," he answered promptly. "Chicks dig doctors. Surely you know all about that."

I agreed, modestly. "Sure, but you've gotta be careful. You just can't go around telling every beautiful woman you meet you're a doctor. Suppose you meet one who wants a free pap smear. What are you going to do then?"

Buster shrugged. "Smear her pap?"

"And another thing," I went on. "A pediatrician is not a foot doctor, he's a children's doctor. A foot doctor is a podiatrist."

Buster was painfully embarrassed. "Damn! I always get those mixed up."

One hour before I was scheduled to go off duty, Carl Hogue arrived in his usual brusque, chain-smoking, coffee-toting breeze. "Hello, Dr. Stone," he said when he walked by.

His sudden appearance was something of a mystery. "What's up?" I asked Margaret Holt. "Has he got an emergency, too?"

"Lee Bob Parker asked him to come," she told me. "One of his patients died and he wants Dr. Hogue to cosign the certificate."

"Two doctors for a death certificate? Is that Alabama law?"

Mrs. Holt smiled cynically. "That's Trafford law. In past years we've had a few problems with Lee Bob being a little quick on the trigger with DOA's and the like. We just want to make sure, and make it legal at the same time.''

"You mean Parker's pronounced people dead when really. . ."

"That's right," she said. "Lee Bob's had Benbow Hutchinson deceased officially at least three different times I know of. And every time the old man coughs or sits up or starts swearing just as they're pulling the sheet over his face. This regulation about two doctors signing the death certificate is Benbow's doing. He thinks Parker is out to get him and wants to make sure that when he dies, he dies—and not before.''

"Not a bad idea," I said thoughtfully. "Has Lee Bob ever made this . . . this miscalculation and gotten away with it?''

"Not that we know of," Nurse Holt said.

At 1:45 Shelly got another call and left me watching the late movie alone. I stayed past quitting time on a hunch: the emergency call came from Grady Convalescent Center and I suspected it might be a DOA. Little did I know what and in what manner I would suffer for my good intentions. Signing the death certificate, in retrospect, would have proven infinitely simpler than the task that lay, quite literally, on the sheet before me.

The patient was Hyland Bashaw. Age: seventy-seven. Weight: two hundred and ten pounds. Height: five-five. Disposition: bellicose. He complained of urinary bleeding and a chronic shortness of breath when trying to sleep. As she wheeled him in, Shelly whispered, "He's a real doll." He was. Catheters bring out the ugliest side of the human personality; it has been said they are the embodiment of humiliation. Hyland had been saddled with a catheter for a month; he was miserable.

"Goddamn hospitals," he mumbled. "I hate them. More people die in hospitals in this country than anyplace else.''

"Quite possible," I said amiably. "You've got some bleeding down there, right?''

Hyland grumbled in the affirmative. I told Buster to remove the catheter while I went to check on Louise Rhodes' cast.

"How's the leg?"

"Sore," Louise said. "Did Thomas go home?"

"Yes, a couple hours ago."

"You sure he went home?"

"He didn't say exactly, but I assume that's where he went."

Louise frowned balefully. "That son-of-a-bitch."

Remembering the patrolman's words about Louise's deft touch with the paring knife, I urged moderation. "I'm sure he went home. Let's not get ourselves all worked up again."

Louise snorted. "I bet he's at Loretta's place. Her husband's off in Nashville on business. I'm gonna kill that man when I get out of here." Buster crashed into the examination room, eyes wide and voice tremulous. Fear had drained the color from his normally tan and robust features. "Otis, come quick! Emergency!"

"What's up?"

Buster's arms hung limp and hopelessly at his sides. His lips moved but he did not speak. His eyes fixed downward, as if on his shoelaces, perhaps on his belt buckle.

"What is it?" I demanded.

"I've done something terrible!" he said hoarsely.

I trotted off to the E.R. behind Buster, leaving Louise Rhodes to plot unspeakable violence against her boyfriend Thomas. There in the corridor lay Hyland Bashaw, peaceful enough and obviously quite alive. A blanket was drawn up high to cover his shriveled neck. I looked to Buster for an explanation. He pointed wordlessly in the general direction of Hyland's crotch.

Gently I peeled back the sheet. Instantly and with great horror, I spotted the problem. It lay motionless on the sheet between the old man's skinny pale legs: Hyland's penis, unattached. Completely disconnected. Untethered and unfettered. On Hyland's pudgy lower abdomen a dark circle of clotted blood marked the spot it had so loyally occupied for nearly eight decades.

At this point it became most important to conceal the panic, and most important to conceal from Buster the awful truth: that in my meager career of practicing medicine, I had

82

never seen, or even heard of, anything like this. Buster was slow but he was not a bona fide moron. He recognized the look on my face for what it was—terror.

"What did you do?" I whispered frantically. "Did you yank it off or what?"

"No! Honest, I went to remove the catheter like you told me and . . . the guy's dick fell off!" Tears came to Buster's eyes, "Please don't tell my old man."

My first impulse had been drilled in from med school days: when the chips are down, get the patient on fluids. "Nurse! Get an I.V. going on Mr. Bashaw and hurry!" I hollered.

"What now?" Buster cried.

"Go get your father. He's down in Mrs. Rhames' room."

"No, no. Please, not that," the orderly moaned pathetically. His hands went to his face and he cringed away.

"For God's sake, Buster, I'm not going to rat on you. I need your dad's advice on this at once." They hurt, those words did, but they were spoken in a moment of numbing disorientation. "The important thing is to stay calm."

Hyland craned his neck towards the foot of the stretcher.

"What's the matter?" he asked. "What's the matter down there?"

I eased him back into the reclining position. "Nothing, nothing, Mr. Bashaw. You let us take care of this, okay? It doesn't look too serious at all."

I grabbed Buster by the arm. "Stay here with the old man. I'm going to make a few phone calls. We'll go get your father as a last resort. This whole thing looks sort of bad for both of us." Buster needed no convincing.

I got on the phone to Jackson Memorial in Miami. Several doctors and friends were on duty and I fished uselessly for information about Missing Penises. Several thought my call was a practical joke and used the occasion to bring me up to date on the latest hospital gossip. "This is serious," I would implore. "This guy's penis fell off. That's right. It just fell off. No reason. Now, what can I do about it?"

"Sell him a new one."

"Glue it back on."

"Make a dashboard ornament out of it."

"Give it to his wife."

"Put it on a Christmas tree."

No, the graveyard shift at Jackson Memorial was not helpful. A few finally admitted they had heard of penises severed in automobile or industrial accidents, but never knew one to just fall off. "Write a paper on it," a former colleague suggested enthusiastically. "Or better yet, let me write a paper on it. It will guarantee my assistant professorship."

Disheartened by the lack of advice compounded by a lack of compassion, I returned to Hyland Bashaw and found Margaret Holt shrieking at the sight of the old man's condition. "Dear God!" she let out. "What have you done to this poor man?"

"Shut up!" I said, and dragged her aside. "Don't scare the old guy. We mustn't let him look down. Ask one of the young nurses or aides to come over and talk to him. That way his eyes won't wander too far south."

In desperation I summoned Carl Hogue from his postmortem conference with Lee Bob Parker down the hall. The three of us approached Bashaw's stretcher; there was no time to warn the two other doctors. I gritted my teeth and flipped back the sheet over the old fellow's torso. Immediately Parker crumpled against the wooden hand rail. "Jesus!" he hissed. "How horrible."

Hogue remained composed. He said nothing. Parker crept outside for some fresh air while Buster and I stood back to watch the senior physician's examination; it called for a most delicate bedside manner. "Get me some alcohol," Hogue called to Mrs. Holt, "and some cotton swabs."

Then he went to work on the mass of coagulated blood several inches below the navel. Ever so gingerly, he dabbed the blood away. Lo and behold, there it was, tucked up in the flabby abdominal cavity, the Real Penis.

"Eureka!" Hogue said wrily.

"Urethra!" I declared with a thankful sigh.

As Hogue explained it, the catheter had acted as a plug.

Blood from the urinary tract clogged up and hardened over Hyland's organ, which in turn had retreated up inside the old man's belly. The culprit lying on the sheet actually was an imposter, a crusty mold that had formed over the original. The resulting facsimile fooled the entire staff, scared the shit out of me, and nearly gave Buster Hogue an arrythmia.

"What's going on down there?" Hyland repeated. Fortunately, the old guy couldn't see over his belly so he missed all the commotion.

"Everything is fine now," Hogue assured him.

"Carl? Is that you?" Hyland asked. "Good, I thought I recognized your voice. Thank God you're here. All this screamin' and yellin' and carryin' on, I didn't know what was going on."

"Don't worry. We're going to stop this bleeding tonight and you'll feel better."

Hyland's gray head sagged back on the flat hospital pillow. "Thank God you're here," he wheezed. "I was beginning to worry. Not that I don't trust young doctors, Carl, but that fellow who was here before, Dr. Stone? Somethin' about him made me nervous."

MARIE DUGGAN ARRIVED THE SECOND WEEKEND IN September. All efforts to dissuade her backfired. "I know you just want to protect me," she would say. "You must not want me to see what horrible conditions you're working under." The stronger my objections, the more stubbornly she insisted on this self-styled mission to the netherlands of America's southern cultural tundra.

Once it was clear that Marie was unstoppable, I made a weak show of good intentions. "Of course you'll stay with me," I offered lamely. Of course she accepted, but not without romantic ramblings. With that, the focus of the problem shifted from Marie to Shelly Farmer. Shelly and I did not share apartments but we shared everything else, and, as I feared, the intrusion of a lithe blonde nurse into the picture did not sit well with the lithe blonde ambulance driver.

"The story of my life," Shelly lamented in a rare maudlin moment of self-pity. "I'm always getting shafted by old girlfriends and wives. I need to find a bereaved widower, someone I can trust."

No amount of reassuring, cuddling or repentance eased the tension; as Marie's date of arrival neared, Shelly grew distant and downright nasty. Her desperation surfaced in a frightening way the night she flirted openly with Buster Hogue, who backed away, confused and suspicious.

The night before Marie's plane was due, I made one last attempt at a truce.

"She's only staying three days. . . ."

"And three nights!" Shelly snapped.

"What can possibly happen? I told you she's just an old friend. I don't feel anything for her."

Shelly snickered mordantly. "And I suppose you're deeply in love with me, right? I mean, why else would you spend the weekend with another woman?"

"I'll sleep on the couch."

"You don't have a couch."

"I'll sleep on the floor."

"Why don't you just get her a room at the motel?"

"Shelly!" I bristled. "She's a nurse. As soon as she lays eyes on that place she'll be able to see it's a health hazard."

"Your place isn't exactly the Waldorf."

"Isn't there anything I can do to make you understand?"

"Understand, yes. Forgive? Never."

Marie's plane landed on a cloudy Friday night in Montgomery and the reunion was dreadful, right out of a soap opera. Admittedly, I worried that seeing her again might rekindle some of that old fire (which was never really much more than a spark), but I was acutely disappointed. I saw Marie step off the plane and all I could think of was my cat. As far as I knew, he was the only one of our original threesome who was happy and free. He was crazy, too, but that comes with the territory.

Marie and I embraced perfuntorily and she even managed to squint out a few tears on my shoulder. I hoped my insincerity was not as obvious as hers. I secretly suspected she would have preferred in the middle of a sob to bite deeply into my clavicle; for my part, I would have preferred to spin her around and march her right back aboard the jetliner. Her luggage, we found out, was already on its way to Houston.

We returned to Grady in darkness. Marie spent five minutes telling me how pale and emaciated I looked, and I spent five minutes telling interesting anecdotes about Trafford Memorial. That still left ninety minutes of driving so I flipped radio stations to break the silence.

"I hate country western music," she said suddenly.

"Oh. It's not too bad. I'm getting used to it."

Marie made a funny face. "You have been here a long time, haven't you?" It was going to be a long, tense three days.

"How's the job?" I asked strategically.

It paid off. Marie was more than happy to fill me in on the life of a newly registered nurse. She liked the hospital but hated her supervisor, liked her patients but hated bedpans, loved the salary but hated the hours. The edge in her voice was a clue that something was left out.

"Anything else?"

She slid over next to me. "I feel funny talking about it to you. You're a man."

"You want me to call Barbara Walters?"

Her voice fell. "All I meant is that some things are easier to discuss with other women."

"Like sex."

"Now that you mention it, yes. I've only been working there a couple months and already . . ."

"The doctors are hot for you."

Marie drew back. "How did you know?"

"I'm a doctor." I laughed. Marie said nothing. "Don't you ever watch television? All the doctors do is save lives and chase nurses."

"It may be funny to you, but I'm really worried," she said indignantly. "Some of the men are very . . . attractive. Smart, witty, good-looking. . . ."

"Rich!"

"Otis! Stop it. That isn't it at all. It's just that sometimes it's difficult not to be charmed."

"So be charmed. Go out with them, Marie. Make some friends," I said gently. "I'm not kidding. I wish you would."

Her eyes narrowed and she moved not so subtly back to the passenger side of the front seat. "You sound like you've already taken some of your own advice. Have you got a girlfriend here, in Alabama?"

"They do have women here."

"Have you been screwing around?" she demanded.

"How do you like the new upholstery? Melvin gave me forty percent off."

Finally we entered Grady. I cut my speed to thirty-five knowing full well that, thanks to past favors, I would not be ticketed (I had treated the police chief's daughter, gratis, for a rather delicate condition about which I was sworn to secrecy). My heart jumped, then, when I spied flashing red lights in the rear-view, growing larger on the highway behind me. I pulled off the road and waited. State troopers and the local constabulary favored blue flashers, so I concluded that, unless they were using ambulances in their speed traps now, this was no cop.

"Must be an accident," Marie said incisively. Universally, this is the standard line when one sees an ambulance, a hollow declaration that affirms the presence of disaster. "Must be an accident." That covers it all, from head-on to heart attack.

"It looks like the ambulance is slowing down." Sure enough, the wagon groaned to a stop, window-to-window with the Charger, and there sat the Richard Petty of rescue medicine.

"Shelly, I hope this isn't your idea of a joke," I shouted over the siren. "There's a law against turning those things on without cause."

"Hey, I'm the law student, remember?" she hollered back. "We got an emergency back at Trafford. Dr. Parker needs you right away. He sounded shook up."

I waved her on, guided the Charger back onto the road and trailed the ambulance into town. "Shit, this is my night off," I grumbled unethically.

"It must be important if another doctor asks for your help."

"Not this doctor." I glanced at her. "It could be anything from a sprained ankle to constipation. Nothing's too easy for Lee Bob Parker."

Puzzled, Marie maundered on about other things. "I can't wait to see your apartment. If it's anything like your place in Miami, I've got a lot of housecleaning to do."

"Oh, I'm much neater now," I lied, remembering how Shelly helped me tidy the place on Wednesday. Marie would be most disappointed. Perhaps I should have kicked over some furniture, left some food out to spoil, or lured the cockroaches out of exile before her arrival.

When we drove up to Trafford, Shelly was nowhere in sight. Humming a bit from its hundred-mile-an-hour cruise, the ambulance rested in its usual berth.

"Is this the hospital?" Marie asked.

"Yep. Trafford Memorial."

She surveyed the homely one-story edifice. "This is the service entrance, right?"

"Nope. Through those old doors is where I work. The emergency room. Come on, let's go see what's up."

The stretcher wasn't in the corridor; apparently the patient had arrived by private transportation. Parker had panicked, and sent Shelly to bird-dog the highway for my car.

"Where's the patient?" I asked a black-haired nurse who sat at Mrs. Holt's usual perch. "Shelly said it was an emergency."

Numbly the woman pointed toward the examining room. Lee Bob Parker met me on the way in. His spindly frame trembled but his voice was firm, from practice. I pictured him at home before the mirror, posing authoritatively as he delivered a diagnosis of which he had no certainty.

"What's the trouble?"

Parker looked defeated. "You're too late. He's dead. Carl's dead."

I pushed my way into the room. Hogue was stretched out rumpled and gray, quiet as a bloated mudfish. Buster cried in the hallway and Nurse Holt screamed hysterically for oxygen. I had arrived in the thick of things. "Heart attack?" I asked. Someone screamed back in the affirmative.

"He's dead, Otis," Parker repeated solemnly.

I shoved the skinny physician out of the way and hurried to Hogue's side. His pulse was irregular but it was a pulse. How Parker missed it I'll never know. In addition, Hogue's blood pressure was barely audible. Mechanically I started barking out orders. "Get the cardioverter! Then oxygen at five liters per minute and I want an I.V. D5W stat with a slow drip so we can get some medication in there." Mrs. Holt scampered off to fill the order.

Parker inserted himself between me and Hogue. "I swear his breathing stopped a few minutes ago. I thought he was dead. I even massaged his heart."

Again I displaced the bumbling doctor. "You're full of shit," I said indelicately. "You probably massaged your own heart. Now stay out of my way before I knock you down."

Mrs. Holt returned, calmer, with the cardioverter. "Should we shock him?"

"Right away."

"Yes, hurry," Parker said absently.

After I shocked Hogue, the cardiac monitor showed a normal sinus rhythm. His blood pressure rose to 100/80. The nurses' station at the end of the main corridor monitored a cardiac care unit with four beds. Buster stopped weeping long enough to help Mrs. Holt and me wheel his father down the hall to a fortuitously empty bed. Carl Hogue had suffered his first heart attack.

He was hooked up to the cardiac monitors; his condition would be scrutinized, if all went as planned, by one of the two duty nurses watching video screens at their station. At the first sign of an arrhythmia, an abnormal heart beat, they were to call me. Twenty long minutes after going into ventricular fibrillation, Carl Hogue was safely tucked into bed in a quiet, closely guarded corner of Trafford Memorial. The king was asleep in his kingdom. His condition was stabilized.

Still, I insisted on a 24-hour nurse. Trafford, nay Grady County, could not afford to lose Carl Hogue. Tyrant that he was, his recovery was most important. Handing over Hogue's patients to the terrifying spectre of Dr. Lee Bob Parker was like allowing a five-year-old child to take crayons and "touch up" Raphael's "Sistine Madonna."

On the matter of Lee Bob Parker, my intentions were direct: get rid of the bastard. Unfortunately, Buster Hogue had

91

the same idea but his methods were more neanderthal. I walked out of coronary care to see the two grown men locked in combat on the white-gray tiles, squinting and grunting like twelve-year-olds. Margaret Holt awkwardly attempted to wedge herself between the two wrestlers, but all she gained for her efforts was a bloody nose and two chipped fingernails.

Luckily, Shelly Farmer heard the commotion and together we managed to separate the white-clad combatants. Buster seethed and struggled. Humiliated, Lee Bob cowered and swore vengeance in a court of law. "You assaulted a doctor," he said, pointing a bony finger at the muscular orderly.

"You pronounced my father dead when he wasn't. You're a quack! You're so damn jealous you can't wait to see him die! You should have been a vet. You're incontinent."

"That's incompetent, Buster," I said.

"Buster, please," Mrs. Holt interjected, trying to soothe the doctor's son. "Mistakes do happen."

"I know. Everyone in this town has been declared dead by Lee Bob at one time or another. Sooner or later he'll get it right."

Parker lunged at the boy, but Shelly's arms—bolstered by months of hauling heavy stretchers—restrained him easily. "Next time you need a doctor, don't call me!" Parker retorted.

"That's what I tell everyone," Buster shot back. "Next time you need a doctor, for God's sake, don't call Lee Bob Parker. Not unless you want to die young."

Were it not for Carl Hogue's critical condition I might have been amused by the hostilities. But, somehow on my day off I had managed to wind up in the middle of a crisis and, worse yet, in control. Parker, the senior physician behind Hogue, obviously was in no shape to administer medicine (except to write himself a prescription for Valium). Mrs. Holt was still spooky as a wildcat, running back and forth between nursing stations to keep her eagle eye on Hogue's coronary monitor.

For now, at least, it was up to me. The diagnosis was routine and the treatment mundane: wait and watch. I wrote orders covering the next three days which included drawing daily blood samples for enzyme tests. The Demerol was to be administered every four hours for pain as needed, as were five liters of oxygen. At sixty-nine, there was no telling what sorry condition the old doctor's heart was in.

At nine o'clock I finished with him. Parker went home in a huff, his professional pride irreparably dented by the taunts of a mere orderly. We consulted briefly on Hogue's condition: Lee Bob stubbornly insisted on listing it as "grave" until I curtly informed him Hogue was nowhere near the condition of the original diagnosis—dead. "He's out of the woods," I said. Parker gave up. After all, on what grounds could he attack my judgment? If it had been left up to Parker, Hogue would have been icing over in the morgue downstairs.

It would take years before Trafford Memorial could forgive Parker for this sin. Maybe they never would. My snubbing him and stealing the case from under his nose was the least of his worries. Buster Hogue was still dangerously livid.

Marie was pacing the waiting room when I emerged from the coronary unit. "All finished? Pretty quick job. I guess all those nights in the E.R. at Jackson Memorial were good practice."

"Yeah. Practice."

As we stood to leave, a middle-aged fellow in a pepper-colored 1958 suit strode across the room. "Are you Dr. Hogue?"

"He's down the hall. What do you want?"

"I need to see Dr. Carl Hogue and another doctor, Otis Stone. I'm a special agent with the sheriff's office."

Marie gave a worried look, obviously unaware that in these parts "special agent" status was awarded all deputies who outgrew their original uniforms. Still, the man appeared so officially stern I found myself pondering over my collective misdeeds. Except for a few deliciously illegal—and unreported—activities in the privacy of my own apartment, I had done nothing that would bring a deputy to the hospital. The alternative to confronting this junior Jack Webb was to lie about my identity. Shelly Farmer changed all that.

Tucked in my belt was a small rectangular electronic gadget known informally as the "beeper." Staff doctors carry them so they can be notified in restrooms, taverns, and on golf courses in case of emergencies. My metallic friend split the air with a howl. Mystified, I waited for the message.

Shelly's voice (probably originating from a dark phone booth on some street corner) was hard as ice. "Otis, she's not bad looking and she seems friendly enough. But if you sleep with that bitch tonight, I'll be inside the ambulance with Buster Hogue tomorrow." Click.

I grinned weakly. Marie stared at the magic box and the sheriff's agent scratched his head. "You must be Otis Stone," he decided. "This is for you." He handed me one of the two stiff legal envelopes.

"Who was that?" Marie whined. "Was she talking about me?"

"No, no. You know what probably happened? One of those late night radio talk shows had transmitter trouble. That's happened before. Why, I've gotten stations in St. Louis with this darn thing."

"How'd she know your name?" wondered the deputy.

"Maybe it was for me," I stammered. "Probably one of the other doctors got his wife to call up as a practical joke."

"You've got weird friends. If that was a joke it was pretty tasteless," Marie declared in her very sternest insulted virgin voice.

The beeper screamed again but this time I hit the "off" button just in time. I sat down and ripped open the deputy's message. My stomach turned over. There in unmistakable legalese was a subpoena requesting my presence at a deposition: the parents of Jake Benton, the gunshot victim whose leg had been amputated, were suing the church for its careless supervision of the riflery range. The church had reciprocated by filing suit against Trafford Memorial Hospital, Carl Hogue, and the assisting physician (me) for "the sum of $50,000 actual damages and the sum of $1 million in punitive damages."

"What does it say?" Marie piped. "Is it an award or something?"

"No. It's a lawsuit. It says the sole reason Jake Benton's femoral artery was severed and the sole reason his leg was amputated was deficient medical care. I can't believe it!"

"Good God, Otis, you're being sued. Two months out of internship and your very first malpractice suit."

Marie wrung her hands.

"Where did that goddamned deputy go?" Voices echoed down the corridor and there, one-on-one, stood Margaret Holt and the sheriff's agent. She had planted herself in front of Hogue's room, feet firm and apart. The deputy's shaven head bobbed up and down as he spoke. "I know. I'm sorry, but I got a job to do."

"Don't let him in!" I bellowed, tearing down the hall.

"Too late," Mrs. Holt said angrily. "He talked his way past a new nurse." She glowered at the pudgy lawman. "I hope you're satisfied."

I rushed past them into coronary care. A sallow limp replica of Carl Hogue lay motionless under the blankets. Even his craggy nose seemed flaccid. His eyes were half-closed but his mouth moved distinctly. "Bastard," his lips said. His cheeks reddened. "Son of a bitch."

The monitors instantly registered tachycardia, a bad sign. Soon the ailing doctor closed his eyes under the dull curtain of Demerol and his heart beat slowed.

I pried the wrinkled, moist subpoena from his right hand and stuffed it in my jacket. Hogue drifted off into a foggy, fitful sleep.

THIS AUTUMN WAS A BAD TIME FOR A DOCTOR TO be sued for medical malpractice. Not that there is ever a good time for it, but this particular season was notable because so many insurance companies were jacking malpractice rates right out of sight. When pressed for an explanation, sober-faced company spokesmen invariably would cite the rising number of lawsuits being filed against physicians, not to mention some astronomical jury settlements in favor of the crippled, maimed or vegetablized plaintiffs.

Among the members of the urban medical community, fear was rampant, for it was in the Big City where Evil Lawyers lurked. Among members of the legal community—whose members were being accused of scalpel-chasing—indignation was rampant. The lawyers maintained that too many incompetent doctors were getting away with everything, murder included. Doctors countered with the argument that patients were being goaded into baseless lawsuits by unscrupulous attorneys hungry for a substantial cut of the damage awards.

So Carl Hogue, Otis Stone and Trafford Memorial became one set of litigants in one of some 20,000 malpractice suits filed in the United States that year. Most were settled out of court; three out of every four that went to trial were decided in favor of the defendants.

But, when a doctor lost . . . oh boy! It could—and often did—cost his insurance company and hospital millions.

As provincial as Grady County was, Trafford Memorial

was not untouched by the malpractice crisis. The symptoms were common enough: in order to compensate for obscene insurance premiums, doctors raised their fees; in order to avoid even the suggestion of negligence, Trafford staff members indulged in all sorts of "preventive medicine" which reached the height of absurdity when a girl with a broken forefinger received not one, not two, but five X-rays of her hand. The upshot was simply that everybody suffered, especially the patients' pocketbooks.

The summer had witnessed an unprecedented blitz of malpractice publicity, including the obligatory *Time* and *Newsweek* cover stories. From a public relations angle, then, Hogue and I were being sued at the worst possible time— and by a church! I fancied the same consequences for the humble physician who had treated Christ for puncture wounds in the hands, but forgotten to administer a tetanus shot. No jury in the world would decide against God.

As far as actual legal processes, we officially were being sued by the Mission Christian Church. The church was being sued by Jake Benton's parents, who charged negligence in supervising the rifle range where their son was shot. Apparently the church lacked adequate coverage and was advised by some clever lawyer to countersue the hospital and the physicians (who always had the money to cover such indiscretions). The church's lawsuit stipulated we were liable only if it lost to the Benton's, and since the odds in this case heavily favored the family, we were in big trouble. The church maintained that the medical care received by Jake Benton in the emergency room fell far below "the standard of care in the community," an allegation so laughably nebulous that it downright frightened the hell out of Trafford's attorney.

Carl Hogue was in no mood or physical condition to discuss a legal tightrope act, so the hearing was mercifully postponed ten days. Three days after Hogue's heart attack, the hospital board convened to consider three important items: Carl Hogue's illness, a lawsuit pending against Trafford Memorial, and an urgent request by administrator William E. Anderson for a permanent emergency room physician.

Dan Satterwhite opened with melodrama. "As you are all aware, Dr. Carl Hogue suffered a heart attack last Friday night right here at the hospital. I have authorized the treasurer to purchase a wreath and send it to Carl's room as a gesture from the hospital board."

Buster Hogue stood up angrily. "Wreaths are for funerals. My father's not dead. A box of candy or even a get-well card would do just fine."

Satterwhite reddened. "Ah, yes. Certainly, Buster. Whatever you say. Our intentions were heartfelt, I assure you. . . ."

"Everybody is trying to get rid of Dad," the young man blurted. "He's not going to die. Dr. Stone says he's gonna be fine." The young man, tears puddling up in the corners of his eyes, looked mournfully to me for some kind of confirmation.

"That's right," I finally said. "With lots of rest and close supervision, Dr. Hogue will be able to resume a light work load in about six weeks."

"He'll be fine," murmured Buster, obviously paranoid. He had convinced himself that Lee Bob Parker's erroneous death judgment in fact had been a calculated plot. With Parker looking on, he rushed to defend his father's chances for recovery. Harry Defoe, the pecan farmer, gingerly interrupted. "We understand, Buster," he said sympathetically. "But I'd still like to hear Dr. Parker's report on your father's condition."

"Why? You just heard Dr. Stone say he's gonna be okay." Buster shouted. "What do you need his lousy opinion for?"

Dan slammed down the gavel. "Please calm down, son," he admonished. "It is our standard procedure to consult the senior physician, even if it's not his case."

Outrageous protocol: Word of Parker's near-disastrous misdiagnosis had spread through Grady like a bad rash, yet here these nine solemn board members pretended to seek out the old man's counsel. Parker took advantage of it. He wore a new blue suit, double-breasted with a vest, and an anemic broad tie. Reading off my chart, he delivered a moving recitation of Hogue's vital signs, medications and daily progress. "His chances of recovery are excellent, provided he gets plenty of time for a full recuperation," Parker announced, "and on that issue I must disagree with my young colleague. I believe Carl needs at least three months of total rest and no work."

Collectively, the board members gasped. Three months without Carl Hogue could ruin Trafford; faithful patients would flee to Selma and Montgomery. Others would simply expire. What naive confidence some of the rural folk had come to have in modern medicine had been gained primarily from Hogue's expertise. Without him, many of the newly enlightened would revert to jasper and root and linament.

"I believe we need an interim Chief of Medicine," Parker went on, "someone to take charge while Carl is recuperating, a doctor with the background, with . . ." and here he gave me a disapproving scowl, ". . . experience."

While Satterwhite was gullible, he was not stupid when it came to Lee Bob Parker; Benjamin Turlington, the grocer, not only was stupid, but a bosom pal of Parker's to boot. It surprised no one when he followed the cue and said, "I move that Dr. Parker take over as chief of medicine."

Satterwhite hammered the gavel so loud Buster fell off the edge of his chair. "Wait a darn minute, Ben. We've got a difference of medical opinion here and I want to recheck the facts. Now, Dr. Stone, you said six weeks?"

"That's a good estimate based on Hogue's progress these past few days, which were critical in a case like this. Still, I'm not a fortune-teller so I can't say with absolute certainty he's out of the woods."

"Do you think the board needs to appoint an interim Chief of Medicine until Carl gets better?"

"No, sir. Myself, Dr. Parker, Dr. Gleason and Dr. Drake—between the four of us we'll manage. For my part," I gritted my teeth, "I'd be more than happy to look after some of Carl's patients both here and at his office."

Satterwhite was pleased. "That's reassuring, to say the least."

In his own stubborn way, Parker was a battler. Indecisive as he was in emergency situations, he made a solid stand at this meeting. His audacity was matched only by an absence of logic. "I don't like to get personal," again with a nod in my direction, "but we shouldn't forget the second item on today's agenda which is delicately related to the first. Of course, I'm talking about the malpractice suit filed against Dr. Stone and, wrongfully of course, Dr. Hogue. Should news of this action get around town—and I fear it will—confidence in Trafford Memorial and in our physicians would suffer irreparably." Parker sat down and the room buzzed. Ted Moeller, a used car dealer whose marriage to Dan Satterwhite's sister had landed him a spot on the board, raised a hand.

"I'd sure like to know about this malpractice business," he said.

Were Hogue able, he would have seized such a moment to mount an impressive counteroffensive, detailing in his own impervious way the complex nature of Jake Benton's injury, the inarguable necessity for amputation and, thus, the complete nonliability of the hospital and its staff. My talents, whatever they are, do not include the oratorical arts. As best as I could, I recounted the Jake Benton saga and concluded with the motive for the lawsuit, i.e., that Mission Christian Church obviously was unprepared to handle a huge court settlement and chose instead to involve the hospital. It was an unfortunate tactic, dragging a reputable house of worship into the public forum. I paid dearly for it.

"I'm a proud member of that congregation," declared a red-faced Ted Moeller, "and I can truthfully tell you, Dr. Stone, that the Mission Christians have done more for the young people of this fine county than the entire Boy Scouts of America."

"Amen!" sung out Joel Andrews, the pharmacist. "Hayrides, carnivals, turkey shoots, and one year we even chartered a bus down to a Saints' game. That church has done nothing but good for this town. It shouldn't have to suffer a

100

financial catastrophe just because one fool kid points a gun at another.''

"Then who?" I demanded bravely. "Should the hospital and the doctors pay simply because they can afford it? Even if liability rests with the church?"

"Can't you settle out of court?" Ted Moeller asked. "Compromise ain't exactly dishonorable, you know. I've made a life out of it. Man comes in and offers me five hundred dollars for a six-hundred-dollar-car and we settle at five seventy-five. That's compromise.''

"That's piracy. And if you settled this case out of court, the insurance rates around this hospital would double or triple," I pointed out. "And when the insurance rates go up, so do the fees."

"It's just don't seem right to make a church pay," Moeller grumbled.

"Sure don't," chimed in Joel Andrews. "They've been putting money away for that new bowling alley, too. Ten lanes. Gonna be open to the whole congregation.''

Dan Satterwhite ignored the rabble, concentrating instead on mashing imaginary ants with a pencil eraser. The man who engineered the debate, Lee Bob Parker, waited like a buzzard for the thing to die. When the shouting eclipsed ninety decibels, Parker realized his point would be lost so he leapt back into the thick of it.

"Gentlemen, please! It's not a matter of liability. That will be settled in court. It's a matter of, well, public relations. The malpractice controversy would go thoroughly unnoticed if Hogue were able to handle his normal work schedule. His reputation is impeccable and his stature in this community is secure. As for Dr. Stone, the people hardly know him. He's been out of school barely one year and already he's being sued for malpractice. What will prospective patients think about that? Most doctors, like myself, practice thirty or forty years without incident.''

I grabbed Buster before he could lurch from his chair. The veins in his neck stood out like rivers on a brown roadmap. Shelly reached over and handed him one of her legal textbooks. "Read the chapters on libel and slander," she whispered. "Maybe you better take a look at the section on assault, too."

Harry Defoe looked nervously over to the chairman, but Satterwhite made no move to mediate; he just sat there like a cow, poking away at the lectern with his pencil. Some of the nurses began to titter, a sure sign someone better do something. Pride and common sense were battling over my ego: pride won. As I rose to defend my meager medical background, a savior voice rose from the public seating section of the hearing room.

"I know what I think, Dr. Parker." It was Hollis Rhodes, gout victim and donor of the 200-pound hog. "I think I'd rather have my own blind grandma doctor me than you. I also think Dr. Stone is one of the best doctors I ever knowed. He made my aches go away for the first time in years, and that's somethin' you never could do. He's a miracle man, I'm tellin' ya."

The big man's simplicity was heartwarming. For once I felt good about Grady. Well, maybe not good, but certainly glad, glad that some of it had been worthwhile.

Hollis' softspoken indictment reduced Parker to incoherency and gave the board a perfect excuse to vote down the motion to replace Carl Hogue. Satterwhite dutifully stuck to the agenda, so the malpractice issue was rehashed. The only additional information was a memorandum to the board members from Carl Hogue, as dictated to loyal Margaret Holt. Satterwhite attached his tiny reading spectacles and delivered Hogue's message as if it were a major policy decision:

"I intend to fight this lawsuit all the way," Hogue began. "It is unfair, malicious and slanderous, to Trafford Memorial, to myself and even to Dr. Stone. Please retain the finest attorney available. The reputation of Grady's community health care is at stake here. We cannot back down."

Satterwhite folded the letter. "I guess Carl has made his position clear. I am instructing the treasurer to voucher funds to retain the hospital's attorney for special services. I trust we won't bicker anymore about this malpractice thing. We're all on the same side now."

"There goes the church bowling alley," Joel Andrews sighed.

The final item, Anderson's proposal for a full-time emergency room physician, was hardly well-received. The status quo always is hard to topple, particularly when a new man like Anderson implies change is overdue, and imputes inefficiency to the old methods. "I've gone back over the records. At least six times this year the duty nurses were unable to locate the doctors on call. On three occasions Dr. Hogue covered for Dr. Parker, who neglected to take his electronic receiver to the Elks' meeting. Several other times, no doctors were available in the E.R. for several hours. Four patients who might have been saved died."

Moeller, a shifty little fellow whose eyes never focused on anything, ignored Anderson's argument. "I'm talking about budget. At fifteen dollars an hour for five or six days a week, we're talking about $33,000 a year. I don't see where that money comes from."

"If you'll read the memorandum, I've listed the possible sources for such a new salaried position. The contingency fund is the best bet until next year's budget is drawn up."

And so it went, back and forth in an interminable duel between fiscal and physical needs. "One reason for the competitive salary is to lure good physicians," Anderson explained.

Harry Defoe, sympathetic but typically unhelpful, grimly predicted that top-quality physicians would "overlook the career possibilities here. They can make twice as much money in private practice. Where are we going to find a doctor to fill this job?"

"Dr. Stone has promised to locate for Trafford a first-class physician before he leaves in January," Anderson told the board. "With his connections—he went to Stanford, you know—I'm sure it will be no problem."

Rubbish. Utter nonsense. But Satterwhite and his underlings were impressed. They drafted a resolution: if I could find them a doctor, they'd find room for him in the budget.

It crossed my mind to prepare them for the worst, to come clean and relate my fears that no young doctor in his right mind would come to Grady to work in Trafford's sparse, melancholy emergency room. A person doesn't spend eight years in school to give tetanus shots, set broken arms and pry jelly beans from tiny noses . . . or does he? Was it possible to find a country boy or country girl tired of urban medicine?

Ted Moeller cornered me after the meeting. "Don't make any wild offers to these young fellers. If you can get 'em for less than thirty-three thou, for God's sake, do it. Better yet, if you know any old-timers lookin' for a good place to retire, mention Grady. Hell, they might even work for peanuts, just to keep in practice."

"Oh, you're a sharp one," I said.

"I didn't get where I am by throwin' money away," Ted confided. "You got to be tight-fisted."

"How old do you want this doctor to be?"

"Sixty, maybe seventy if he's real spry."

"Don't worry," I said. "I'll give him a tune-up and roll back the odometer so no one will know."

"Good boy," Ted winked.

Marie Duggan's immediate departure was the first priority on my personal agenda. I declined her offer to stay another week ("I'll just call in sick.") and helped her pack. Her cosmetic case was still somewhere between Houston and Montgomery; the trip home would be risky, she said, but she thought she could make it without Revlon's assistance.

As it turned out, I was unable to ferry Marie to the Montgomery airport. A snakebite victim showed up in E.R. shrieking that a "killer cottonmouth" had accosted him in the Alabama River.

"What were you doing in the river this time of night?"

"Gigging frogs," he answered.

The U-shaped wound showed numerous tiny punctures instead of the two deep fang holes customarily inflicted by poisonous vipers. When I raised the possibility that a harmless water snake was the culprit, the boy's mother flew into a frenzy and produced a large jar. Inside was a tangled mass of brown skin and pink meat, the battered remnants of her son's reptilian attacker. On this evidence, I was instructed to identify the snake and effect the proper antidote for its bite. As the minutes ticked away, Dennis Allen's wound changed little: no swelling, no discoloration or other symptoms of a poisonous snakebite.

"It was only a water snake," I decided after a close examination of the serpentine corpse. "You'll be fine."

"We're not moving from this hospital," Mrs. Allen announced. "My boy has been bit and you're going to do something about it. Come on, Doctor! Can't you see he's real sick?"

"How long does it take for cottonmouth poison to kill you?" Dennis asked studiously. He looked down at his foot to make sure it had not rotted off.

I was called to the telephone at the nurses' station. It was Marie. "You're late," she said. "I've got to be going or I'll miss my plane." Her voice was choked, well-rehearsed.

"I'll be right over," I said. "Had an emergency here, but I didn't forget you. Hang on."

"Oh, don't bother," Marie replied sweetly. "I found a ride with Shelly, that ambulance driver. She offered to give me a lift all the way to Montgomery."

"Good-bye, Marie."

THAT IT WAS ONLY DR. HOGUE'S FIRST HEART AT-
tack was a minor miracle in itself. He smoked too much,
drank too much, worked too much and worried about Buster
too much—all of which made him a prime candidate for the
Big H. How he made it all the way to age sixty-nine before
collapsing with myocardial ischemia will remain a medical
mystery. "Death is Nature's way of saying, 'slow down,' he
used to joke before his heart attack, which carried a portentously similar message.

For a man like Carl Hogue, the extended period of con-
valescence was more agonizing than the heart attack itself
because his practice, his patients and, consequently, his reputation were all in the hands of another doctor. He was
benched, knocked out of commission, and confined to the
sidelines. Meanwhile, the world of medicine marched on
without him. He was irked by the fact that the people of
Grady continued to get sick in his absence. Patients Hogue
had not seen in years showed up at his office or in the emergency room; he was baffled, so frustrated he even began
reading Frank Slaughter novels. His position as Medicine
Man in this simple tribe was in jeopardy. The miracles
Hogue had worked so deftly with penicillin and cortisone
and valium were being worked no less impressively by a
neophyte.

The hearing for the malpractice suit was scheduled for the
same day Carl Hogue was released from the hospital. We
both gave depositions, answered some elementary questions

106

and were dismissed from the judge's chambers. Our attorney casually mentioned that it might take years for the case to come to trial. "So relax," he said, "and try not to worry. I've never handled anything like this, but from what I read it looks like the litigation will take damn near forever. I'll keep you posted."

To Carl Hogue, the malpractice suit was an insulting nuisance, minimal in importance compared to the immediate fate of his medical practice. As we left the hearing, I for the hospital and Hogue for his bedroom, the old doctor warned, "I'll be back in three weeks. See if you can manage until then without killing off any of my patients."

Then came the long-awaited confrontation between Hogue and Dr. Lee Bob Parker at Hogue's gauche colonial semi-mansion. Lee Bob took along a nurse, ostensibly to check on Hogue's medical progress; it was merely a precautionary measure, in case Hogue got violent. At any rate, the nurse was banished to a hallway for ninety minutes while Hogue railed at Parker for trying to kill him. Trembling and green with nausea, Parker stumbled from the meeting and weakly informed the nurse, "Dr. Hogue is progressing excellently."

Among the staff members at Trafford Memorial it was generally known that Buster Hogue was advertising in his own clumsy way for some kind of "hit" man, if not to do away with Parker at least to inflict some sort of humiliating calamity on the skinny malpractitioner. Publicly, Buster denied knowledge of any plot.

"I hate the son-of-a-bitch but I'm no murderer. 'Course, I can see where an Alabama court might rule it justifiable. . . ."

Parker soon got wind of Buster's clandestine solicitations and went to the sheriff, Rooster Bootman, who laughed heartily.

"Hey, that's pretty funny, Doc. Listen, while I got ya' here could you gimme somethin' for the piles? I been runnin' speed traps for two weeks down by the Eisenhower Bridge and I mean to say my ass is killin' me!"

Parker's only alternative was to arm himself with an old target pistol and avoid Buster Hogue whenever possible.

Meanwhile, Carl Hogue was disobeying strict medical orders and making a nuisance of himself. One day I physically removed him from his office and put him to bed; that night he reappeared in the emergency room sucking on cough drops and dressed in a brown Hoover-era bathrobe. "My wife's watching some damn movie on television. 'Midnight Cowboy'—I hate westerns," he griped. "No law says I can't sit here in the waiting room."

Mrs. Holt had neither the heart nor the courage to expel Grady's senior physician so Hogue was tolerated; that he was thoroughly ignored by us didn't seem to bother him a whit. Familiar patients clustered about him like groupies pawing at Mick Jagger.

I was preoccupied repairing some nasty lacerations on a raccoon hunter who had paid, in spades, for the thrill of the hunt. His arms and hands were striated in red, the bloody legacy of having reached for a coonskin hat before it had ceased being a raccoon. Hogue was on his tiptoes, watching from a distance, as I bathed the scratches in disinfectant.

"Am I going to get rabies?" the hunter cried.

"Please, put down the shotgun," I begged. Buster moved in swiftly and pried the polished double-barrel from under the man's right arm. He removed the shells and propped the weapon safely in the corner. The hunter watched longingly.

"Am I gonna catch the rabies?"

"I don't think so. Was the animal behaving strangely?"

"What do you mean?"

"Did it try to get away or did it run up to you?"

The hunter scratched at his moist mustache. "Don't know. Couldn't tell if it was runnin' away or not, least not with all my dogs on top of it."

"Have you got the carcass?"

"Not exactly." The hunter reconstructed the scene of battle: his dogs, "the best in the county," treed the ring-tailed varmint not one hundred yards from the truck. The hunter arrived, fired a shot into the branches and knocked the raccoon to the ground. Assuming it was dead, he grabbed for the carcass, which immediately bit and clawed the living daylights out of his arms and hands.

"That's when I went out of my head," the hunter related sadly. "I just started firing and reloading, firing and reloading. Killed two of my best dogs."

"And the raccoon?"

The hunter gingerly stuck a bandaged hand into his red woolen jacket and pulled out a scrawny banded tail. "Here's all that's left. My boy's gonna tie it to the truck's antenna."

"Might as well," I said. "It won't do us any good. We need the head of that animal and unless we find it you're in for some rabies shots."

"Billie!" yowled the hunter to his son. "Get your ass out to Cutter's farm and find me that coon's head."

Billie edged close to me and whispered, "Is my daddy all right?"

"Do what I say before I break your hairless butt!" the hunter screamed. "You want your pappy to start foamin' at the mouth? You want me to die of the rabies?"

Billie scampered out the door, hopped into the bright-blue pickup and roared off toward the unhappy hunting grounds. I cautioned his injured father, Gary Murdock, to calm down. "We'll decide what to do when your son gets back. We'll need the raccoon's head to send to the county lab for a rabies check. Chances are it didn't have anything wrong with it, just an understandable case of bad temper."

Murdock blanched. *"Distemper?"*

"No. A *bad* temper. Get it? Wouldn't you be just slightly irritated if someone shot you out of a tree, so a half-dozen slobbering mutts could chew your ass up?"

But Murdock's troubled mind wandered to other worries. "Doc, I got to ask a favor from you," he said plaintively. "Could you look at one of my dogs? He got messed up real bad."

Carl Hogue and Margaret Holt laughed together as Gary Murdock dragged a trembling, wet-nosed black-and-tan hound into the emergency room's surgery section. I spent

109

thirty minutes suturing some deep cuts on the dog's flanks and picking shotgun pellets from its floppy left ear; all the while, Gary rested on his knees and praised God for letting Beaver (the dog) survive the night's costly ordeal.

Afterward Hogue chuckled. "Still think this rural medicine is a cinch, huh?"

"I wish you'd go home and get some sleep."

"How can I sleep knowing Otis Stone is still at large?" he cracked, a sure sign that some of that nice Hogue nastiness was returning.

My attention was diverted suddenly to the sight and sound of an hysterical person in shortie pajamas groping his way through the doors of the emergency room. In lukewarm pursuit was a woman still draped in her cotton nightgown. "Stop him!" the lady called down the hall at me. "He's gone crazy!"

I collared the subject and set him gently in a wheelchair. "I'm blind! Are you a doctor? Are you a doctor? Help! Call an ambulance," he babbled, "I'm blind!"

"Settle down. You're at the hospital now."

"Oh, good. Thank God. Call a doctor! Call a specialist!"

"Please calm down and tell me what exactly is the matter?"

"Are you deaf? I am blind." He paused to rub his eyes dramatically and shake his head from side to side. "I said I'm blind. Can't you hear me? Oh no, don't tell me I'm mute, too. Can't you hear me? Can *anybody* hear me?"

"I can hear you!" I yelled back. "You're not mute."

Obviously in a hurry to return home, the woman took me aside and explained the situation. Her next-door neighbor, Frank Gianoco, had knocked on the door in the middle of a "super" Sean Connery movie and calmly announced he was blind.

"I didn't know what else to do," she said. "Figured there must be a psycho ward here at the hospital where you can keep him."

"Why do you think he needs psychiatric counseling?"

"He ain't blind," she whispered.

I approached Mr. Gianoco and introduced myself by name. "When did you first notice your blindness?"

Much to the relief of the E.R. staff, Mr. Gianoco quieted down and told his story. "I was watching that James Bond movie on TV when all of a sudden, just as Ernst Blofeld was about to dismember agent 007, everything went black."

"Sure it wasn't the picture tube in your set?" It was Carl Hogue, unable to resist. I scowled and tried to look annoyed. Hogue shuffled back to the waiting room. Frank had stumbled helplessly around the house, screaming fruitlessly for help and breaking pieces of expensive Ethan Allen furniture before finding his way out the front door, through the picket gate, over a six-foot thorny hedge, past his neighbor's vicious terrier to her front door.

"Miraculous!" I exclaimed, peering into his reddened eyes with an ophthalmoscope. "Your retina is normal. Your eyes react quite properly to light. Everything looks fine in there."

"Thank you," Frank replied, "but I still can't see a thing."

"Tell me again. How did you get to the hospital tonight if you can't see?"

"Mrs. Shavers brought me," said Frank, pointing across the corridor exactly to the waiting room where the good neighborly Mrs. Shavers sat, cutting coupons out of an old Redbook. Obviously Mr. Gianoco was not blind, but he did have a problem.

"I've got just the thing for you," I said. "Miss Daily, get me a five cc syringe with a 25-gauge needle."

Out of the corner of my eye I caught the withered, robed figure of Carl Hogue plodding vigorously in my direction, doubtlessly primed for his patented, pedantic version of "professional consultation." Illness had not blunted his manners. "What kind of injection are you going to give him?" he demanded. "Don't you know he can see perfectly well?"

"Of course. That's why I'm giving him a saline placebo."

"Why don't you just kick his ass out of here? He's wasting

the hospital's time and money. The world is full of cranks and freeloaders like this.''

"I wouldn't say he's normal, would you? For him, this blindness *is* a problem, even if he's not blind. Don't you see?'' Finally it has happened, I thought to myself, the illogical has begun to make sense. "I'm going to give the saline a try.''

Hogue threw up his hands and scuffled back to the corner, certainly longing for the day when Trafford's controls were firmly back in his clutches. To Carl Hogue, Gianoco's masquerading as a sick person was a criminal offense, punishable by the most severe verbal abuse.

Mr. Gianoco, for all I knew, could have been a borderline schizophrenic. Even a first-year med student knows Rule Number One: handle with care. "This medication is the latest in antiblindness medicine,'' I told Frank. "You should notice some improvement almost immediately.''

Gianoco shielded his eyes from the sight of the hypodermic, gritted his teeth and took a deep, noisy breath. "I'm ready, Doc, so fire away.''

Five minutes after the placebo injection, Frank was rubbing his eyes, peering around the room. "It's working,'' he said, awed. "I see lightness. Shadows. Your striped necktie. . . . ''

"Just as I thought,'' I said with supreme confidence. "We'll be giving you one injection every hour for the next five hours until your eyesight is completely restored.''

Apprehension clouded Frank's face. "Five more shots? Couldn't I take this medicine orally?''

"No! Besides, Nurse Daily here needs to practice her intramuscular injections. . . .'' Gianoco gasped and covered his arms. "And don't worry about the money. Your insurance will cover everything,'' I said. "You *do* have blindness insurance, don't you?'' Gianoco shook his head dismally and closed his eyes.

"Can I go now?'' asked Mrs. Shavers. "I've still got time to catch the end of the movie.''

"Go ahead," I said, out of Frank's earshot. "And thanks for bringing him in. Has he ever acted unusual before?"

"Just one night about six months ago when he came over and insisted I listen to this two-hour speech on 'The Papal Menace.' "

"I see."

"What did he have? Some kind of retardation?"

"No, nothing like that. It's a condition called hysterical blindness."

Mrs. Shavers laughed as she walked out the door. "Damn right it was hysterical. Hilarious is the word."

Then I heard Frank at the top of his lungs praising God. "Doctor, come quick! It's a miracle. Thanks to modern medicine, thanks to your skilled hands and thanks to the grace and goodness of the Almighty, my eyesight has been restored! I can see again!" He thrust his bald, egg-shaped head at my face. "Look at my eyes. Are they not cured?"

I fetched the ophthalmoscope and went through the motions of a cursory optical examination. "The news is good, Mr. Gianoco," I proclaimed. "One more injection ought to do it."

Frank winced. "No, Doc. I can see just as good as ever. It's a miracle." He raised his arms and cheered, an action that once again brought the angry shuffling of Carl Hogue's slippered feet.

"Get that maniac out of here," he growled. "One of Parker's patients is down the hall trying to pass kidney stones and she thinks the world's coming to an end. This racket is going to wake the whole hospital."

But Frank Gianoco already was gone. At the mere suggestion of another injection he fled Trafford, leaving in his wake a roomful of bemused nurses and twenty-two dollars in unpaid hospital bills. Later I asked Shelly if she had ever before encountered Frank. "Not him," she answered, "but we've got a few other nuts in this county who pay regular visits. What makes a fellow act like that?"

"Don't ask me. If I knew that I'd be making sixty-five bucks an hour as an analyst."

"Well, if it's attention he's after he'd do better flashing at Girl Scouts," she remarked.

Anne Daily, a short nurse with straight black hair and big brown eyes, timidly approached to congratulate me. "It was wonderful the way you treated Mr. Gianoco," she said. "Too bad they didn't have medicine like that when Helen Keller was alive."

"But it was only a placebo."

"Don't be so modest." She handed me a pink telephone message: an illegible name preceded by an illegible phone number. "A man named Todd Froehling."

"It looks like 'Toad Fire Engine.' "

Anne looked at the note. "I'm sorry. Can't you read my writing?" She laughed nervously. "I thought doctors could read *any* handwriting."

"What did Mr. Froehling want?"

"He said he's 'interested in the job,' whatever that means."

"It means," I said jubilantly, "Trafford might have itself a brand new doctor!" One week had passed since I invested a hundred bucks of the hospital's contingency funds placing want ads in strategic urban newspapers. This Todd Froehling character actually seemed interested, even with the word "Alabama" brazenly included in the advertisement. What was he running from? I asked myself. How deep was his desperation? I headed for the telephone but stopped in my tracks. There, a shotgun cradled in one arm, was Billie Murdock. "Hey, Doctor, look at this!" he grinned, hoisting by one ear the bloody slack-jawed head of an ex-raccoon. Four paces behind Billie, Benbow Hutchinson looked up aghast from his wheelchair, then lapsed into a wheezing spell. When Billie set the vermin's head on an empty stretcher, Benbow's eyes closed and his chin fell to his chest.

GARY MURDOCK WAS NOT RABID. HE DID FROTH AT
the mouth, but it happened only when he chug-a-lugged a
can of Schlitz the day the county lab tests came back negative. The husky hunter rejoiced wildly for a week.

For finding the raccoon, Billie was promised a new shotgun. Two weeks later it was discovered that the boy had
killed a *second* raccoon, beheaded it and returned with the
evidence. In the chaos that fateful evening, no one had bothered to explain to him *why* a raccoon head was necessary for
his father's recovery, so Billy had attributed it to some kind
of modern witchcraft and figured any old raccoon head would
do just fine. Apparently neither of the ill-fated varmints carried hydrophobia.

Benbow Hutchinson was not so fortunate. Complaining of
minor chest pains, the old man had been rushed to Trafford
by his paranoid housekeeper. The sight of Billy's raccoon
had triggered genuine coronary insufficiency. We put Methu-
selah on nasal oxygen and hustled him into intensive care.
To no one in particular, an exasperated Margaret Holt asked,
"What? Dead again? He's becoming a nuisance."

Not a single nurse gave him a fifty-fifty chance of lasting
through the night; they drew straws and the loser sat at the
old guy's bedside until morning. Trafford's varicose super-
man was indeed a problem for those who longed to see the
hospital renovated. To them, Benbow was a reupholstered
couch or a new pharmacy. For eleven years, promises of "the
Hutchinson money" kept staffers like Mrs. Holt from going

insane with depression. Even in a tranquilized euphoria beneath the blue oxygen tent, Benbow would not have rested so placidly had he known what terrible ambivalence governed those who controlled his medical destiny. Of course, if looks could kill, the old man would have been DOA two years earlier.

"I know how they feel," Shelly commented. "Maybe it's true. Maybe the future of the hospital is more important than Benbow's life."

"I can't agree," I said, purely for the record. "At least I'm not supposed to agree."

"So don't. I understand. But it happens everyday and you know it."

"What happens?"

"Doctors play God. They let some patients live and others die. It happens all the time. Remember the Karen Quinlan case? Most doctors would have quietly pulled the plug like her parents wanted."

"I can't agree. I'm not *supposed* to agree."

"Thataboy, Hippocrates," Shelly muttered.

A week after Benbow's coronary, Todd Froehling arrived momentously from New York. A tall, pock-marked, humorless fellow, Froehling wore a perpetual snarl on his lips. Still, I was forced into a diplomatic show of courtesy because it would be disastrous to offend or repulse a possible successor. At the airport I sized him up as a fellow who yearned to escape, a fellow so forcibly oppressed and so savagely beaten down by the Big City he'd do anything for peace.

"What made you decide to answer the ad?" I asked during the return trip from Montgomery to Grady.

Froehling scowled. "Good question." Uneasily his eyes took in the Alabama countryside. "Got a lot of clay down here, don't you?"

"Oh, it's not bad at all," I said quickly. "Besides, it's better than smog. Where you from?"

"Brooklyn. That's how come I just got off a flight from La Guardia, remember?"

"I meant *originally*. Where were you born?"

116

"Born in Jackson, Mississippi. I was raised in Atlanta."

"Really? Then you're used to clay."

Froehling grimaced. "No. Not at all."

"Funny, though, you don't sound Southern."

"If I was born in Nairobi, would you expect me to speak like a Masai tribesman?"

When we finally pulled up to the hospital, Froehling made no attempt to hide his disappointment. "You're kidding!" he groaned. "This place is worse than I thought. Doesn't it even have a parking lot?"

"At the main entrance. This is Emergency."

"You can say that again."

Unfortunately, our arrival had coincided perfectly with that of Eileen Robinson and her solicitous mother Marjane. They shoved us out of the way in their mad dash for the E.R. Being from New York, Froehling was not easily intimidated. "Dumb bitch," he growled charmingly and followed me into the hospital.

Instantly, I realized this was not the night for Todd Froehling to visit Trafford Memorial, not if he was ever to accept a position here. His face bore a curious disbelief. "Is this a ward?" he asked. "I know. It must be one of those therapy sessions. TM, right?"

"Sit down and I'll give you the grand tour in a minute." I confronted Marjane Robinson and her eight-year-old daughter. "What's the trouble?"

"I'm Marjane Robinson and this is my little girl Eileen."

"The nurses have got all that information. Now what seems to be the matter?"

"It's not me, Doctor, it's my little girl. My little girl is very sick." Mrs. Robinson stepped aside so I might take a professional look at Eileen, whose big brown eyes wandered playfully around the examining room. Her pulse was fine, as was her temperature and blood pressure. Her throat, ears and eyes looked normal. She even giggled a normal giggle when I tested her knee reflexes.

"What's the matter?" I asked her.

117

"Nothing," Eileen whispered. "Momma says I'm real sick."

"Do you feel sick?"

"No, but I can't tell Momma. She'll get mad."

I took Mrs. Robinson by the arm and led her down the hall. "She looks fine to me. What seems to be the matter?"

Marjane reddened. "How the hell should I know? *You're* the doctor."

"Has she vomited? Had any dizzy spells? Has she fainted or fallen down lately? Have you noticed *any* sort of symptoms?"

Marjane faltered. "I don't know anything about symptoms. She just doesn't *look* right. A mother can tell these things. A mother knows, Doctor."

"Doesn't look right," I repeated, pretending to write this nebulous observation on Eileen's blank chart. "How," I ventured politely, "does she usually look?"

"Different."

I pointed at Eileen's bewildered face. "Even her cheeks are rosy."

"Her cheeks have never been rosy. She's always been a pale child," Mrs. Robinson said gravely. "Did you give her a blood test?"

"No, ma'am."

"A urine test?"

"I don't think that is. . . ."

"How about X-rays? Where are the X-rays?"

"For what? A brain tumor? Or maybe a broken neck? What's the matter with you, lady? Your daughter is perfectly fine!"

Marjane shook her fist. "I'm her *mother!* I know my daughter and she doesn't look right. We're not leaving here without a complete physical examination."

Todd Froehling was enjoying the squabble. "Is this an emergency ward or an outpatient clinic?" he asked with a thin trace of a smile.

"What do you suggest?"

"Kick her out."

118

"Hey, this isn't New York."

"It's a good thing," Froehling said, "or we'd have that witch locked up on the sixth floor by now."

"We don't have a sixth floor," I smiled. "We don't even have a second floor."

"Where do you put the crackpots?" he asked.

"Oh, we have a psychiatric ward," I answered in an hasty attempt to recoup Trafford's tattered prestige. "Well, it's not really a ward."

"How big is it?"

"One room. I'd let you see it but there's a very nasty fellow in there. Recovering from a hemorrhoidectomy."

"Unreal." Froehling laughed acidly.

"Why do we need a psychiatric ward, anyway?" I said cheerily.

Mrs. Robinson obtrusively managed to answer my question. "Is it because we're Lutheran? Is that why you won't treat my daughter? Call Dr. Hogue! I demand to see Dr. Hogue before Eileen goes into a coma!"

"Dr. Hogue is sick. He won't be back for several weeks," I said. "Speaking of sick, we've got a hospital full of very sick folks and you're waking them all up. Please be quiet."

Marjane swallowed hard. Her black eyes drilled tiny holes in my forehead. *"You!"* she panted. "You don't know who I am, do you? I'm Mrs. Rayfield Robinson."

"Good for you."

Eileen whined. "Momma, stop yelling. I wanna go home." The curly head shook as the little girl began to cry. Marjane smothered Eileen in her arms.

"Don't worry, honey. Momma will protect you from that mean old doctor. Don't you worry." Mrs. Robinson glowered. "See what you've done? You'll be sorry, mister."

Mrs. Holt intervened anxiously. "Wait, Mrs. Robinson. We'll do the blood and urine tests if you want."

"The hell we will," I argued thinking this would demonstrate for Todd Froehling the assertiveness exercised by Trafford physicians. "The girl is fine. Let them go home." And go home they did. Eileen must have weighed ninety

119

pounds but Mrs. Robinson protectively lugged her out to the big family Oldsmobile. Pained and defeated, Mrs. Holt watched them leave.

"Do you know who that was?" she asked distantly.

"A nut."

"That's Mrs. Rayfield Robinson. Her husband is the state senator from Grady." Mrs. Holt patted me on the shoulder. "I guess it isn't your fault. How were you to know?"

"Know what?"

"Just how important Ray Robinson is to this hospital." Mrs. Holt walked slowly back to her station. Absently she picked up a stack of unopened envelopes and sorted them into three piles. Something had happened, I told myself shrewdly. I've done something terrible. So terrible Mrs. Holt can't find the strength to chastise me.

I persisted out of curiosity and masochism. "Just because she's the wife of some redneck politician doesn't mean she can use this emergency room like it was her own private clinic."

Mrs. Holt patiently put down her envelopes. "Her husband is the chairman of the Health and Urban Resources Committee. Can you guess which committee votes funds for Alabama hospitals?"

The curtain of fog lifted. By offending Marjane Robinson I had virtually assured Trafford a smaller piece of the HURC pie. Marjane was at this moment doubtlessly raising hell with her husband about the rude, inconsiderate treatment at Trafford Memorial. Rayfield would respond gallantly, lopping thousands off Trafford's ledger.

"That's political suicide," I said. "The voters wouldn't stand for it."

"There are more voters in Selma. Selma is also in Rayfield's district," Mrs. Holt noted. "Every year Selma gets twice as much as Trafford Memorial. Things could be worse next year."

Froehling pulled me to a neutral corner. "You didn't tell me your job included playing politics with these hillbillies," he said. I assured him the ugly Robinson incident was an

120

exception, probably already forgotten by the insulted party. Froehling didn't buy it, not for a minute.

Understand, his early impressions of Trafford Memorial were something short of outstanding. Nor did the tour of the hospital offer much promise. He took notes scrupulously in a brown appointment book and punctuated each observation with stinging sarcasm. "Fifty-two beds. Eight obstetrical, ten pediatric and thirty medical and surgery. Plus four in coronary care. Sure this isn't just the wing of some big hospital?"

"Don't forget the morgue and medical records room downstairs," I said.

"Lord, don't tell me you keep the bodies and files together?"

"No, don't worry. There wasn't enough room in the filing cabinets. Would you care to see our ICU?"

Froehling arched his eyebrows. "Intensive care? You bet. Is it in the lobby or the cafeteria?"

Now furnished with an EKG unit, portable respirator, heart monitors and oxygen, Benbow Hutchinson's room, number forty-seven, had officially become intensive care. We tiptoed in. Benbow didn't stir; his eyes sagged shut.

"This is it?" Froehling wanted to know.

"Catch the view." I pointed to the pond. "The patients can actually see bass jumping out there sometimes."

"Big deal. What's the TV doing here? I've never heard of a television in ICU. This old guy goes for the Saturday morning cartoons?"

"Mr. Hutchinson is sort of special."

Froehling leaned over and studied Benbow's face. "Is he alive?"

"He's eighty-seven. Besides that, he's got severe coronary disease."

"Bet it's costing $200 a day to keep him going," Froehling speculated coldly.

"Two hundred and forty, but who's counting?"

"What a waste," Froehling said. "The old buzzard's in a coma."

"No he's not!" wheezed Benbow, lifting a wrinkled eyelid. Froehling stumbled backward. "Dr. Stone," the old man whispered, "get this bastard out of here."

Genuinely shaken, Froehling managed a meek apology.

Benbow laughed gruffly and his right eye drooped shut again. "Dr. Parker sent you, didn't he?" he asked, slipping off into dreamland.

Todd Froehling saw too much of Grady's wildlife for his own good. Marjane Robinson and Benbow. It was a cinch he'd retreat back to Brooklyn and regale his medical colleagues with tales from down under. "Didn't see much in the way of emergency medical care tonight," he remarked as I left him at the motel.

"Just a bad night," I answered lamely. "You should see the place when there's a bad wreck on the Eisenhower Bridge. Talk about excitement!"

I was stunned when Froehling called the next morning to accept the job. "It's going to be a tough challenge," he allowed, "but I'm kind of looking forward to it."

Shelly was ecstatic. "Call Anderson and tell him the good news. He's got himself a new sucker." She planted a kiss on my cheek. "You did it, Otis!"

"I can't believe it either." I sipped a cup of coffee and paced the apartment. "It doesn't make sense. After last night, why would anyone take a job like mine? You think Froehling might be psychopathic?"

Shelly held out the telephone. "Call Anderson."

As I reached for the receiver the phone rang. Froehling, I thought morosely. Changed his mind already. Goddamn New Yorker. "Hello," said a female voice. "I'm Dr. Froehling's wife. May I speak to my husband?"

"He's staying at a motel. Would you like the number?"

"I'll just leave a message," said Mrs. Froehling, who sounded remarkably pleasant for a person married to the sour doctor. "Tell him Cynthia died so he won't have to come back tomorrow for the heart surgery."

"I'm sorry . . . about his patient, that is. Can I ask what happened?"

"Sure. She got run over by a milk truck."

"That's terrible."

"Yes, it is," said Mrs. Froehling. "But I blame Mrs. Demetri. It was her fault."

"Ah, the babysitter."

Mrs. Froehling laughed. "No, Mrs. Demetri was Cynthia's owner. You know, she never kept that puppy on a leash."

SO TODD FROEHLING WAS A VETERINARIAN.

That explained why he wanted the job so badly: anything beats giving enemas to poodles.

He was just the first in a long procession of losers who came to answer the newspaper ads. Investigating each applicant was a fascinating, albeit time-consuming, sport. Jerome Regan was running from a medical malpractice suit in St. Louis. Leroy "Swifty" McCutcheon was dodging a Phoenix bank. Peter Swineburn was hiding from an ex-wife. The best of the bunch, Earl Bottoms, turned out to be a med student who had been axed for cheating in his third year. None of the applicants were exactly what the board had in mind.

Four weeks after Todd Froehling boarded a plane back to New York, Trafford Memorial still lacked a full-time emergency physician. For those of us who were ambulatory and sober, the work load grew unmanageable. The only doctor offering his services was Lee Bob Parker, and no one wanted him around. Carl Hogue was still recuperating, but not as fast as anticipated. As for the other doctors, they made it a point to see their patients and only their patients.

November was a horrible month in the emergency room. Carl Hogue was partly to blame; first, because he wasn't around to share the load and, second, he *was* around to quarterback from the sidelines. Emphatically banned by my orders from the E.R. unit, the persistent old man took his case all the way to William E. Anderson, who capitulated readily.

Every night at seven Hogue would show up with a stack of paperback books and TV fan magazines.

"Please, Dr. Hogue, go home."

"Eh! Worried, Stone? A good doctor has confidence in himself." Then the bulbous nose would implant itself amidst ratty pages captioned "Dino Leaves Wife for Joey Bishop."

On one such night, Dr. Earl Halberstam called from the San Jose City Hospital. The purpose: a briefing on the progress of The United States vs. Juan Jiminez, M.D. Uncle Sam had come to his senses, Halberstam reported optimistically, and granted the Brazilian doctor his visa.

"He can leave as scheduled in January."

"Two months? That's wonderful," I crowed. "I can't wait."

"We can't wait either, Dr. Stone. Jiminez is so preoccupied with personal problems that his work here at the hospital is lagging badly. We may have to replace him."

"But *I'm* his replacement."

"Of course you are," Halberstam soothed, "but until you get here we're in a real bind. Jiminez spends half his time down at the Federal courthouse and the other half with his dying mother and pregnant wife."

"I thought you told me his family lived in Brazil."

"No, no. I said he had a *girl* in Brazil. That's why he wants to go back. See, he's divorcing his wife here in the States. . . ."

"Never mind."

"Now, Otis, don't worry," Halberstam said. "We're just going to take on somebody part of the time, maybe from one of the Oakland hospitals. You'd be surprised at the number of doctors looking to relocate at smaller hospitals like ours," he continued. "Just today I interviewed a fellow from New York. Name was Froehling."

"Just don't give my job away," I pleaded.

Halberstam laughed. "Take it easy. I didn't hire him. The first clue was all that animal hair on his coat. Then when I showed him OB-GYN, he said it was the most modern spay ward he'd ever seen."

Two months until freedom—it seemed impossible. What else would go wrong? Juan Jiminez could unexpectedly win the Nobel Prize for research on viral warts; San Jose City Hospital would offer him a nice, fat contract, fly his paramour up from Brazil and forget all about Otis M. Stone in Grady, Alabama.

I said good-bye to Halberstam and promised to be on his doorstep January 10th. No sooner had I hung up the receiver than the first emergency of the evening arrived in two well-dressed parcels. One was the celebrated All-State fullback of the Grady High School Boars, blond and muscular Don Singer. The second package was his date, a pert strawberry blonde draped with a long pink gown. Her name was a wet one: Lilac Kirkpatrick. They entered arm-in-arm, exchanging twin looks of grave concern.

"We need a doctor," Don announced nervously.

"Over here," I said. He led Lilac into the examining room. Something—either the bright surgical lights, or the lima bean color of the tiles—frightened the girl and she buried herself in Singer's arms.

"I'm scared," Lilac whined.

"Don't talk!" he yelled. "Whatever you do, don't talk."

Grady High School schedules only two significant social events each year. One is the Autumn Formal and the other is the Spring Prom. Those who behave themselves at the November extravaganza are encouraged to attend the finale in May. Those who do not behave are delegated to get the beer, drive to Gresham Pond and wait for their classmates. Don and Lilac were *the* couple: football star and head cheerleader. They had been "going together" for almost three months. Tonight would have made it official, Don related sadly.

"What happened?"

"She swallowed a pin. Actually, it was kind of funny. When we got to the gym she gave me a corsage . . ." (here Lilac nudged Singer and he produced from his coat pocket a mutilated white carnation.) ". . . anyway, she put the pin in her mouth."

126

"Boutonniere," said Lilac instructively.

"What?"

"It's not a corsage. It's called a *boo-ton-ear*."

"Shut up," Don scowled. "Don't talk anymore until the doctor looks at you." He turned courteously back to me. "That's it. She just swallowed it."

"How? Did she gulp it down or did she inhale it?"

"I really don't know," Don replied. "Does it matter?"

Lilac spoke. "I swallowed it. I'm sure. I was fixing the boutonniere into Don's buttonhole when Mr. Cormier—that's our civics teacher—he said Don's zipper was down." Lilac covered her mouth, muffling a snicker. "That's when I swallowed the straight pin."

Don reddened. "I told you to shut up."

Buster Hogue, my sidekick on Friday nights, didn't even know what an otolaryngologist was, much less where one could be procured on a weekend. Nurse Holt suggested I call a hospital in Selma. Carl Hogue suggested an old friend of his, now retired in Montgomery. Buster suggested I hold Lilac Kirkpatrick upside down by her feet and shake. After much coaxing, I was able to persuade the ear, nose and throat man at a Selma clinic to make the trip over, but only after assuring him the pin was still lodged in Lilac's esophagus, and had not passed into the stomach, where nature would take over.

"A forty mile trip," he griped, "just because some pretty debutante gobbled up her date's corsage."

"Boutonniere," I corrected.

Don and Lilac sat rigidly together. "How long?" he asked.

"At least an hour. Relax."

"How can I relax with a two-inch pin in my throat?" Lilac fretted. She looked at her thin gold wristwatch. "The formal's half over already."

Don stood up and made a sidewise motion with his head, the way jocks do when they've got something manly to talk about. "Is she gonna be okay? I mean, like, we were gonna drive down to Gresham Pond after the dance and . . ." he fidgeted, ". . . and get it on. You follow me?"

"No, thanks. I've got other plans."

"Doc, you know what I mean. Once they get the pin out she'll be okay, right? I won't have to worry about . . . about hurting her."

"Ask the throat doctor," I advised clinically, "and Don, pull up your fly!"

Carl Hogue put down his book, a two-hundred page history of the Mafia in Wisconsin, and motioned me over. "Otis," he said avuncularly, "I've been doing some thinking about this malpractice thing. The lawyer said it might take years to reach court. Maybe, just maybe, we ought to settle. We would save ourselves and Trafford Memorial some money, in the long run."

The suddenness of Hogue's about-face forced me into a nearby chair. What he said made sense for him. He had nothing to lose by settling out of court; in fact, it might prove less embarrassing than a court trial. His patients would never desert him; Carl Hogue was above reproach. Clearly he was not worried about his future, but rather about his past, about his hard-won reputation.

"It's an annoyance," he said matter-of-factly. "I'm not worried about legalities or even the financial liability. I'm convinced I did the right thing for that boy."

"And me?"

"Of course, you did the right thing, too, Stone. You did exactly what I told you." He smiled apologetically. "I'm not so young and idealistic anymore. I've got other things to worry about. I don't want any lawsuit to ruin my legacy here."

Shrieks from another carload of wounded crazies drew me back to the examining room. "We'll talk about this later," I promised Hogue, "but I'll tell you now: I'm not going to settle. I'm going to fight it."

Hogue just sighed. "Don't be a hero," he said.

That night I had another dream: the phone is ringing. It is a call from San Jose City Hospital. Dr. Halberstam. Good news? Let's hear it. Oh, I see. Juan Jiminez just discovered a cure for leukemia? Wonderful. You've appointed him Assistant Chief of Medicine? What about me? The position is no longer open. Why? It wouldn't look proper for the hospital to hire a physician who is being sued for malpractice. No, I *don't* understand. How did you find out about the lawsuit? Ah, an anonymous phone caller who identified himself as a Mafioso from Wisconsin. I see. Maybe next time? Sure.

Shelly shook me awake. "You're dreaming, Otis. Wake up! We gotta go."

"Shit, what a nightmare. What time is it?"

"Five-thirty. Trafford called. Looks likes they got another one for you."

"But Parker is on call tonight."

"Parker is missing!"

"What?"

Shelly nodded. "The sheriff is questioning Buster now. They haven't booked him."

"That means they haven't got a corpse . . . yet."

At the hospital, Duane Moultry paced like a wildcat. His brown hair lay like a sloppy nest on his head. His eyes were red and bloodshot. He wore a pair of jeans and the top to fire-engine red pajamas. His son, Duane Jr., sat on the edge of the stainless steel examining tables, swinging his stubby legs and picking happily at his nose. A trickle of dark blood meandered out of his left nostril toward his lips. His father paled. "Lord, help us! He's hemorrhaging."

Through a drowsy fog of disjointed medical jibberish I tried to convince Duane Sr. that his son was not mortally ill. He refused to be reassured. "He's still bleeding. Can't you do something? What kind of doctor are you?"

A very short-tempered one. "Have it your way." Through an otoscope I explored the crusty inner recesses of young Moultry's nostrils. "Just as I thought!"

Duane Sr.'s eyes widened. "How bad?"

"Acute. An acute case of nosepicking, the leading cause of nosebleeds in America today."

The elder Moultry cocked his head suspiciously. I had him.

"Your son has become another grim statistic, Mr. Moul-

129

try. Oh, he'll live to lead a normal, happy life—thanks to the miracles of modern medicine. But each year literally millions of youngsters are tragically stricken with nosebleeds.'' So dramatic was my liturgy that even little Duane stopped picking and listened studiously.

"You see, Mr. Moultry, this trip to the hospital could have been avoided had your family been able to recognize the Seven Warning Signs of Nosepicking."

Moultry nodded fervently. "I heard about them on a radio talk show."

"I'll go over them again. I advise you to listen closely and memorize them. Number One: does your child cry at the sight of Kleenex? Two: is he able to fit unusually large objects, like a garden rake, up his nostrils?"

"That's Junior, all right."

"Does he *try* to catch colds just so his nose will run? Does he miss meals. . . ."

"Dr. Stone!" the sharp voice belonged to Nurse Barnes. "That isn't why the Moultrys are here."

"Go on about them seven warning signs," Duane Sr. implored.

"Later. Tell me why you're here."

He pointed at Junior. "Damn kid eats everything. Swallowed up twenty-three hundred dollars."

"In bills?"

"Coins."

"He must have been up half the night. What did he do, break into the piggy bank for a bedtime snack?"

"Actually Duane Jr. swallowed only three coins," Mrs. Barnes noted. "They happened to be worth twenty-three hundred dollars. You can see why Mr. Moultry here is very anxious to retrieve them."

The X-rays were encouraging: three bright discs registered clearly in the boy's large stomach. At the sight of the coins, Duane Sr. grew agitated. "Damnation! See that?" He pointed to the largest disc. "That's an 1801 silver dollar. Those two little jobbers over here are pennies. In mint condition, too. They been out of circulation for sixty-seven years.''

''Not anymore,'' observed Mrs. Barnes.

Moultry tapped a chunky brown finger on the X-ray. ''What are you going to do now? Operate?''

''Nope. We're just going to wait. There's no need for surgery, Mr. Moultry. Those coins aren't going anywhere but out. If you want, I'll prescribe a stool softener to help your boy through the next day or so.''

''A laxative?''

Duane Moultry finally understood the full consequences of his son's appetite and what indignities it implied. ''I get it,'' he said sourly. ''Junior's gonna shit out those coins.''

''Right you are.''

Moultry wrung his hands. ''What if they accidentally get flushed down the john or something? Then I'm out twenty-three hundred bucks.'' He began to pace back and forth. Suddenly, he stopped and pointed menacingly at the little boy. ''Don't you go to the bathroom without your Pappy, you understand? Don't you go *near* a toilet without tellin' me.''

''You've got about twelve hours,'' I said helpfully. ''That gives you time to think of a way to get the coins back.''

Duane Sr. grimaced. ''Guess I'll use a coat-hanger to fish 'em out of the john.'' He made a face. ''Hey, you don't think they'll lose any of their collector's value up there in Junior's tummy?'' He laughed nervously. ''I'll just wash 'em off real good. No one will know . . . they won't lose their shine or anything?''

''I doubt it. Let me know how it works out.''

Moultry slung the boy under his arm like a sack of oats. ''Jesus H. Christ,'' he swore on his way out, ''why couldn't I be a stamp collector?''

Meanwhile, the search for Dr. Lee Bob Parker had expanded unenthusiastically to the Selma area where Parker was last seen, buying a new seven-iron at a pro shop. Buster still was in the custody of the Grady County Sheriff's Office, where his father was arguing unsuccessfully for the boy's release. The authorities couldn't very well charge Buster with murder because Parker legally was only a missing person. So they went back in the files and found nine unpaid traffic tickets with which to justify Buster's confinement.

When I got home from the E.R., Shelly was entertaining a sheriff's deputy in my apartment. He stood up and introduced himself as Jim Marshall. My knees trembled: he looked and spoke exactly like James Arness.

"What can I do for you, Marshall Deputy?"

"It's Deputy Marshall, Dr. Stone. As you know, we're looking into the possibility that one of your associates, Dr. Lee Parker, has met with foul play."

"I know what you're thinking," I interrupted courageously, "but Buster Hogue was with me at Trafford Memorial until two this morning. I'm his alibi."

"And I suppose he's your alibi, too? Very tidy."

"What are you talking about?"

"Some of the nurses and staff aides at the hospital seem to remember you and Dr. Parker arguing loudly on several occasions. Did you hate him?"

Shelly butted in. "You don't have to answer, Otis, until your attorney is present."

"I don't have an attorney."

Shelly flashed me a cunning look. "*Of course* you do. Remember, in Washington? Your brother Benjamin."

"The shoe salesman?"

Shelly covered her face and groaned. "Call an attorney, Otis."

"That won't be necessary," said Deputy Marshall, rising. "I got what I came for. I'll probably be back. We might need to talk to you downtown, Dr. Stone."

Downtown? Downtown where? The courthouse stood between a coin laundry and a pet store. "If I were you," said the deputy, "I wouldn't leave town." He swaggered out the door as if he'd been sitting on his nightstick.

Shelly and I opened a beer and pondered the unseemly situation. Parker's disappearance was just one more annoying problem, one more unwelcome complication, one more untimely roadblock between me and California. Should the hapless quack turn up dead, every newspaper in the Southeast would dispatch an investigative reporter. Should Parker's body be found in some macabre mutilation—strangled poetically, for instance, by his own stethoscope—the incident would certainly find its way into the national tabloids. My name would figure prominently in the speculation, no two ways about it. I thought of Sam Sheppard.

"Maybe my brother needs a partner in the shoe business," I wondered aloud. I looked to Shelly for solace. "What has Buster done?"

"Otis, don't forget that *you* are a suspect, too," said the law student. "You've had your share of fights with Lee Bob. Remember last Tuesday with the secretary?"

"How could I forget? That maniac wanted to put sutures in a half-inch paper cut! Any decent doctor," I said defensively, "would get angry in a situation like that."

Shelly patted my arm. "I know, honey. But you *threatened* him in front of a dozen witnesses."

"So what? It was just a tongue depressor. What could I possibly do, gag him to death?"

"You still *threatened* him, Otis."

I fell asleep and instantly found myself on Death Row. To one side of me is a three-hundred-pound homosexual rapist. In the other adjoining cell is an anti-Semitic axe murderer. Rumors about the "new man" on Cell Block D bounce off the cold yellow walls. "What's he in for?" one con is heard to ask. "Murder One," says another. "Offed a doctor."

"He's ba-a-d!" whistles another inmate. "You heard of the Boston Strangler and the L.A. Slasher? This dude's known as the Grady Tongue Depressor. Gags people to death. Say ahhh. . . ."

As I stand trembling before the parole board, Shelly wakes me.

"Wake up! I heard it on the radio. They found Lee Bob's car outside of town."

133

IT COULD BE SAID WITHOUT CONTRADICTION, AND
often was, that Lee Bob Parker had no taste. He drove a
Cadillac that cost $14,000. He boasted that it cost so much
because it was custom-made, but the real reason it was
custom-made was simply that General Motors had the good
sense *not* to build a green automobile with cherry red inte-
rior. And that is what Parker wanted; no other combination
of colors would do. He scoured the country for a green and
red Cadillac and one day even drove all the way down to
Mobile. Melvin Dryden had heard a rumor that a green and
red Caddy was being sold by a dealer down that way, but
when Parker arrived he found it was a repainted car with a
Studebaker engine and 167,000 miles.

So he wrote directly to Detroit and in three months the car
was delivered. Parker's wife Beulah hated it, but he pacified
her by giving her the old tan Mercedes (which she promptly
drove into a tractor).

Lee Bob's car was easy to find, even for Sheriff Rooster
Bootman. Parker was the only doctor in Alabama, possibly
in the continental United States, who affixed a magnetic sign
to the side of his automobile which read: "L.R. Parker,
M.D." and listed his office phone number. When the medical association charged him with advertising, he blandly
countered with the argument that the sign merely helped his
patients keep track of him in case of emergencies.

Bootman was roaring east on Highway 80, drunk out of
his mind, when he spied the green Cadillac parked crookedly

on the south side of the road. Forgetting everything he had ever learned about emergency driving, the sheriff promptly slammed down hard on the brakes and slid sideways off the highway. Before passing out, Rooster had managed to activate his siren and radio for a backup.

It was eight-thirty when Shelly and I arrived. Four squad cars encircled Parker's Cadillac, which rested at an angle about ten feet from the right-of-way. Three deputies and a single burr-headed highway patrolman prowled around the auto, squatting periodically and peering underneath as if hunting for clues. No one went closer than ten feet.

"No trace of the doctor," Shelly whispered after conferring with one of the cops, a buddy she'd met on an ambulance run. "They're waiting for the lab men to check for bloodstains and fingerprints."

We sat in the sun on the hood of Shelly's car, swatting gnats and eyeing the lawmen, who sternly eyed us back. "Lee Bob was drunk," I speculated. "His car broke down so he decided to walk back to town."

"No, he would have turned up by now," Shelly said.

I pointed a half-mile down the road toward the David Eisenhower Bridge. "Not necessarily, my dear Watson. Dr. Parker could be lazing in the Alabama River at this very moment."

Shelly shook her head. "I don't think so, Otis. He loves this car more than he loves his wife. He would never have abandoned it out here. I'm afraid something serious has happened. Maybe he was ambushed or kidnapped."

"By what, a bear? The only persons who knew that Parker went to Selma were his wife and his golf pro. Besides, I'll bet there wasn't a soul within miles of here when Parker stopped, except for a few coon hunters."

One of the cops got bored and walked over to chat. "Foul play," he said grimly. "No doubt about it."

"How do you know?"

"First of all, there's more than half a tank of gas in the car."

"Maybe it was the transmission," Shelly said.

The cop studied her. "With all due respect, Miss Farmer, that happens to be a brand new Cadillac. Ain't got but four thousand miles on it. My cousin owns one and in two years it's never been in the shop. Never."

"What else makes you think there's trouble?" I asked.

"The keys are still in the ignition, and the car is locked. What kind of guy would lock the keys inside the car?" Nobody answered. The cop summarized his conclusions. "It's murder, all right. Just don't have a corpse, yet, but we will!" He fiddled around in a back pocket and fished out a small brown notebook. "Lemme ask ya' something," he said amiably. "Who'd want to kill Dr. Parker?"

Shelly looked at me and I looked at the Cadillac. "Besides the AMA, the nurses' association and a couple hundred patients, no one."

The cop pursed his lips. "Yeah, it's a mystery to me, too."

The lab man from the county sheriff's office arrived and ritualistically puttered around the car, dusting for prints and tweezing hair samples from the red leather upholstery. "Nice car," he said, depositing one of Parker's less glorious golf scorecards in a plastic evidence bag. "Nice car," he repeated, "but I never have seen one quite this color. I wonder, Dr. Stone, was the victim color-blind?"

At noon, William E. Anderson's nervous voice came over Shelly's car radio as the Trafford administrator was interviewed by a local newsman. "We have the deepest faith that Dr. Parker will be found alive and unharmed," he intoned. "Trafford Memorial Hospital is offering a $100 reward for any information leading authorities to the body—eh, to Dr. Parker."

By now, a motley busload of volunteers was combing the area eastward from Parker's car to the river. The men wore snakeboots and carried high-powered deer rifles on their shoulders as they trudged through the dense acreage. At one o'clock, Gary Murdock—the nonrabid raccoon victim—emerged from a thicket on the north side of the highway with an eight-point buck draped over his shoulder; he tossed it into his truck and drove home for the day.

"Let's go," I begged Shelly. "They'll be out here all afternoon and I don't think they're going to find anything."

"Just a little longer," she said. "It's very important I'm here when they find him."

Her concern took me by surprise. "Since when did Lee Bob Parker mean so much to you?"

"Don't be so crass. I've known the man two years," she said defensively. "Besides, the *Mobile Register* offered me fifty bucks for a photo of the cops bringing the body out of the woods. . . ."

"Mercenary!"

"And it looks good for *you* to be here, Otis. Don't forget, you're a suspect. This way they can see you've got nothing to hide."

I shivered and found myself saying, "God, I hope he's alive."

"Me, too," Shelly said. "This town can't afford to lose another doctor."

We left at four, an hour after the volunteers had given up. Melvin Dryden's tow truck dragged Lee Bob's precious emerald Cadillac away and the cops went home. That evening, the front page of the *Grady Guardian* blared, "No Trace of Parker's Body." Unintentionally, the town seemed to be getting back at Lee Bob for the time he prematurely pronounced Carl Hogue dead. Nobody gave Parker a prayer.

That night Buster confessed.

His statement, read by a deputy over the local radio station, was typically disjointed. "I did it. I know it was wrong. Can I go home now?"

Shelly heard the broadcast and burst into tears. "Poor Buster!" she cried.

"Wait a minute!" I shouted. "Listen." And, sure enough, there was more.

Impassively, the deputy read the remainder of Buster's "confession." He had stated: "I went to Parker's house and saw the car in the driveway. All the lights were out. I knew that putting sugar in the gas tank screwed up the pistons, but I didn't have any sugar so I had to use a couple of bottles of

137

that low-calorie sweetener. It wasn't real sugar, I swear. I poured it into the tank, threw the bottles in some bushes and ran away."

For Buster it was a valiant try. Sabotaging Parker's Cadillac was the closest thing to gangland crime the young man would ever do. He was promptly charged with three counts of petty mischief (one for each bottle) and released on thirty-seven dollars bond. We found him at home, characteristically remorseful and reflective.

"Hot damn!" Buster hooted when he saw us at the door. "I did it! I got sprung."

"Did you kill Dr. Parker?" Shelly asked tactfully.

"No, girl," he replied, stung by the accusation. "I just dumped that low-cal stuff in his gasoline. That's all, I swear."

Carl Hogue chuckled uneasily. "It was just a prank, right? Something you picked up at one of those damned liberal colleges I sent you to, right, son?"

"That's right," Buster said, after mulling the notion and finding it plausible. "One of my sorority brothers taught it to me."

Shelly left the room for a moment and Buster leaned over to tell me this revenge business isn't half what it was cracked up to be. "I hope they find him," he said. "One way or another. Just waiting here, not knowing, is like having the clap." I took him at his word and left him alone with his father.

Precisely twenty-eight hours after his mysterious disappearance, a befuddled Lee Bob Parker stumbled out of a swamp on the south side of Highway 80. He flagged down a trucker, hitched a ride into town and immediately went to the sheriff's office to report his car stolen. Failing to recognize the tall, miskempt fellow holding a seven-iron, the desk officer went ahead and took Parker's report. It was only when another deputy, one of the doctor's bursitis patients, recognized him that Lee Bob was prevented from slipping unnoticed into the night.

Parker's version of the ordeal was published two days later in a special edition of the *Grady Guardian*. It was a rich example of Lee Bob's flair for the dramatic. "The car wheezed and rattled to a stop on the highway," he was quoted. "I knew something was wrong, so I climbed into the back seat and hid. Pretty soon a vanload of drug-crazed hippies parked nearby. Four of the biggest, dirtiest ones dragged me from the car and tried to rob me. But, using my golf club, I fought them off and managed to escape into the woods. There I collapsed from exhaustion until I awoke two nights ago."

Of course, no one believed a word of it. The doctor who examined Parker after this tortuous adventure happened to be Carl Hogue, who easily wrangled the truth from him.

Buster's vandalism, it turned out, had worked like a charm. The sugar-coated Cadillac had indeed sputtered and died, leaving its owner infuriated. The hapless Parker had never before looked under its hood, but he tried . . . and tried. Failing to locate the proper release switch among the Caddy's myriad of dashboard gadgets, Parker decided to open the trunk as a distress signal—only to find the keys locked fast in the ignition switch.

"He was hungry, but the only thing he had on him was a pint of scotch," Hogue related merrily, "so he drank the whole damn thing in an hour. That's when he got up the courage to go trailblazing with only a seven-iron for protection. He stumbled into the woods and passed out, not thirty-five yards from the car. When he woke up, he thought he'd been sleeping only a few hours. He saw his car gone and hitched back to town for the cops."

Parker was sorely distressed when the true version of his "abduction" leaked out among his peers. His initial buoyancy upon learning that the green and red Cadillac wasn't stolen turned to rage when Parker received the towing and repair bill from Melvin Dryden. The invoice was instantly mailed to Buster Hogue, who instantly mailed it to his father, who instantly consigned his son to twenty menial hours of weekly overtime at Trafford.

At first, Buster was undisturbed by the new longer work schedule because a pert new nurse was making the hours pass very quickly. In the course of two amorous days, he had managed to sneak into Shelly's ambulance three times, so his mood was cheerful—until the circus came to town.

Bill Kelley's Bijou Big Tent visited southern Alabama every two years. Grady was traditionally the third stop. Bijou Bill unleashed an advertising blitz—a two-column display layout in the *Guardian*—a full six months before his arrival. The entire county was properly geared for a rural Mardi Gras by the time Kelley's six tractor-trailer entourage steamed in from the east. For the kids, the big attractions were a roller coaster, a shooting gallery, a ferris wheel and a thrill ride known as the Flying Upchuck.

For the men, the attractions were Cindi, Stormy and twin dwarves named Tammy and Tululah. They slept during the day, presumably to save energy and stay out of sight. At eleven each night the Big Tent closed to women and children; the kids, gooey and tired, piled into the trucks and station wagons so Mom could drive home. The husbands would dawdle, wink at each other and crack a few beers until eleven-thirty when the lines formed at one of Bijou Bill's "extra special tents."

Buster Hogue dearly wished to attend one of these legendary performances. Margaret Holt, however, was not about to have Buster filch on his overtime duties.

"Talk to her, Otis," he petitioned. "I just want two hours off. Is that too much to ask?"

"I'm going to the circus."

His face turned to rubber. "What? You can't do that to me."

"It's my night off and I'm going. Don't look so depressed. Bijou Bill's been in town only two days and already I've treated five men who think they got the clap."

Buster blanched. "Really?"

"See you later."

He grabbed at my sleeve. "Will you at least let me know how the show is? Please?" He winked spastically.

"I'll do even better than that, Buster. I'll bring you back a kewpi doll."

Whether motivated out of boredom, lechery or curiosity, my mind was made up to see firsthand what all these farmers and factory workers were whispering about. Bill Kelley's circus was a regular carnal celebration, the most exciting thing to happen in Grady since I had arrived.

At eleven-thirty sharp, I stood in line behind a tough-looking pecan farmer and his eighteen-year-old son. Over the dingy yellow tent was a sign heralding Bijou Bill's Harem Dancers. The barker was Bill himself, a stubby man with curly sideburns, leathery jowls and Richard Petty sunglasses. "Step right up and get your fancy tickled! Cindi will thrill you. Stormy gives a whole new meaning to the words 'Big Top,' and Tammy and Tululah will titillate you beyond your wildest, kinkiest fantasies. Step this way and hand the man four dollars, just four dollars for the hottest, sweetest belly-dancers in the entire Southeast United States!"

The eighteen-year-old grinned at his father. "Goddamn!" he laughed. "This is going to be great, just great!" His father didn't laugh at all, just slapped the boy hard between the shoulders and told him to keep his eyes and mouth open.

Reluctantly I shoved four bucks at the seedy ticket-taker and made my way past a couple of mongoloid bouncers into the stale tent. The stage, fashioned from warped plywood, stood six feet off the ground. In the absence of seats, the convivial customers milled around and pretended the place didn't smell like elephant shit, which it did. At midnight, Bill Kelley himself swaggered onstage in a green vest with a brown bowler hat. He wasted no time with formal introductions.

"The rules are simple: You hurt the performers and our highly trained security personnel will remove you from the premises. In other words, if you grab too hard you get your head broke!"

The first act was an ill-tempered woolly monkey named Pierre who masturbated furiously in time to a Mitch Miller record. The men cheered wildly, threw money and giggled until spit dribbled down their chins. The music stopped, but Pierre intently continued his routine until Bijou Bill thumped him sharply with a cane; then the wiry monkey obediently scooped up all the nickels and pennies and loped offstage.

The next headliner was "Sensuous Cindi," ninety pounds of emaciated belly dancer who lacked both a belly and the smallest trace of dancing prowess. When she doffed her majorette costume, two men grabbed her ankles and yanked her into the audience. She giggled politely, warded off a few well-placed gropes and scrambled back onstage. By the time Cindi wiggled through her finale—a Latino rendition of "Jingle Bells"—she was coughing uncontrollably.

Billed optimistically as "the South's favorite sex kitten," Stormy Daze mewed her way through a stultifying pantomime of "Hey, Big Spender" before she began to entertain the rowdy onlookers with graceless nude acrobatics. Each ticket-holder was literally given a taste of Stormy's talents while I, for purely sanitary reasons, edged discreetly to the rear of the tent. Like Cindi, Stormy was hacking most unsensuously and at one unfortunate juncture interrupted a headstand to spit offstage. Both girls appeared weak and dispirited, a condition I initially attributed to their depressing occupations.

My opinion changed at the comical arrival of the twin dwarves, Tammy and Tululah. Bill Kelley gave them a generous introduction as "the dynamic duo," but even the debauched audience realized the two girls were in no shape for their arduous, albeit imaginative, embraces. As the last hollow bars of "Me and My Shadow" played through the foggy sound system, I cornered Bijou Bill outside the tent.

"What's the matter with these girls?" I asked.

"Sorry, buddy, no refunds! See the sign?"

"I don't want my money back. I'm a doctor at the hospital here in town. Those girls are coughing badly. They look terrible."

Kelley motioned for one of the bouncers to move in. He was a big, flabby fellow with no hair and a flat, twisted nose. As he lumbered towards me, I jabbed him in the gut, forcing the air from his lungs. He choked for breath and backed off.

142

"Keep Igor away from me," I told Kelley. "I'm only trying to help. If those girls are sick, every guy in this county could be in bad shape by the time you leave Grady."

"It's just the flu," Kelley said impatiently. "It's been going around the circus. I think we caught it up in Buffalo. Everybody's got a little cough, that's all."

"Any chest pain?"

Kelley scratched his head. "Yeah, I guess a couple of the fellas mentioned something like that. But, it's just the flu. Don't be such a good Samaritan, okay?"

"How about excessive weight loss?"

"No!" Kelley growled.

Then Igor spoke, no mean feat. "What about Girtha?"

"Who's Girtha?" I wondered.

Kelley slapped Igor and sent him off somewhere to cry. "He don't know what he's talkin' about. Girtha was our Fat Lady for about two years till we had to fire her. She went on a diet or something. Anyway, what good is a fat lady that weighs a hundred and fifty pounds? Who's gonna pay to see *that* when they can watch their wives at home?"

Convincing Bijou Bill to permit me to examine his troupe was no small task, but he relented as soon as I started calculating aloud the cost of having to replace an entire cast of circus performers. We piled into an old blue bus: Cindi, Stormy, the twins, Samson the Strong Man, Franco the Lion Tamer, two clowns, a juggler named LeRoy, Pierre, the self-abusive monkey, and Kelley himself. A fellow named Roy with elephantiasis drove.

Nurse Barnes and Buster Hogue ran outside when they heard the bus rattle up to the emergency room.

"It must be a football team," said Mrs. Barnes.

"Or the Salvation Army," mused Buster.

I climbed out first, followed by Cindi and Stormy, both shivering in their phosphorescent G-strings. The rest of the unsightly entourage straggled through the parking lot with a chorus of hoarse coughs and nervous cursing.

Mrs. Barnes bolted inside to phone Margaret Holt and alert

Carl Hogue. Buster stood there stupefied, eyes hopping from one performer to another.

"Otis," he finally said. "I was only kidding. You didn't have to bring the whole goddamned circus."

CARL HOGUE WAS ONLY FIVE DAYS BACK IN THE
saddle and already his bedside manner was being tested in a
tense and bizarre situation. Clustered sullenly in his beloved
waiting room were eleven sick circus performers and a per-
verted monkey. Civility not being Carl Hogue's strong suit,
he found it impossible to treat these strange people without
insulting them. So badly lacking in diplomatic finesse was
Dr. Hogue that were he a United Nations delegate, the United
States would certainly be at war with continental Europe.

"Get these freaks out of the hospital," he ordered.

Bill Kelley had stuffed himself into an uncomfortable high-
backed chair (the legendary uncomfortability of all waiting
room furniture is, I am certain, part of a master design to
discourage attendance) when Hogue made this first deni-
grating remark. Despicable as he was, Kelley decided to defend his dignity. He squeezed himself out of the chair and
rose to his feet.

"Just a moment, sir!" he said dramatically. "I will not
have these professional performers debased in such a callous
fashion. I don't know who you are and I can't pretend to
care. The fact is, Dr. Stone here himself requested our presence to determine the cause of a rather persistent—and possibly serious—cough that has been hampering my employees
in recent months. We are here only because we were assured
by Dr. Stone that our conditions warranted it. Honestly, do
you think high-paid dancers like Cindi here—who once

145

worked with the Rockettes!—enjoy this kind of public humiliation?"

Cindi obligingly straightened her G-string, blinked innocently and shook her head.

"Of course not!" Kelley boomed. "We are here to receive medical assistance which, I was led to believe, you people are paid to administer."

Hogue turned to me. "Who is this asshole?" he grunted.

"His name is Bill Kelley. He's in charge of the circus. I asked him to come down here because his people are sick. I want to run a couple of tests."

Hogue nodded sarcastically. "Oh, they're sick, all right. I couldn't agree more." He pointed at Roy. "That fellow's got elephantiasis. What the hell do you plan to do about *that*?"

Kelley winced and put a finger to his lips. "Quiet!" he whispered. "Roy doesn't even know he's sick. He actually believes he's a big celebrity."

"How do you explain to him why his arms and legs are enlarged like tree trunks?"

"By telling him he *is* the Abominable Snowman of the Himalayas. I guess he believes it after all these years 'cause he never asks any questions." Kelley smiled paternally at the bloated, dark-skinned man. "He's as gentle as a lamb."

I reviewed for Hogue the reasons for my concern: the chronic coughing, chest pain, weight loss and night chills. "I'm not making any predictions, but I'll guess it's either mono, pneumonia or TB."

There was not much to offer in the way of argument, so Hogue tapped his foot and tugged impatiently at a fleshy part of his neck. "This isn't a free clinic, Stone. We've got *real* patients who depend on us, patients who pay their bills and our salaries. How do you think this town is gonna feel about having a hospital full of circus freaks?"

"I don't care," I said. "How do you think this town is gonna feel when they all come down with infections after a day at the circus?"

146

Hogue surrendered gracelessly. "Have it your way. Margaret, get a chart started on each of these clowns. . . ."

"Beg your pardon," Kelley corrected him, "but only Bobo and Bebe are clowns. LeRoy is a juggler and Franco . . ."

"I'll be at home if you need me," Hogue said to Mrs. Holt as he walked toward the doors.

Trafford had no bona fide emergency admissions desk. The next best thing was the nurses' station, manned on this particular evening by the head nurse herself. To Margaret Holt, then, fell the wholly unenviable task of quizzing the eleven vagabonds for personal details. Normally, admitting patients was an annoying, but elementary, bit of paperwork; on this night the task would assume horrifying proportions. So foul became Mrs. Holt's mood that for the first time in recent memory her tongue was silenced, her piercing hawk-like eyes dulled, and her foreboding, flaring nostrils deflated.

"What's your name?" she asked the first patient.

"Samson," replied a hulking, fuzzy truck of a man who wore a cheap, gold ring in his nose.

"Full name?"

"Samson the Strong Man."

Mrs. Holt bit her lower lip. "Your *real* name?"

Samson looked to Bill Kelley, who nodded. "Yes," said the strong man with renewed conviction, "that is my real name."

"Address?"

Samson chuckled. "Which one? Biloxi? Carrollton? Savannah? Jackson? Baton Rouge? The circus moves around quite a bit, don't it, Bill?"

Bill nodded and Mrs. Holt wrote: "Transient."

"Occupation?"

Samson stood up and flexed both meaty arms. "Strong man!"

"Age?"

"I dunno. Put down twenty-five."

"Where were you born?"

"Persia," grinned Samson. Mrs. Holt glared hatefully in my direction.

"Please," I intervened, "we need to know your real place of birth."

The big man frowned. "Raleigh, North Carolina."

"And your real name?"

Samson's forehead wrinkled. "Do I have to?"

"Please. We won't tell a soul."

"Jules," he whispered painfully. "Jules LeBreque."

And so it went, each interview more arduous than the last. By the time dutiful Margaret Holt would finish with the troupe two hours later, she would willingly agree to record as Roy's occupation: snowman, abominable.

The cacophony of hacking and coughing and moaning filled the hospital. I prepared to begin the first distasteful procedure which, unfortunately, required that Buster and I roam about to each suspected carrier and collect sputum.

If there is one substance more potent, or more repulsive than ordinary spit, it is sputum. And sputum is what Buster and I sought, for it is from this humble, vile substance that modern medicine men can discern many valuable clues. The circus performers each suffered from what is known euphemistically as a "productive" cough; that is, a nasty, wet barking that finds its origins somewhere in the fertile recesses of the human lung. If there is infection lurking down there, the sputum will tell the story.

With a great show of courage Buster and I made the rounds, gathering in sterile cups the viscous products of those productive coughs. The results were gratifying, a sputum collector's dream. It took a full three hours to stain, examine and diagnose the slides. What I found was not at all encouraging: evidence of tubercule bacillus in nine of eleven cultures. Under a microscope, the guilty devils appeared as slender curved rods tainted pink by the stain; med students know them as "red snappers."

At my emergence from the lab, the waiting room dissolved in pandemonium. A circle of anxious, grotesque faces closed in, each begging for a personal diagnosis, each etched in fear. I recognized one of the faces from an earlier encounter: Mrs. Rayfield Robinson. She screamed something about "appendicitis" but her voice was drowned out by the shouts of the circus sickies. I managed to corral Bill Kelley and drag him into the doctor's quarters. I slammed and locked the door behind us.

"The news is not good," I panted. "It looks like some of your people could have tuberculosis."

Kelley rolled his eyes, wavered slightly, then fell back onto a cot. "My God! My God! How long do they have left? I want to make their final days as pleasant as possible. I might even cancel our week in Selma."

To quell his unwarranted generosity I waved both hands. "It's not that serious. I don't think any of them is going to die. They just need rest and the proper medication."

Kelley's eyebrows squirmed. "Oh? You say they're not going to die?"

"I doubt it. But what I want to do is get chest X-rays on each of them, including yourself. Unfortunately, our X-ray machine is broken and we're waiting for the technician to get back from a fishing trip. It may be a few days."

"A few days?" Kelley toyed with his fuzzy sideburns. "You've got to understand, Doctor, I'm operating a business here. A circus may look like it's all fun and games but it's backbreaking work. We can't just quit for a few days. We got to be in Jackson by Friday."

"If this is TB—and I'm reasonably sure it is—and it goes untreated, well, then your whole operation is in big trouble. Start shopping around for a new ringmaster."

Kelley hardened. "It's just the flu, like I said."

"Then let me take some X-rays. Don't forget, you're in the thick of this thing. Even if you don't give a damn about the health of your performers, I know you care about your own."

Kelley twitched. "Wait a minute! Didn't you say . . ."

Kelley tried another scheme. "How about if you give *me* one of those X-rays now? If it looks like I got TB, *then* the rest of the kids can get one. How about it?"

"No deal. It's everyone or no one."

"Then I'm going elsewhere," Kelley announced defiantly, "to get a second opinion."

"Where?"

"Jackson's as good a place as any." And with that, Bijou Bill marched into the waiting room to inform the troupe that there was nothing to fear but exorbitant hospital bills. "Come on," he said with a wave of his chunky arm, "let's go back to the circus."

Realizing some sort of drama was in order, I jumped up on a counter, slipped breezily on a piece of old gauze and fell off again. This ballet successfully recaptured the performers' attention. "Wait!" I shouted from the cold tile floor. "Don't go! Not unless you want to take a chance with tuberculosis."

Instantly the room hushed. Tammy looked at Tululah. Tululah looked quickly away, stubbing her nose on Franco the Lion Tamer's kneecap. "TB?" cried the flesh-peddling dwarf. "Little sister, are we gonna die?"

"I said it looks like some of your people have tuberculosis. If you'll remember, I made each of you cough up some sputum. I examined each slide under a microscope; nine of eleven showed signs of the disease."

"What about mine?" Kelley asked. "Was mine negative or positive?"

I said nothing, but bowed my head and inhaled momentously.

"How much," asked Bijou Bill, "are these X-rays going to set me back?"

"Seventeen-fifty apiece."

With a nubby brown index finger he drew imaginary numbers in the air and multiplied. "Jesus, that's almost two hundred bucks. I didn't make half that much tonight at the fairgrounds!"

"It's a worthwhile investment."

One of the clowns helped me off the floor. "That was a pretty good pratfall, Doc," he said cheerily. I couldn't really tell if he was smiling or crying under the thick greasepaint.

150

"Tell me," said the clown, "are you sure this isn't just a virus or something?"

"I don't think so. I want to take chest X-rays."

Samson seized Bijou Bill Kelley by the neck and began to strangle him. "Why didn't you tell us the truth?" he bellowed. "Were you going to let us die?"

Buster and I rescued Kelley before he could pass out. The group was assembled and the plans for X-rays were explained. A few members of the circus gang continued to insist tuberculosis would always be fatal.

"If that's the case, then why would I start you on this medicine tonight?" I held up a bottle of isoniazid and, as it so often does, the mention of the medication by name did much toward convincing the patients of my competency.

That hurdle surmounted, the next problem was locating Ralph Waters, an itinerant technician who serviced five small hospitals in southern Alabama. Luckily he was in Selma, only forty-five minutes away and the bass weren't biting. He promised to stop in Grady the next morning.

"It looks like you'll be spending a few days in our fair town," I told the assembly, by now weary and despondent. "Take it easy, go back to the campgrounds and enjoy yourselves if possible."

"Hell, we got shows to perform," Kelley said gruffly.

"No you don't. I won't have you infecting the entire county."

"Who's gonna stop me?"

"The health department," I said.

The crisis miraculously was kept under wraps by the hospital. The X-rays were taken, and the bad news was spooned out. Each of the X-rays revealed varying degrees of tubercule infiltration in the upper lobe apices of both lungs. The disease was at an unpleasant stage—cold sweats, coughing and weight loss—but it still could be arrested with diligent treatment. Isoniazid alone was prescribed for each of the performers but two, Franco the Lion Tamer and dancer Stormy Daze, who were put on triple therapy (three drugs) because their cases were more severe. Additionally, every county health department along Bijou Bill's circuit was alerted. Bill Kelley's band of dancing gypsies was disconsolate to learn that treatment lasts for a long time. I had no doubt that they would continue their public careers—"Show business is the only thing we know," LeRoy had explained—but the regular dosage of antituberculous drugs would greatly lessen the chance of transmission.

Before Kelley finally pulled up stakes and pointed his caravan toward Jackson, Mississippi, he delivered one final, grateful peroration. "Dr. Stone, I just want you to know I have no regrets about paying this fine hospital this six hundred dollars and fifty-three cents for the conscientious health care we have received. The lives and well-being of my employees were at stake"—here he smiled benevolently in Samson's direction—"and no price is too high for their safety. I thank you." He bowed, shook my hand, nodded as his Big Tent cronies proffered polite applause. Then he leaned toward me, muttering under his breath, "You'll be getting a bill for three hundred bucks!"

"What for?"

"Pierre."

"What about Pierre?"

"He died, that's what. Old Roy was worried that Pierre caught TB from one of the showgirls so he poured a whole bottle of the goddamn medicine down the little guy's throat. Next morning we found him, stiff as a board with his tiny cock in his ape hands."

"Ah, always a showman," I said wistfully.

"Don't be a wiseass. It takes years to train a monkey like Pierre. He was worth a solid forty bucks a night in small change alone."

Soon after Bill Kelley's departure, the bad news leaked out among Grady's loquacious citizenry. It began with an innocent phone call to Nurse Barnes from a reporter, *the* reporter, for the *Grady Guardian*. He wanted to know why the circus had been detained, why the performances were halted, and why the entourage had hightailed it out of town so suspiciously. Not wishing to induce panic by fueling the TB rumors, Mrs. Barnes charted a new course; she told the reporter that eleven performers had contracted venereal disease and were being treated with massive doses of penicillin by Trafford physicians.

Unfortunately, the circus affair was one instance where a lie was worse than the truth. Every truck driver, farmer, mechanic and construction worker in Grady County showed up for treatment, each demanding anonymity. Twelve hours after the story broke out, as it were, Trafford Memorial ran out of penicillin.

This forced Carl Hogue between the proverbial rock and hard place. He chose honesty. He issued a statement through his secretary: "It was erroneously reported in today's newspaper that certain members of a visiting circus were being treated for venereal disease at Trafford Memorial Hospital. That was a mistake caused by a clerical error. In fact, some eleven members of that circus *were* receiving treatments, not for any venereal disease but for pulmonary tuberculosis." As expected, everyone who had attended Bijou Bill's Big Tent stampeded the emergency room, all of them certain that lethal bacteria were multiplying like poisonous rabbits in their lungs. Three days after Bill Kelley's departure, Trafford was working up an average of thirty-seven X-rays a day.

The remunerations generated by this panic drew a laudatory memorandum from administrator William E. Anderson. It was addressed to Drs. Stone, Hogue and Parker—in that order. It commended us for "boosting the hospital's radiology income forty-five percent in a matter of days."

"It is rewarding to know," Anderson wrote, "what can be accomplished when our three most dedicated physicians work together. If the good work continues and the profits from this source keep rising, some of these long-sought renovations can be effected. I don't know what you fellows are doing, but keep it up!"

That same day, the first Monday in December, Anderson dashed off another memo. This one was directed confidentially to "the desk of Dr. Otis Stone," a curious notation because I had no desk at all. Its tone and substance were considerably different from the X-ray memorandum. It read: "Senator Rayfield Robinson wrote me a most emotional letter in which he complained bitterly of the rude and inconsiderate treatment accorded his wife and daughter during recent visits to Trafford's emergency room.

"Mrs. Robinson said that on one occasion you refused to treat her daughter and insisted over her objections that nothing was wrong with the girl. After this episode, the senator reports, his wife was so upset by your manners—or lack of them—she was confined to bed for three days with regular doses of Valium."

As I skimmed Anderson's note, Shelly sat down next to me on the cot. "Could you get me a cup of coffee?" I asked weakly, without looking up from the neat hospital stationery.

"The most recent episode," Anderson went on, "occurred last week when Mrs. Robinson came to the emergency room with a suspected case of appendicitis. According to her husband, Mrs. Robinson was ignored in favor of two midgets, a man in a loin cloth, several strippers and a monkey.

"Without his directly saying so, I got the impression from the senator's correspondence that he is disenchanted with the way we do things around here. He intends to make his doubts known next year when the subject of hospital funding comes before his committee. This development is most disturbing. Perhaps you have an explanation."

FOUR DAYS AFTER THE CIRCUS PULLED UP STAKES,
Carl Hogue collapsed again. This time the attack struck as
he shopped for groceries in a supermarket; Hogue fell face
first into the frozen foods and it took two full minutes for the
other customers to realize he wasn't just reading the price on
the Boston cream pie. Then he was rushed to the emergency
room at Trafford Memorial.

Parker was on call that afternoon, but one of the nurses
saw him slip out of the lobby at the arrival of Shelly's ambulance. It was just as well: Hogue was still very much alive
and very conscious. It is doubtful he would have stood for—
or laid down for—another critical examination from Lee Bob.

Hogue was admitted quietly, given Demerol for the pain
and immediately hooked up to the EKG machine. An I.V.
was attached and lidocaine was administered. All in all, just
a routine heart attack for the E.R. crew at Trafford. But coming so soon after his last myocardial infarction, Hogue's onset
was a bad sign—bad for him because it meant his heart tissue
was damaged; bad for me because once again I was relegated
to long days at Hogue's office, treating patients who trusted
no one but the craggy master himself.

Besides Hogue, the person who most vehemently resented
my intrusion into his august oak-paneled edifice was Jeannie
Montraine, Hogue's faithful nurse and admirer for twenty-
four years. Nothing about me or my behavior suited Mrs.
Montraine, whose favorite maxim was: "I've never met a
good doctor younger than forty-five years old." She was a

tall woman, heavy of bosom, possessing nightmarish yellow hair and a yen for bright red lipstick which invariably veered off the runway of her upper lip. She was loud, stern, officious, stubborn and devoted, not to mention condescending and short-tempered.

The day after Hogue's second attack, I settled in at his desk, flipping through the appointment book.

Mrs. Montraine stuck her head in the door and scowled. "Don't get too comfortable back there," she cracked. "He'll be back on the job in no time. Hey, don't open those drawers!"

"I'm looking for a pencil."

"*I'll* get you a pencil. I'll get you *five* pencils. Just stay out of Carl's desk."

"I'm gonna be here for a few weeks, Mrs. Montraine. Don't you think it's going to be somewhat time-consuming, having to ask your help every time I need a prescription pad or a patient's file?" Innocently I let my foot wander to the deep drawer on the bottom right of Hogue's desk. It slid open easily to reveal an electric coffee maker and a box of Titleist golf balls. "Ah, top secret!"

Mrs. Montraine flushed. "You're a rude, disobedient young man," she flared, slamming the door as she stormed out. Hogue had trained her well. The patient who had arrived first—and who had been sitting there since seven-thirty—waited two hours before Mrs. Montraine finally escorted him into the examining room.

"How come you didn't bring him in sooner?" I demanded.

Mrs. Montraine was indignant. "He had no appointment. I don't know how you do things in Miami, Dr. Stone, but around here people need an appointment to see the doctor. Eight other patients had appointments and they came first."

Will Landrum trembled. "I'm sorry, ma'am. I can go home. It ain't no emergency."

"Don't be silly," I said, motioning for Mrs. Montraine to make her exit. "What's the matter this morning, Mr. Landrum? You feel poorly?"

Will shook his head. His gray eyes sparkled and a mischievous smile lighted up his face. "Give me your hand," he said quietly.

My instincts told me to back off. Once, in kindergarten, a red-haired bully named Vincent Jones had made the same request. "Give me your hand," Vince said, his tone of voice suggesting it was either my hand or a few teeth. I complied. Vince grinned, cupped his hand over mine, then pressed my fingers together in a fist. "This is for you, Stoneface," he said warmly. Upon opening my hand, I laid eyes on a truly impressive creation: sixty-four pieces of chewing gum married together into a moist, gray forbidding wad. How Vince had chewed all that gum in one morning I'll never know, but it took three weeks to remove it from under my fingernails.

"You don't have gum in your hands, do you, Mr. Landrum?" Puzzled, Mr. Landrum said no, no gum. Cautiously I extended my left hand, regretting that there had been no time to don gynecological gloves. "Close your eyes," said Mr. Landrum excitedly, "please."

Reluctantly, I shut my eyes and felt something inserted into the ball of my hand. Landrum patted the top of my wrist twice and said, "Okay, you can look now."

Folded neatly in my hand were several dollar bills. "Thank you, Will, but you can give this to Mrs. Montraine when you leave. I haven't even examined you yet."

Landrum giggled like a small boy with a naughty secret. "That ain't for the examination, Doctor. There ain't nothin' wrong with me today."

"Then what's it for?"

"Me. It's for me," he said simply. "That money is for my birth." Reflexively, I punched the office intercom and asked Mrs. Montraine to fetch Landrum's records. Obviously he was a psychotic of some sort who harbored some Freudian birth canal fixation. "Let me get this straight," I stalled. "This money is the doctor's fee for your delivery?"

"Right."

I counted the cash. "Four dollars. It's only four dollars, Mr. Landrum."

He scratched his head. "Damnation!" he exclaimed. "I almost forgot." He fished into his brown trousers. "Here's fifty cents. That evens it up, don't it?"

Scanning over his records, I could see nothing in Will Landrum's past to indicate any psychological aberrations. For want of a better strategy I played along. "So this is the obstetrical fee, is it? Um, when exactly would you like to be born, Mr. Landrum?"

He cocked his head. "Uh?" He looked down to check his body. "I *am* born, Doc."

"Then what's the money for?"

"My birth." He saw the confusion in my eyes. "Let me explain. See, when I was born, my daddy couldn't pay the doctor bill. When he died a few years back he left a note, said he owed Doc Hughes four dollars and fifty cents for deliverin' me. This here's the four-fifty."

Awash with guilt, I apologized to Landrum. Closer examination of the medical files proved him correct: fifty-six years earlier, his father, Haney Landrum, wrote Dr. Hughes an I.O.U. for four-fifty. Now Will had come to make good on it. "Doc Hughes died before my daddy could pay him back," Will said sadly. "Dr. Hogue was just a young fella back then, but he remembers my dad. He took over Doc Hughes' office."

"I'll put this in the proper account, and I'll be sure to tell Dr. Hogue you came by."

Will sprung to his feet. A great weight had been lifted from his shoulders. The poor fellow had lived his life knowing that his own birth was a family debt. "I feel alots better," he said. "Don't ever like to be beholdin' to nobody."

I scolded myself for suspecting the worst and blamed the gut reaction on my year at giant Jackson Memorial in Miami. There it was not unusual to meet up with two or three bona fide psychotics, paranoids and perverts every night in the emergency room. One time a fellow demanded an emergency operation to remove a high-powered radio transmitter which the FBI had installed up his rectum. Another night I was confronted with a fanatical woman who insisted there was a spike in her head; sure enough, she had hammered a four-inch masonry nail through the top of her skull, missing the right hemisphere of her brain by a scant tenth of an inch. Could I really blame myself, then, for thinking Will Landrum had wanted me to reenact his coming into the world?

Over the days as Hogue's proxy, I grew more impressed with his patience and stamina. Despite the personal antipathy between us, I marveled at the old fellow's schedule; on some days he saw nearly seventy patients. No wonder he was grouchy. Who wouldn't be irritable after twelve hours of flu shots, throat cultures, diarrhea and urine samples? Such a regimen also served to explain a hardhead like Mrs. Montraine, who seemed to revel in the daily dramas and traumas of Hogue's congregation. She gloated when patients panicked to learn Hogue was sick; she snickered when they asked to see my diploma from med school. Patients would often demand her presence to supervise the techniques of this new young doctor.

One patient was truly excited to learn I was standing in for the ailing Carl Hogue. Her name was Judy Lydell, a 32-year-old bus driver and part-time psychic. In sixteen years she had single-handedly done more for Carl Hogue's financial well-being than any other patient. Judy showed up every Wednesday, rain or shine, and every Wednesday it was something new. Not once, according to Hogue's records, had her illness proved anything more than imaginary—but her determination and unbounded certainty were extraordinary.

The first time I treated her had been a few days after Hogue's first heart attack; then, Judy had exhibited unbridled delight at the chance to convince another physician of her impending death. On that particular Wednesday she had complained of an irregular heartbeat. "My heart stops beating," she told me, "sometimes for thirty seconds at a time." The next time it was something else: her knees. She greeted me, an edge of excitement to her voice. "Ah, Dr. Stone! Good to see you. Dr. Hogue must be sick again."

" 'Fraid so, Mrs. Lydell. What's the problem this morning?"

"I'm feeling real badly, Dr. Stone. Think you better check me into Trafford. Been having some terrible pains in my knees. Sure wish there was a knee specialist here in Grady."

"In the knee joints?"

"No!" she snapped. "So don't you tell me it's arthritis. The pain's not in the knee joints. It's in the *knees*. Besides, I'm only thirty-two. That's too darn young to get arthritis. Said so in *Reader's Digest*."

"What was the name of the article, Mrs. Lydell?"

" 'I Am Joe's Arthritis.' "

"That's what I thought. Sit down here on the examining table."

She hoisted herself up and raised her brown cotton skirt. "There!" She made a face and pointed at her right knee. "There it goes again. Lord, I bet it's cancer. Better call Trafford and get me a room," she moaned.

"So it hurts right here?" I pressed firmly on the patella. Nothing in the way of spasms, discolorations or bruises was evident at either kneecap. Thinking back to the malpractice suit, I wondered about getting X-rays—just in case Mrs. Lydell had really injured her legs.

"Lord, it hurts! Right on the kneecaps, Dr. Stone. It's murder!"

"Hmmm. Maybe you've been on your knees too much. Have you been doing a lot of praying lately?"

Mrs. Lydell eyed me. "Ain't no such thing as too much praying, Dr. Stone. That ain't the problem, no sir! Besides, we got brand new pews out at the Mission Christian Church. Wouldn't hurt you a bit to come out one Sunday and pray with us, either."

"I got real bad knees."

"Yeah, I bet. What you gonna do about my cancer?"

"I don't think it's cancer, Mrs. Lydell, but I'll schedule some X-rays for you, if you want."

She shifted uncomfortably. "Don't you have some pills or something?"

I rang for Mrs. Montraine and she showed me down the hall to an empty consultation room where she excoriated me for spending five full minutes with Judy Lydell. "We got a kid with tonsilitis out there, Dr. Stone. We don't have time to worry about a crock like Judy. What is it this week, emphysema?"

"Her knee caps. Cancer of the knee caps."

Mrs. Montraine was relieved. "Why didn't you say so?" She went to a medicine cabinet and withdrew a plastic pillbox full of fat pink tablets. "Placebo," she whispered conspiratorially. "These pink ones are Dr. Hogue's 'cancer pills.' We've got three or four patients who take them regularly."

"Think Judy will go for it?"

"Always has in the past. Just give her these, tell her to take three a day for ten days, and change her diet."

"Diet? What's wrong with her diet?"

"Same thing that's wrong with *her*: nothing. But the more mumbo-jumbo you give her, the easier it is to get rid of her."

Judy was delighted with the pills, but slightly suspicious. "These look like the same ones Dr. Hogue gave me three weeks ago for my osteomyelitis."

"Did they work?"

She brightened. "Like a charm!"

"Good," I said, "because these are made by the same pharmaceutical company. Take one every eight hours. Additionally, I want you to change your diet. No eggs or dairy products for two weeks."

"I knew it!" Judy proclaimed. "Damn carbohydrates will do it every time. Read about 'em in *Reader's Digest* last month." She thanked me effusively for the attention, referred me to an article called "I Am Joe's Cholesterol Deposits" and left peaceably. I saw two more patients, both with viral infections, then took a moment to call Shelly.

"Nothing today, either," she reported. "Otis, maybe newspaper ads aren't the best way to attract physicians down here."

"I can't afford network advertising."

"You got a letter from that girl in Coral Gables," Shelly said. "Want me to open it?"

161

"No. Just put it on the counter by the refrigerator."

I could hear Shelly rattling the envelope. "Hmmm. No perfume. Maybe's she's mad at you."

"She's got a new perfume. It smells like stationery."

"You also got a letter from your sister."

"Don't open that, either. Sure there's nothing about the job at Trafford?"

"Nothing," Shelly said. "Sorry about that."

Anxiety was setting in. If January 10th arrived and there still was no one to take over my night duties at Trafford, then the whole county was in trouble. If only Hogue's heart condition would improve, the outlook would be so much brighter, I thought.

In the meantime, I was running myself ragged, working Hogue's family practice by day and the graveyard shift in the E.R. at night. The extra money was most welcome, but there was no place to spend it. At Grady's two ratty indoor theaters, "Gone with the Wind" and "Jaws" were still playing, just as they had been last summer when I arrived. The only civilized recreations were hunting, fishing, church-going and sex. I hated hunting, Shelly hated fishing and we both hated church-going. My ridiculous work schedule was threatening to make a chore out of our only hobby.

If nothing else, my twin duties as family practitioner and emergency room physician offered a valuable chance to look at both medical situations and compare. Family practice was more personal; it permitted more backgrounding, closer study and diligent follow-ups for the patients. The emergency room, on the other hand, was relatively free from office monotony. And it was economical for the doctor—no office expenses, no overhead, no problem collecting fees (Trafford took care of that). Moreover, the emergency room required quick-thinking and well-honed lifesaving techniques. Without a doubt, the E.R. was a more exciting place to spend eight and often more hours, even in sleepy Grady County.

This is not to say private practice exists without its particular crises. A case in point: Kitty Lane. Everyone in town and almost everyone in the county knew about Kitty, except me. She showed up during my second week as Hogue's stand-in; she told Mrs. Montraine she'd been suffering from a hacking cough.

Kitty had long blonde hair, thick eyelashes and a rather healthy chest. She couldn't have been more than twenty-five. "What are you staring at?" she asked when first I propped myself in the doorway to the examining room. "Nothing. It's just that, well, it's not too often a female patient—any patient, really—will wear a negligee to the doctor's office."

"Like it?" Kitty winked.

It was only later, after questioning several bachelors including Buster Hogue, that I learned the full legend of Kitty Lane. Born the daughter of a well-to-do cotton farmer and an aspiring artist, Kitty had grown to consider Grady County her territory. She went off to college in Atlanta at age sixteen and returned four years later with a bachelor's degree in British literature and an acute case of nymphomania.

Since then, Hogue himself had refused to examine her without Mrs. Montraine's impenetrable protection, and he was deeply afraid to refer Kitty to Lee Bob Parker—afraid Lee Bob would interpret the referral as a gesture of conciliation. Grady's doctors were old doctors, old-fashioned and Calvinistic and thoroughly unaccustomed to advances from nubile aggressors. Though fancying myself neither old nor old-fashioned, I was scared shitless of Kitty Lane. Afterward I nearly fired Mrs. Montraine for not warning me.

"Listen to my cough," Kitty had said, shedding the negligee and baring her chest in one gracefully erotic motion. In medical school future doctors are taught to react to these situations with professional distance and passivity, taught to say little and to pretend to notice nothing. Whoever formulated that particular bit of advice completely overlooked the design of the modern stethoscope, which requires the doctor to poise himself a minimum of eight to ten inches from the zone to which he is listening. Eight to ten inches was nothing for Kitty Lane. As I listened to her heart, she grabbed my head with both her hands and pulled it to her bosom—the first and last time a patient has ever done so.

"Hear anything?" she whispered.

"Oh, just your heartbeat," I mumbled self-consciously into her breasts.

"Sure it isn't *your* heart, sugar?"

I extracted myself, stood up and straightened the ever-important white jacket. "Sounds fine to me, Miss Lane," I announced clinically.

Kitty coughed a cute, quiet little cough. "There I go again. What *am* I going to do about that? You don't suppose I might have caught tuberculosis from that awful circus, do you?"

"I doubt it. Let me prescribe some decongestants and a cough suppressant to help you sleep at night."

"Sleep" and "night" were two words never to be spoken in front of Kitty Lane. Medicines, she informed coyly, were *not* what she needed after the sun went down. I bolted for the intercom and shouted for Mrs. Montraine, but Mrs. Montraine had vanished, had crept off to Gresham Park with her egg salad sandwich. Nothing, not even a cardiac arrest, could bring her back to the office before the lunch hour officially ended at one p.m.

"Please," Kitty implored, "listen one more time." She grabbed the bell of the stethoscope and yanked me toward her tan, ample cleavage. I raised my hands—merely to cushion the impact and separate our bodies—only to feel them make warm contact with Kitty's nipples. "That's better," she said. "I feel better already."

For a slender hundred-pound woman, Kitty was strong. She managed through a series of intricate maneuvers to pinion me in a rather pleasant half nelson from which we struggled awkwardly until I landed, finally alone, in one of the chairs. Kitty promptly planted herself in my lap and wrapped her arms around my head; all protestations, no matter how curt and professionally cold, landed on deaf breasts.

Visions of Mrs. Montraine barging in, then reporting the orgy to her boss, inspired another attempt to bring the examination to a halt. My right hand managed to locate a prescription pad and I fought desperately to scribble a request for Actifed. But I found myself writing with a cotton swab instead of a pen.

Finally, I located a ball-point and managed, in a fashion that would have made Houdini proud, to complete the prescription. As I signed my name to it, the phone rang. By the fifth bell I had struggled to my feet and fought my way past Kitty into Hogue's office.

"Where the hell have you been?" It was Hogue. His tone was bellicose so I knew he was feeling better.

"Boy, am I glad you called. Kitty Lane is in the examining room and I'm scared to go back in there."

Hogue laughed unsympathetically. "I didn't mean to interrupt you. Ha, wait till she tries to palpate for a hernia."

"I don't wanna wait. What do I do?"

"Do what I did. Tell her you're a eunuch."

"Come on. She's got a cough. At least she says it's a cough."

"Then give her some expectorants and get on to the next patient. That's a doctor's office, not a massage parlor." Hogue had a grand old time teasing me about Kitty's ravenous sexual appetite, until the lady herself appeared at the door, negligee intact, apparently ready to renew the hunt.

"Carl, you better tell me the best way to handle this. Fast!"

It must have dawned on Hogue what was about to occur in his office, *his* sacred, austere office, right before the watchful eyes of Ebbet Hughes' portrait. The thought of such irreverence mortified him. "Stone, do something! Didn't they teach you how to handle this sort of thing at Stanford?"

"Didn't they teach *you*?"

"They didn't have nymphos back when I was in med school," Hogue said.

Kitty sat down in a red leather chair. I cupped my hand over the receiver. "I'll be with you in a minute. Very important phone call."

"I've got it!" Hogue exclaimed. "I remember now. Tell her Bobby Dean is looking for her."

"Bobby Dean?" I repeated, wondering what mystical effect mere words could have toward taming Kitty's desires. She heard the name and stood up, stiff and anxious.

"What? Excuse me, Dr. Stone, but what did you say?" I pretended to converse with Hogue and ignored Kitty's concern.

"Did you say Bobby Dean? Is that what you said?" Kitty cried. "Is that him on the phone? Please don't tell him I'm here." And before I could answer she fled, her feathery nightie trailing behind in a perfumed breeze. Bobby Dean, it seemed, was Kitty's current boyfriend and a sensitive fellow, even for an alligator poacher. The last man Kitty had been caught fooling around with ended up in a Selma emergency room with a hunting knife protruding from his buttocks. Naturally Bobby had been perturbed, what with all the foul rumors that Kitty was two-timing, sometimes three-timing him. So he had threatened to break her fingernails off if he ever caught her with another guy.

"No wonder she ran," I remarked. "Thanks for the tip, Carl."

"Can you imagine being her gynecologist?" he mused. "The reason I called—wait a second. . . ."

"Carl? Everything okay?"

"Yeh. Margaret Holt just popped in. Said to give you a message. Some guy named Sherman Flowers is waiting to see you about the E.R. job. Said he's a doctor from New Orleans."

"Wonderful!"

"Flowers, huh?" Hogue snorted. "Sounds like a faggot to me. Another young one, I suppose. You trying to infiltrate this town with damn liberal doctors, aren't you?"

"Any doctors would do just about now," I answered. "Parker's never around, and when he is he makes you wish he wasn't. Gleason and Drake are too old to play golf. They've got no more than ten patients each at Trafford. The rest are yours, and frankly, you're in no shape to look after them. Grady is hurting."

"We'll survive," Hogue said. "Always have."

166

"How are you feeling?"

"Not too bad. Had a little touch of angina this morning but I took some nitro and I feel better. How are you and Jeannie getting along? She's a real gem, isn't she?"

"A gem."

"Actually, what I called about is this lawsuit. I saw this Fred Trumpe fellow today. He's the guy Anderson hired to defend the hospital in this malpractice business."

"And?"

"The Mission Christian Church settled out of court with Jake Benton's family. They admitted, more or less, culpability."

"In the shooting?"

"No," said Hogue. "In allowing Jake to come to our hospital. Bastards are still trying to sue us."

"How much was the settlement?"

"Forty thou."

I whistled. "That's a lot of bake sales."

"Trumpe says Trafford's going to fight the countersuit."

"So am I."

"I wouldn't recommend it," Hogue said. "It might take years. It's gonna hang over your career like a raincloud, Otis. You don't have the money to pay off a big settlement."

"I've got malpractice insurance."

"Settle," Hogue urged. "Settle and get it over with. You can get off with just a few thousand, I'm sure. They don't want you, they want the hospital."

"Is that what your lawyer said?"

"Yep." Hogue coughed. He was breathing hard and his voice sounded tired.

"Don't do it," I said. "The operation was necessary. You did a great job on that kid's leg. Don't let these guys scare you. By giving in, you're just ensuring more malpractice suits against other doctors. Don't make it any easier for these lawyers."

"I already have," Hogue sighed. "Signed the papers this morning. Nothing to it."

"How much?"

"Five thousand." He laughed cynically. "Don't panic, Stone, you can probably get out of this mess for less if you'd quit being such a stubborn, idealistic asshole. Besides, it went for a good cause. If I'm gonna lose, I might as well lose to the church."

I thought of Judy Lydell's knees. "I'm gonna fight it," I told Hogue. "I'm not gonna pay for those new pews."

SHERMAN FLOWERS WAS A PERFECT SOUTHERN
gentleman. Smooth. Courtly. Rosy-cheeked. Impeccable
haircut. Charming accent. Even-tempered. I don't know why
I liked him.

We sat in a booth at the Bear Bryant Bar and Grille, formerly the Rebel Saloon, formerly Millie's Billiard Palace.
Sherman drank bourbon, of course. I drank beer. For a fellow born and raised in busy New Orleans, he seemed oddly
at ease in the redneck honky-tonk.

"We had to live in the city," he explained. "My daddy
was a grain inspector at the port." He paused and seemed
to concentrate on the words to a Charlie Rich song. A girl at
the bar had punched it on the juke box for the third straight
play. Flowers just smiled. "Well," he said finally, "it ain't
Pete Fountain."

"Why'd you answer the ad?"

He shrugged. "Curiosity. To be honest, I didn't even know
about the job until I picked up a copy of the *Times* at the
drug store here in town. I was just passing through on my
way East."

"Job hunting?"

"How'd you guess? I got a couple offers up in Boston."

"Why are you leaving New Orleans?"

"Boredom. I finished my surgical residency two years ago
and I been looking for another city ever since. After my wife
and I divorced, well, I just decided to split." Flowers drained

the last few copper drops of bourbon from his glass. "How about you? Why are you here?"

He listened with bemusement to the story of the disabled Charger, Mel Dryden's extortion and my subsequent decision to endure six months of southern Alabama medicine. "I'm leaving next month," I said with what I hoped was convincing forcefulness. "I've accepted a job out in California."

"Hmmm, just like that. Then I guess you're not married," Flowers surmised.

"No. I'm not ready for that kind of responsibility." I thought of Marie Duggan's final letter, the first "Dear Otis" rejection in many years. For maximum impact she had dropped the big bombshell in the first sentence and used the rest of the letter to fire tiny, well-aimed mortars.

"By the time you get this letter I'll be in Johannesburg, South Africa," she began, "and my journey there has nothing to do with Albert Schweitzer or medicine. I've gotten married, Otis.

"I came to the painful conclusion that our relationship must end. I thought those few days I spent in Grady might change one of our minds, but obviously it did not. You've made your decision to stay there, despite the anguish it is causing me and your family.

"Just when I was feeling most depressed about Us, I met a wonderful man here at the hospital. He's a surgeon, Otis, and a very famous one. He's written three books and was even on the Merv Griffin show once. We fell in love almost immediately and were married last night on his yacht in Biscayne Bay. I was going to invite you, but when I remembered how seasick you get. We plan to honeymoon in Acapulco, but first Reginald must fly back to South Africa to perform a gallstone operation. The patient is the doorman at the American Embassy. Isn't it exciting? I never dreamed marriage could be so much fun.

"Oh, it won't be easy to forget you, Otis, but I'll find a way, I must. You see, we're two different people. You're you. I'm me. I hope you understand." (That part I understood.)

"Wish me luck, okay? I'm not crazy about the idea of keeping house with all those baboons and rhinoceroses prowling around, but I've made up my mind to try. Failing that, I can always go back to nursing. Love, Marie."

I suspected the baboons and rhinoceroses of South Africa were in many instances less menacing and more civilized than some of the patients downtown Miami coughed up. From Marie's letter, I inferred she was relieved to leave nursing. That decision had apparently been given more weight than her marriage, for I had found out in my sister's letter that Marie had been consulting with Elizabeth by mail about the problem.

"Her temperament is ill-suited for the stress of hospital work," my psychiatrist sister explained, "so I advised her to get a job in a private clinic. As you know, it can be lucrative work. But she's a mixed-up girl. She doesn't know what she wants, only what she doesn't want . . . and she doesn't want Grady, Alabama. She got a good look at the town, such as it is, and decided you weren't ever going to leave—no matter what you promised about glory in San Jose. So Marie decided to marry this surgeon and go to South Africa. You really blew this one, little brother!

"As for me, I've broken up with Brad. While the Rams were making the playoffs this year, Brad was making it with a nineteen-year-old cheerleader. Don't worry, though. I handled the situation calmly and terminated our living arrangement simply by having the locks changed. I have since become friendly with a basketball player named Darren. He is six-foot-ten and in desperate need of overcoming an Oedipal complex. Wish me luck on this one. Be sure to call when you get to San Jose—*if* you get to San Jose. Love, Liz."

Sherman Flowers listened impassively to the story of Marie Duggan's defection. "Marriage can be a real can of worms," he said afterward.

"Speaking of which, there isn't anything the hospital board should know before considering your application, or is there?" Three beers had vanquished my sense of propriety. "I'm sorry. What I meant was . . ."

Flowers laughed and held up his hand. "I know what you mean. The answer is no. I'm clean, honest. I'll give you twenty-five references."

"Ten will do."

He grinned. "Jesus! I'm talking like I've already made up my mind about this job. I haven't even seen the hospital yet."

"Well, you're about to." I watched Rooster Bootman escort Thomas Dixon into the bar. The man whom I had suspected of breaking Louise Rhodes' leg was now in somewhat of a bind himself. Though tight-lipped and expressionless, it was painfully evident from big Tom's paled face and wobbly knees that something was terribly wrong.

Bootman scanned the patrons until he spotted me in the corner booth. He pushed Dixon across the room toward our table and waved. "There's Dr. Stone now, Thomas. Don't give me no goddamn trouble, y'hear? You need some looking after," I could hear Bootman lecturing. I stood up to meet the two men.

"How are you, Sheriff?"

"Jest fine," he said with a yellowish smile. "The little lady's got herself a touch of the gout, though. 'Preciate it if you'd give her some of that stuff you gave Hollis."

"No problem," I said amiably.

Bootman nudged Dixon. "Go on now, Tom. Tell the doctor what's wrong."

Dixon looked at me sullenly. "Nothin's wrong, Doc."

"Damnation!" yelled the sheriff. "Why are you so stubborn? Show Dr. Stone what's the matter 'fore you bleed to death!"

Thomas' arms were folded tightly in an "x" over his chest. When the sheriff's coaxing turned to threats, the big man sheepishly let his arms droop to his sides and revealed the nature of his discomfort: a gaping pair of sewing shears imbedded in his chest. The left side of his green flannel shirt was brown with dried blood, except the base of the scissors which was moist and oozed bright red.

"Damn fool won't tell me how it happened," Bootman clucked. "Says it was an accident. Says he was cutting out paper dolls for one of Louise's kids when the shears slipped. You believe that shit?''

"I don't really care *how* it happened, Sheriff. I'd say we better get Mr. Dixon to the hospital pretty soon.''

Trouble was, Mr. Dixon didn't *want* to enter the hospital, not for anything. Both parents had died after long illnesses at Trafford so big Tom was not in the least inclined to take a chance there. Fortunately, the loss of blood had left him so weak that Bootman, Sherman and I were able to wrestle him into the squad car. He quit struggling only when we got him on the operating table at Trafford Memorial.

Luckily for Thomas, the blades of the scissors had entered at an angle between ribs. Miraculously, his left lung was not collapsed; most of the damage was done to fat and connective tissues in the rib cage. Had Dixon's assailant aimed the thrust a bit lower, the big man would have been dead by the time Sherman and I saw him.

Clipboard in hand, Bootman hovered outside the operating room while I finished sewing up the muscle in Tom's chest. As Buster wheeled the victim toward the recovery room, the sheriff trotted along. "Tell me the truth, Thomas,'' he pleaded. "Who did this to you?'' Dixon just shut his eyes and pretended not to hear. "Dammit, Tom, what am I gonna put on this report?''

"That the whole thing was an accident,'' Dixon grunted.

"You sure Louise didn't stab you?''

"I'm sure. Just ask her.''

Sherman Flowers got a full tour of the hospital. I felt like a Disney tour guide whisking through cardiology, obstetrics, surgery, pediatrics, central supply and the pharmacy. Flowers said nothing, just nodded politely and listened to my spiel. We ended up in the lobby lounging on an old red leather sofa under the dour portrait of Squire Trafford himself, who must have been constipated the day of the sitting.

"What do you think?'' I ventured.

"It's not a bad little hospital,'' Flowers answered diplomatically. "You're underbedded, that's for sure. And some of the equipment is pretty old. You could use a new X-ray unit. Same goes for the surgical lights.''

"I can't argue, but I think I should tell you we're coming into some money very soon.'' I almost choked on those words. It was the same line Marshall Needham had used on me. It worked even better on Sherman Flowers.

"How much?'' he asked intently.

"A lot. Two million bucks. All of it's earmarked for expansion and improved facilities.''

Sherman was pleased. "Well, well. That certainly could make a difference around here.''

"But it won't make Trafford another Massachusetts General,'' I felt compelled to say. "And your salary as an E.R. staff physician won't come close to what you made in private practice.''

"It's not the money,'' Flowers said without elaborating. "If you don't mind, I'd like to hang around a few days and see the place in action.''

He stayed two days, spent most of his time watching the emergency room function, or attempt to function. He saw the full parade of asthmatics, auto victims, pneumonia victims and crocks. Always polite and attentive, Flowers was still too reserved for William E. Anderson, whose high-pressured campaign ultimately drove the New Orleans doctor out of town. Two or three times a day Anderson would corral Flowers with some new offer: more money, an apartment near the hospital, a car, season tickets to the Saints games.

Nothing worked. Flowers was decisively indecisive. Anderson pressed for a definite "yes" or "no"; when that failed, the frustrated administrator coolly ended negotiations to "resume scrutinizing the resumes of all the other applicants.'' In fact, a sixty-year-old urologist from Birmingham was the only other contender for the job. Anderson's desperation was understandable in light of Trafford's most recent trauma: the retirement of Dr. Lee R. Parker.

It had come with numbing surprise and incurred no small amount of panic at the hospital. One day Lee Bob was working his rounds, behaving himself as furtively and fumblingly

174

as ever—and then the next day came a notice in the *Grady Guardian:* "Dr. Lee Parker regrets to announce his retirement from the general practice of medicine." That was it. No explanations. No hint of concern for his patients' future. No ticker-tape parade. Parker was quitting and no one seemed to know why. His own version, leaked to one of the more loquacious barbers in town, boasted of a high-paying teaching position at an Eastern med school. Even the *Guardian* didn't go for it after considering the source.

Parker's veil of secrecy remained intact for exactly twenty hours. It was broken by an urgent phone call from William Anderson imploring me to report at once to his office, a strange request made all the more so coming at four-thirty in the morning. Disheveled and thick-tongued, I listened while the funereal Anderson told of his shocking discovery: that Lee Bob Parker was leaving Grady under duress.

Anderson poured himself a glass of water without offering me one. His hands shook. Sweat beaded up on his thin neck.

"Parker has been named in a very ugly lawsuit," he blurted out. "One of the nurses phoned me with the details about half an hour ago. I don't know how she found out and I don't *want* to know. The point is: I am abandoning all hopes of convincing Dr. Parker to stay. His presence at this hospital is no longer welcome. This lawsuit could be a blight." Anderson studied me. "You don't seem surprised, Dr. Stone."

"Oh, I'm surprised—surprised that someone didn't go after him sooner than this."

"You knew about this, er, problem?"

"Knew about it? The whole hospital knew about it. Hogue knew about it. Gleason and Drake even knew about it and they still played golf with the guy."

"Why wasn't I told?" Anderson steamed.

"Don't tell me you've never heard anyone bitch about Parker's work?"

"It's not his work that worries me," Anderson said.

"Then why is he getting sued for malpractice?"

Anderson screwed up his face comically. "Malpractice?" He managed to grunt out a chuckle. "Do you think I'd be

175

this upset over some little malpractice suit? You gotta be kidding.''

"I just assumed. . . .''

"You assumed wrong. Malpractice is a picnic compared to this. This particular incident involves, ah, an assault.'' He chewed on his lip.

"Against a patient?'' I asked incredulously.

"I'm afraid so. I called you as soon as I found out. I thought you should know. It's going to put the whole staff in a bind, work-wise, not to mention the horrible public relations problem we've got with it.''

The circumstances of the lawsuit were a painful subject for William E. Anderson. In bits and pieces, sometimes near tears, he told me what he knew about Parker's legal predicament.

It had happened at his office. In the middle of a normal busy work day, a patient named Nancy Rawlins came to have a mole removed from her right buttock. The excision was carried out smoothly and without complication. Miss Rawlins paid Parker's receptionist with a check for fifty-four dollars and left—and that's when the trouble started. Parker was doing a throat culture on another patient when he heard the wrenching crunch of steel against steel. Somehow the old guy just had a hunch. He dashed out of his office—leaving the throat swab protruding from the mouth of a bewildered old man—and ran into the parking lot. There, with its abbreviated rear end creased like an accordion, was Parker's precious Cadillac.

What had happened next is unclear. Some witnesses said he hit Miss Rawlins four times, others said he struck her as many as seven. To Parker's credit, he apparently used only the palm of his hand—not his fist. To his discredit, he chose to turn the young woman over his knee and paddle her as if she were a child; he failed of course, to exercise any caution with regard to her recent surgery. Miss Rawlins maintained in her sworn statement that she could not sit down for ten days after the incident.

"Originally she wanted to charge him with rape,'' Anderson related sadly, "but her attorney said she stood a better chance with assault. Parker was arrested later the same day and posted bond. He's a very scared man."

The grievous sins of Lee Bob Parker were less of an immediate concern than the drastic increases in patient loads levied on each of the doctors. The two oldest men, Gleason and Drake, had for years been purging their files by attrition: when one patient died it was merely one less obstacle to retirement; few new patients were taken on. On the other hand, Hogue cherished his supremacy in Grady and was constantly seeking to broaden his political-medical base of support by acquiring new patients.

With Hogue temporarily out of commission, Gleason and Drake asked for—and received—full reign in choosing which of Parker's patients they wished to care for. First draft choices naturally were cases of minor arthritis, asthma, hay fever and acne. The grim prospects by default went to Carl Hogue.

Amazingly, Parker was able to clear up his problems and leave town within the week. Mrs. Rawlins dropped charges when Lee Bob offered nine hundred dollars compensation. He then moved quietly out of Grady one night and reportedly resettled in Raleigh, North Carolina, where he had invested his entire life savings in a Toyota dealership. His quest for a prestigious teaching position failed, as did his hopes for a syndicated newspaper column to be titled, "Take Two Aspirin and Call Me in the Morning." The next time we were to hear from Dr. Lee Bob Parker was the arrival of a postcard addressed "To All The Men and Women of Trafford Memorial." On one side was a color photograph of the scenic fourteenth hole at the Greensboro National Country Club. On the other side Parker had written: "Today was the happiest day of my life. I played nine holes with Sam Snead."

On Christmas Eve, I was working the late shift (as usual) when my parents called at midnight. With two broken legs (not mine) in urgent need of attention, I had little time to chat.

"I can't talk long, Dad."

"Oh?" He sounded hurt. "It's just that the rates go down this time of night. We didn't know you'd be so busy."

"Who," interrupted my mother harshly, "was that girl who picked up the phone in your apartment?"

"Just the answering service," I lied.

"Got a nice letter from Marie Duggan today," my father began. "She said she can get me a discount if I ever need a heart transplant."

"That was nice of her."

"Your brother Benjamin is thinking of opening his own shoe store in Hackensack," my mother announced.

"Great!"

"And your sister is getting a paper published in the *California Journal of Psychiatry*."

"Very good."

"And you?"

"Still waiting, Mother. January 10th is the big day."

"Is your car working?" asked my father.

"Don't worry. I'll make it."

"Have you found that doctor to replace you?"

"Not yet, but we will. Now I've gotta run. We've got a couple of emergencies now. Have a happy holiday."

"You, too," said my father. "Hope the next time we talk you'll be settled in your new job. Call us then."

"Collect!" added my mother.

My beeper squealed and I hightailed it back to the operating room where Margaret Holt was consoling an old woman who had fallen down in her home. The X-rays confirmed the injury as an extracapsular fracture in the neck of the femur, the large bone in her hip. I had two choices: to use either a special nail or an intramedullary prosthesis to fix the bone together. Either procedure required an orthopedic surgeon; there was none to be found in Grady.

"Call Richard Chambers in Selma," I ordered a nurse. "Ask him how soon he can get here to repair a bad hip fracture."

"Mind if I take a look at it?" asked a voice behind me.

I wheeled around. It was Sherman Flowers.

*FRED TRUMPE WAS A MAN FOR WHOM INCONVE-*nience of any sort was extreme misery. He was, after all, an attorney and, as such, felt he should not be kept waiting. Not for appointments, not for lunch, not for fees and certainly not for emergency medical care.

He sat mordantly in the small emergency room at Trafford Memorial while Sherman Flowers stitched up an injured truck driver and I pumped some kid's stomach. For two hours and twelve minutes Fred sat there while blood trickled slowly from his nose, down his cheeks and into the collar of his twenty-dollar shirt. He must have been in some kind of agony.

"This is a friggin' hospital?" he shouted sarcastically at Buster Hogue.

"Please try to stay calm," Buster begged solicitously—and with good reason. It was all Buster's fault, Fred's accident, and, even as dumb as he was, Buster foresaw the awful implications of driving an ambulance into a rich lawyer's Lincoln Continental. The Continental, it turned out, fared only slightly better than Fred Trumpe himself.

"I hope you're insured," Fred kept saying to Buster, "because I'm going to sue the living hell out of you."

"Please," Buster said plaintively, "try to stay calm."

The fact that Fred was Trafford's newly appointed legal counsel gave Buster little solace. When he tried to milk his own hospital affiliation for all it was worth by recounting past E.R. exploits, Trumpe merely seized on Buster's infor-

179

mation as new ammunition. "I'll have your ass fired," the lawyer gloated nasally. "That's what I'll do."

By the time I entered the fracas, Buster's feverish hunt for an alibi had become so desperate he was blaming Shelly for the accident. In a vague sort of way it made sense. "If she wasn't leaving for law school, this never would have happened," Buster said confidently.

"But it was your decision to try out for her old job," I countered.

"But I would never have got it without her recommendation," he argued.

Shelly not being present to defend herself, I steered the debate toward Buster's notorious driving habits and we hollered back and forth until Fred Trumpe piped up. "If you're a doctor and you know what's good for you, you'll fix my damn nose before I bleed to death!" he bellowed by way of introduction. "You've heard of malpractice? Well, I'm seriously considering suing you for *non*practice, so hurry it up."

I took one look at the pulverized probiscus and pronounced Fred the proud owner of a broken nasal bone. I set to work repairing it, chatting with the injured lawyer to take his mind off Buster's reckless driving. It seemed the accident occurred while Trumpe was leaving a very important hearing, a hearing which involved the hospital, the Mission Christian Church, Jake Benton and an itinerant physician named Stone. Fred was far less eager to discuss the routine trivialities of law than he was to expound on his dramatic brush with death.

"There I was, sitting in my car and minding my own business. Hadn't even turned the key when here comes this ambulance on the wrong side of the road. I didn't have a chance to get out of the way. Not a chance!"

"Was the beacon flashing?"

"No! In fact, I'm damn lucky the thing was moving so slow."

"Buster? Driving slowly?"

Trumpe nodded. "Can't very well deliver newspapers going seventy miles an hour, can ya?"

Buster had nerve, no doubt about it. Screwing in the back of the rescue wagon was one thing, but using it as a delivery truck on his paper route was something else. Moonlighting during off-hours was fairly common practice, but Buster had devised a way to do it *during* his regular job hours—between ambulance runs.

"I'll bet Buster just forgot to turn on the siren," I explained to Fred. "He was probably on his way to an accident."

"Yeah, mine," Fred said.

"So, how did the hearing go?"

"Not bad. Saved the hospital a few thousand bucks and did exactly what Anderson wanted."

"And what was that?"

"Settled."

Fumbling, I nearly taped a piece of gauze over Trumpe's nostrils. "Settled?" I stammered. "I thought you guys were gonna fight it all the way."

"I was ready," Fred said, "but then Anderson tallied up courtroom fees, retainers, court costs. . . ."

"And decided it would be cheaper to settle?"

"That's about the size of it."

I handed Trumpe a small mirror. He flinched at the sight of the small pyramid of splints and bandages above his mouth. "It doesn't look too suave," I admitted, "but it'll hold your nose on. How does it feel?"

Trumpe was still scowling at himself. "I got a jury trial this week and I'm gonna make one hell of an impression. Looks like I've been through a barroom brawl."

"How does it feel?" I repeated.

"Lousy," said the lawyer. "If my client gets convicted I ought to make that half-witted ambulance driver do the time."

"Can you breathe okay?"

"Sure, through my mouth." He stood up and smoothed the wrinkles out of his slacks. "This shirt is ruined. I'm gonna make that punk pay for it."

"Hey, I'm just curious," I interjected, "but how did the doctor fare? The one in the malpractice suit."

"The old man, Hogue? He settled."

"No. The other one. The young guy."

Trumpe laughed. "He was the smartest one of the bunch."

"Really?" I could hardly conceal my delight. "How so?"

"Well, he just hung on and hung on and, sure enough, the church dropped his name from the suit. Didn't want to bother with an accessory. Thanks to me, they only hit us for twenty grand. Where's my briefcase? Long as I'm here I may as well tell Anderson the news."

Trumpe stalked out the door and I floated after him, thinking of my wasted ulcer. Buster, who was behaving like a terrified puppy, handed Trumpe his briefcase and apologized no less than eleven times for the inconvenience. I struggled to get my mind out of shock and into first gear. "They really dropped the suit against that doctor?"

"Hell, yes," said Fred. "That happened two weeks ago, which reminds me . . . I oughta get in touch with the guy and give him the big news." He laughed again. "Shoot, a few more days won't hurt. Do him good to make him worry over it. Make a better doctor out of him, right? Ha."

He headed down the main corridor in the general direction of William E. Anderson's office.

"Didn't you forget something?" I called after him.

Trumpe stopped and looked down at his briefcase. "No, I've got everything," he said assuredly and turned away.

"The bill!" I yelled with fraudulent politeness. "Don't forget to see the cashier to straighten that out."

Trumpe charged back down the corridor. "What? For Chrissakes, I'm the attorney for the goddamn hospital. Don't tell me I've gotta pay for a crummy popsicle stick and two snips of tape!"

Buster hurried to Fred's side. "Of course not, Mr. Trumpe. We'll take care of the whole thing, don't you worry. You've been through enough today."

I grabbed Buster by one of his thick arms and yanked him to a neutral corner. "If the peanut farmers can afford to pay for medical care, Fred can," I said sternly. "The best thing you could do right now is to get your butt out of the immediate vicinity."

"But, Otis, he said he's gonna sue me!" Buster whined.

"It wouldn't be worth the trouble."

Buster slunk out a back door for parts unknown and I caught up with Trumpe as he turned the corner in full retreat. "It sure would be embarrassing to put a collection agency after you," I remarked casually. "After all, it's only forty-three bucks. Do you have Blue Shield?"

Reluctantly, Trumpe followed me back down the hall to the cashier's window where Mandy, our ever-cheerful money handler, merrily filled out the foul-tempered lawyer's claim.

"You're a pain in the neck," he said to me afterward. "I'm going to see Mr. Anderson right now. Your lousy attitude is first on my agenda. What's your name, Doctor?"

"Otis Stone."

"Oh?" Fred arched his gray eyebrows. "No wonder you expressed such interest in the malpractice settlement. Pretty cocky, aren't you?"

"Relieved, that's for sure."

"Congratulations, Dr. Stone. You got away with it this time. Good thing I was on *your* side, though."

"It's a good thing you *weren't*," I replied. "Your fee probably would exceed the settlement."

Trumpe wordlessly turned on his heel and briskly marched toward Anderson's office. For about the fifth time I heard my page on the intercom, so I hustled back to the emergency room where Sherman was in urgent need of another pair of hands. During my argument with Trumpe, the E.R. had been invaded by three dozen august Daughters of the American Revolution. Apparently something had gone awry at the afternoon luncheon, some rancid type of food poisoning in the Bicentennial Salad. The result was a stampede of patriotic diarrhetic matrons, each more hysterical than the other. Sherman diagnosed the malady as a strain of salmonella, most likely contracted from infected hard-boiled eggs. We went to work setting up I.V. bottles next to each victim so we could get fluids going and offset any electrolyte imbalance resulting from the vomiting and chronic diarrhea. Every few minutes a squabble would break out between two women frantically fighting for the same toilet in the nurses' lounge.

In the midst of all this regurgitating and chaos, I was interrupted by a strong tap on the shoulder. A tall man in a neat blue suit led me to a stretcher where a middle-aged man lay panting, unconscious. Three other blue-suits surrounded him. With no small amount of shouting I was able to quell the panic among the victim's burly guards. I examined the man calmly and slowly—secretly grateful for a respite from the nauseous D.A.R.—and concluded he was hyperventilating.

"Get me a paper bag," I said to a nurse, who was running with a half-filled pan of vomit from the E.R.

"Did you say paper bag?" asked one of the men coldly. "I hope this ain't your idea of a joke."

"I don't like the way this guy looks," said another with a contemptuous sneer. "His hair's too damn long. Let's call Selma and get an ambulance instead."

Ignoring the insult, I ran to the doctors' quarters and found what I was looking for: a garden variety brown bag used with much success and appreciation by millions of American lunch toters. This particular model belonged to Buster Hogue, but I dumped his knockwurst sandwich on a cot and carried the bag back to the E.R. My haste was impeded by the victim's squad of bodyguards, but I fought my way to the man's side. His eyelids were fluttering and he seemed to be struggling back into consciousness. I placed the open end of the wrinkled bag over his mouth. "Breathe deeply," I said firmly into his left ear. He nodded a hazy agreement. Before long, his breathing steadied and color returned to his cheeks.

"Feel better?" I asked.

"Yes. Thanks a lot," he said weakly. Unlike his entourage, the victim wore a green knit golf shirt, tailored slacks and imported loafers. His silver hair was longish in the back, while his curly sideburns had been permitted to wander down the side of his ruddy face to the jawline.

184

"What happened?" I asked him.

"He started gulping air and then he just keeled over," answered the largest of the four henchmen. "We thought he'd cracked."

"I was out at the skeet range near Gresham and the last thing I remember was downing my fifth clay pigeon in a row," the man said. "Now you tell me, Doctor. What happened?"

Hyperventilation, I explained, was a condition of heightened respiration which actually results in the inhalation of too much oxygen. Putting the paper bag over the victim's mouth simply forces him to breathe the carbon dioxide from his own exhalations, while reducing oxygen intake.

"Amazing," was the cynical response from one of the stern sycophants. "How much do we owe you?"

"For this, nothing."

"Thanks," said the man, sitting up. "I appreciate your quick thinking. I've never fainted before, but I guess I got too worked up over my sensational marksmanship."

"Jogging is better exercise," I suggested half-jokingly. No one likes to be told that jogging is good exercise; there is not a human being in the country who has not heard its virtues extolled by athletic Hollywood superstars and studs.

"I might try it," said the man. "Obviously, I'm in lousy shape if I pass out so easily."

"When was your last checkup?"

Before he could answer, the man was hustled out of the emergency room into a waiting limousine. He waved once from the back seat before black drapes closed across the window. The broad white car sped off on Highway 80.

"Who was that, the Godfather?" asked Sherman.

"Probably some V.I.P passing through Alabama on his way to . . . wherever it is people who are passing through Alabama go."

"You didn't even get his name?"

"How could I, the way his lieutenants dragged him out of here. He's either a Mafioso, a politician or an A.T.& T. executive."

"What's the difference?" said Sherman.

"He could have been royalty," I mused, "in which case I should have offered him the Sacred Bedpan."

"Speaking of royalty, remember the old guy with all the money? The guy you said was giving a couple million bucks to the hospital?"

"Sure. Benbow Hutchinson. He's the fellow we toasted to on the night you accepted the job here."

"Wait here," said Sherman excitedly. "I've got something to show you."

He scurried down the hall, nearly colliding with a distraught D.A.R. victim on her way to the restroom. When Sherman returned, he carried the afternoon edition of the *Guardian*. He mumbled through the first six pages until he found the society section. "Here it is. Take a look."

Immediately my eyes lit on a black and white portrait of Benbow, obviously taken twenty years earlier when he could still keep both eyes open simultaneously. Next to Benbow's face was an eyecatching photograph of a smooth-skinned, long-haired beauty young enough to be the old man's granddaughter. Below the pictures were two succinct paragraphs which foretold of the future, both Benbow's and Trafford Memorial Hospital's:

"Benbow Hutchinson, retired pecan farmer and well-known pioneer of Grady County, and the former Denise Carswell, originally from Reno, Nevada, were married last week in a private ceremony in Montgomery. The wedding was attended by Dr. Earl Gadwell, a heart specialist from Emory University, and two of Miss Carswell's business associates, Fanny Smith and Lurleen McCall. The marriage was performed by Red Dickerson, a justice of the peace.

"The couple plans to live in Grady at the four-hundred-acre estate belonging to Mr. Hutchinson. His new bride plans to continue her career as a professional masseuse and social director for a fashionable health spa franchise in Grady."

The expected outrage was not long in sweeping through the pale corridors of Trafford, or the quiet streets of Grady County. The near-unanimous indignation hinted at a subcurrent of jealousy, as if Benbow had in some rude way been stolen from the townsfolk. For the orderlies, nurses, doctors and accountants of Trafford, Benbow's blissful journey into Denise's arms was but another bitter reprieve from death, another delay in planning the new wing. Rev. Jimmy Bullock, who privately disapproved the union because of the secular ceremony, openly preached an attitude of moderation and tolerance.

"She's a whore," said Margaret Holt conclusively. "Have you seen that massage parlor? Twenty-five bucks for the full treatment, and I *don't* mean a body rub."

"Bite your tongue, Maggie," Rev. Bullock intoned. "It could be worse. Why, I've heard tell the massage parlors in New York charge one hundred dollars for the same thing."

"This might give Benbow something to live for," I speculated.

"Yeah," muttered Mrs. Holt.

"And we were so close," reflected Billie Simmons thoughtlessly, which is pretty much Billie's standard operating condition. "Just the other day I saw old Benbow picking up his Social Security check at the post office. He looked terrible, just terrible."

"Probably just came from the massage parlor," sneered Mrs. Holt. "At age eighty-eight, the body just can't withstand too much s-e-x."

Ugly rumors about the new Mrs. Hutchinson sifted through town like a bad odor. Most of them hinted at a seamy past and an impure present. Rooster Bootman, citing "sources in the law enforcement field," claimed Denise had been arrested for prostitution on numerous occasions in Kansas City. Benbow's paperboy, Buster Hogue, said she paraded around the lush estate in a string bikini, the rump emblazoned with the words "Viva Las Vegas." A bagboy at the Winn Dixie went so far as to admit patronizing the massage parlor and paying for the "full treatment." He proudly told anyone who would listen that his experience with Denise cured his acne pimples for six weeks afterward.

"It's disgusting," Shelly said when I told her of Benbow's

187

marriage. "He's got no business with a gold digger like that."
Her rather unliberated reaction surprised me.

"Do you know her?" I asked.

"No, but Buster does. He told me all about her place on
Route 80. From what I hear, Denise gets more of a workout
in the spa than all the barbells and treadmills put together."

I chalked Shelly's bitterness up to professional frustration.
She had always been one of the more optimistic workers
when it came to Trafford's future, but her optimism had always hinged on the Hutchinson money. Denise Carswell
complicated matters considerably. It looked to Shelly as if
she would be embarking for law school without seeing the
fate of Trafford Memorial resolved satisfactorily.

As for Denise, she didn't seem to mind the lurid gossip
that dogged her footsteps in Grady. On weekends she was
spotted by passers-by as she wheeled Benbow around the
magnolia gardens on the estate. On weekdays she was busy,
too, as business at the health spa boomed as a result of the
rumors. Rooster Bootman, reacting to community pressure,
repeatedly threatened to raid the place until one of his own
deputies was spied running from the spa wearing only a pair
of black laced panties.

At Buster's urging, I decided to visit the new Mrs. Hutchinson and to experience the fleshly delights of the Roman
Solarium first hand, so to speak. I drove out Highway 80 one
afternoon until I came to a tiny storefront building with a
huge red neon sign out front. The windows were painted
yellow and festooned with angular nude silhouettes. As I
walked in the door, I bumped into Dan Satterwhite, the hospital board chairman, who pretended not to recognize me.

"I want the full treatment," I told the pudgy brunette
behind the cash register. She snatched the money from my
hand, popped her bubble gum twice and pointed me toward
another door. I approached cautiously, listened, knocked
twice and entered. I came face to face with a two-hundred-
pound woman with dark red fingernails and bright red hair.
She wore a red two-piece bathing suit that was the closest

thing to a bikini manufactured for women her size. She smiled at me and I caught a glimpse of gold in her mouth.

"Hi, sugar," she said huskily. "Wanna play horsie?"

"I'm looking for Denise."

"My name is Holly. Want the full treatment?"

"Maybe some other time. I'd like to see Denise."

Holly displayed her sensitivity by pursing her crimson lips in a Doris Day pout. "What's the matter? Don't you think I'm pretty?"

Without answering I backed out the way I had entered. I tried the next room, knocked twice and opened the door. I should have waited for some signal: I had interrupted Denise and a customer in the middle of a massage. The man was nude on his belly and he groaned with immense pleasure while Denise's tiny hands rubbed his shoulder. A lewd anticipatory smile brightened his face. His eyes were closed until he heard my voice.

"I'm terribly sorry. . . ."

"Who are you?" Denise asked softly.

"I'm . . . eh, I'm in the wrong room. I'm looking for Holly."

"Sit down," she invited. "I'm almost through."

The customer reddened. "The hell you are. I paid my twenty-five bills and I want the full treatment." He sat up and grabbed Denise by the arm. I realized the situation called for some heroic rebuttal, probably physical and possibly violent, so I instantly bolted for the door.

"Don't go," Denise said calmly, "you're next."

"What about me, sister!" the customer raged.

She threw him a dirty towel. "Put this on." Then she pressed a tiny brown button on the wall. Moments later, a huge bald man with a tattoo on his neck burst into the room, pinioned the terrified naked man and carried him from the premises.

"Creep!" said Denise, referring either to the customer or the bouncer.

Timidly I spread myself out on the massage table. As Denise went to work, I introduced myself as one of Benbow's

189

doctors and she seemed glad to meet me. We started off with small talk about Grady and the hospital; by the time she had worked down to my buttocks, we were deep into a technical discussion about Benbow's heart disease and the causes for it.

"Tell me," said Denise, "is sex harmful when you've got a bad heart condition like Ben's?"

"I'm not sure I can answer that," I said cautiously. "Once might be safe. Twice would be risky. Five or six times a day could be fatal."

"Oh. Just wondering. Benbow says you're a good doctor."

"Well, that's nice," I grunted as she kneaded my lower back muscles. "You're a good masseuse. Where'd you learn?"

"Vegas," said Denise. "Used to be a showgirl. I danced at The Sands one night."

"Really?"

The massage was not worth twenty-five bucks. It was a good massage, to be sure, but the price included a subtle promise that was never fulfilled. It wouldn't have felt right anyway, I told myself, being her husband's doctor. Ethics can be complicated.

Feeling five years younger, I drove away from the Roman Solarium thoroughly convinced that I didn't know a damn thing about Denise Carswell Hutchinson. She was pretty, courteous, intelligent, but guarded. Years of rubbing nude men will do that to a person, I decided.

Benbow's wife was something of a mystery. The fact that she was sixty years her husband's junior, the fact they met at a health food store, and the fact they had married after a twenty-minute engagement—those things just seemed to add an air of impulsive romance to the whole May-December escapade. Denise Carswell Hutchinson could very well see Benbow through the toughest time of his life, I told myself, and maybe it's just what he needs.

Then again, maybe I was wrong. I never got a chance to

know Denise very well. The day after I visited the Roman Solarium, Benbow Hutchinson died. Denise wasn't around for the funeral.

WE STOOD IN A COLD, STINGING RAIN WHILE THE Reverend Jimmy Bullock eulogized Benbow Hutchinson. Upstanding Benbow Hutchinson. Generous Benbow Hutchinson. Compassionate Benbow Hutchinson. Rugged Benbow Hutchinson. Christian Benbow Hutchinson.

Dead Benbow Hutchinson. Margaret Holt and Shelly Farmer cried together in a wet, froggy chorus. Carl and Buster Hogue stood tight-lipped and somber in identical Sears trenchcoats. William E. Anderson and his secretary whispered gloomily to one another. Gleason, Drake, Flowers and I—the other doctors—lined up together, stared at our shoe tops and tried to ignore Bullock's sermon. Dan Satterwhite led the self-conscious contingency from the hospital board; the members dabbed at their red eyes and snorted unmasculine sobs into wrinkled gray handkerchiefs.

All this grief was genuine. Benbow Hutchinson had changed his will.

In the brief ten days of their union, Benbow and Denise had, through some sort of bedroom negotiations, reached an agreement about the young woman's future. The lawyers had been contacted and the will was altered with remarkable haste and at considerable expense. When the old fellow's scarred heart finally fluttered spasmodically to a halt, Denise probably just sighed, rolled Benbow off of her and called the ambulance. The next morning she packed her bags, drove her old Thunderbird to the Roman Solarium and hung a small wreath on the front door. Two days later, a For Sale sign was posted at the Hutchinson estate, much to the delight of realtor Henry R. Henderson, who was in for the biggest, sweetest commission of his thirty-year career.

No one actually saw Denise Carswell Hutchinson speed out of town past the faded city limits sign on Highway 80. She fled in the dead of night. Melvin Dryden serviced the Thunderbird, though. With much drama he recounted how he had put air in two of the tires (twenty-eight pounds apiece), added a quart of oil and installed one new windshield wiper. Denise, who was reportedly wearing a sheer black halter top, wrote Melvin a check for twelve bucks and drove off. It was the last anyone in Grady would see of her. The last person to talk with her was Benbow's lawyer. "You're going to be a millionaire," he told her.

"Really?" replied the long-legged widow.

"We will miss him sorely," lamented Rev. Bullock, "but God called for Benbow Hutchinson and Benbow answered."

"He'd been letting the phone ring for years," whispered Billie Simmons, unmoved.

As we turned away from Benbow's grave, a strong hand clamped down on my left shoulder. I turned to meet one of the blue-suited gorillas who had escorted the hyperventilated skeet shooter into the E.R. a few weeks before.

"Everything okay with your boss?"

"Come on," he said in a tone borrowed from Efrem Zimbalist, Jr. He led me across the rolling, grave-studded hills of the Veterans of Foreign Wars Cemetery to a rusty 1968 Rambler parked under a dead oak tree. The silver-haired celebrity sat in the back seat, puffing a cigar. He wore a rumpled black suit, a thin brown tie, and what looked to be, ugh, flesh-colored socks. I told myself this person could not possibly be the same austere man who had appeared so nattily dressed and suave during the D.A.R. salmonella epidemic. This must be his twin.

"Ah, Dr. Stone!" The man climbed out of the Rambler and pumped my right hand. "Glad we caught you."

"Aptly put. Where's the big white limousine?"

The man laughed uncomfortably. He signalled to his

bodyguards, who immediately began wandering away from the car, safely out of earshot. I guessed that this gesture was a necessary courtesy in underworld etiquette.

"Do you know who I am?" the man asked.

"I don't think so. See, I've only been in town just a few months."

"Of course, and you're scheduled to leave in three days. Am I right?" He grinned with benign smugness. "My name is Ray Robinson. I represent this part of Alabama in the goings-on at the capitol."

"Rayfield Robinson?"

"One and the same." He handed me a cigar. "You don't have to smoke it, just read it."

Inscribed in red letters on the cellophane wrapper were the words, "From One Good Ol' Boy to Another. Best Wishes from Senator Ray."

"What happens when you give this to a lady?"

"Haw!" Robinson slapped his knee. "My boy, the women get julep glasses, of course. You smoke?"

I shook my head no.

"Then you won't mind if I take this back." He snatched the cigar out of my hand. "These'll come mighty handy in November, y'understand. Election time. I don't suppose you'll be here for the election."

"No, sir."

"Too bad."

"How are you feeling? Any fainting spells?" I was utilizing a surefire, time-tested strategy: steering the conversation toward the subject of personal health.

"I feel pretty good. That's what I want to talk to you about," Robinson said. "You saved my life, Dr. Stone."

"Nonsense."

"Now, don't be modest. The boys told me what you did. Very clever! Lots of folks in Montgomery wouldn't mind seeing ole Senator Ray with a bag over his head. . . ."

"I put it over your mouth. . . ."

"Whatever. You did save my life, and I wanna pay you

194

back." He reached into his moldy suit and his hand came out with a fat brown envelope. "Take this," said the senator.

I raised my hands, defending as if the package was a letter bomb. "No way," I argued. "I was only doing my job. Keep the money."

"Money? Who said anything about money? I'm a politician, son. I take money, but I'll be damned if I give it away." He slapped me good-naturedly on the back. "Go on. Open the envelope."

Inside was a ten-page portfolio comprised substantially of clumsy clauses, superfluous paragraphs and stilted statutory jargon. Vaguely remembering some civic government courses I once took, I was able to identify the document as pending legislation. The last page, punctuated liberally with dollar signs, appeared to be the state health and urban services budget for fiscal year 1976–77.

"Read it," Robinson ordered.

"Now?"

"Never mind. I'll tell you what it says. It says that Trafford Memorial Hospital is in line for a few more dollars this year, quite a few more than was originally expected. It all goes back to an administrative error. Seems one of my clerks, young fella with tight pockets and an imagination to match, wrote up the original HURC budget wrong." He shook his head disapprovingly. "Actually *cut* Trafford's funding."

"That wouldn't," I suggested feebly, "have had anything to do with your wife, would it?"

"Marjane? Good Lord, no. I do seem to recall her bitchin' about a little run-in with one of the Trafford doctors, but I don't believe the character is still working around here anymore." Robinson winked slyly. "This hospital could use more physicians like yourself, Doctor. It could also use a new medical wing."

My jaw hit my chest. "You're kidding?"

Robinson put a heavy arm around my shoulders. "Whoa! This money is just a start. All I could wrangle for this year is about four hundred thousand dollars. Now, that's got to be approved by the whole legislature, although I venture to say it's got a good chance of passing free and clear." He absently tossed a mangled cigar butt at the headstone of a Confederate soldier. "You're a good man, Stone. I've been doing some checking on you. Anderson thinks highly of you. So do most of the nurses. Even Maggie Holt says she could tolerate having you around for a few years."

"I'm leaving in three days, Senator. I've got an important job waiting for me in California."

"Yes, I know. I'm not going to stop you, although I probably could." He whistled through his front teeth and the hulking entourage appeared as if from thin air. Robinson grunted as he slid back into the car. I noticed the figure of a woman sitting in the shadow next to him.

"Nice to see you again, Mrs. Robinson," I said politely. The senator rolled his eyes and put a finger to his lips. "Sssshh. Ah, this here's my secretary Miss Kentwell. Marjane is home with the kids. Funerals depress her." When all the bodyguards were safely back in the car, I decided to be brave, or more accurately, recklessly bold. "What's happened to that big car and all those fancy clothes you wore when we met before?"

Robinson was slightly annoyed. He lit up another cigar as the driver revved the Rambler's engine to a noisy growl. "It's like this," said the senator, raising his voice over the noise. "There were many, many voters at a funeral like this. Farmers and small businessmen, well, they don't take it too kindly when a politician flaunts how rich and slick and sassy he is. You follow?"

I nodded.

"So you understand why I drive around town in clothes that don't fit and a car that shoulda been melted into scrap metal two years ago. It's easier for the little folks to talk to me. 'Course, on the skeet range or at the country club is another story. I can't very well let all those bank vice-presidents turn up their noses at the old country boy who just happens to be responsible for all those wonderful tax breaks, now can I?"

I saw the woman lean over and say something to the garrulous politician. He whispered back, then patted her bare knee unpaternally. "We've got to go, Dr. Stone. I've already sent a letter to Mr. Anderson with the good news about Trafford's funding. Too bad you won't be around to see that money." He winked at me again. "It's too bad you won't be around to vote, either."

Back at Trafford, there was talk of retribution against Denise Carswell. It was murder, one nurse was saying, because the bitch had obviously planned to kill Benbow with a special kind of kindness, planned to screw him to death. Personally I felt Benbow probably had wanted it that way; that the marriage lasted ten days and ten exhaustive nights was a tribute to the old man's battered heart.

Whether deliberate or accidental, Benbow's death incurred far less palpable despair than the denial of his fortune. I feared for the mental health of Margaret Holt, who had spent the better part of the last decade living and breathing solely for the day when she could reign over a spotless, efficient new hospital wing. After the funeral she had returned directly to her post at the E.R. nurses' station where she doodled disconsolately on a patient's chart for the next three hours.

Buster Hogue was also slow in recovering from Benbow's final crisis. He had been on ambulance duty the night of the fatal infarction. Instead of racing directly to the Hutchinson estate, he drove around the block a few times, stopped to pick up some cigarettes for his latest girlfriend, pretended to lose the address, and generally took his sweet time getting there. Had Benbow not already changed the terms of his will, Buster's sluggish performance would have drawn praise from hospital observers, but as it turned out his procrastination only put the seal on Denise's devious scheme. Or so it seemed. The autopsy showed Benbow was probably a dead, albeit happy, man before his head hit the pillow. Still, Buster berated himself publicly for days afterward. His favorite line: "If only I could have saved his life, he might have divorced

197

that witch and given the money back to Trafford.'' (Fat chance.)

The news of Senator Rayfield Robinson's largess did less for the morale of hospital employees than I had anticipated. It was a long way, Mrs. Holt noted cynically, from two million dollars to four hundred thou. Billie Simmons wanted to know if there were a clause in the grant commanding all hospital workers to vote for Robinson in November.

Still, by the time Anderson's official memorandum about the proposed fund hike hit the bulletin boards, the staff had seemed to warm to the idea. Mrs. Holt started yelling almost as loudly as in the old days.

The orderlies started drooling. When the X-ray machine broke down, no one complained—save for the old man with the fractured hip who was put on an ambulance to Selma.

Even Sherman Flowers, who had taken the Trafford job with an airtight assurance of two million dollars in renovations, was heartened by the news from Montgomery. Good old Senator Ray had bailed Trafford out.

This good will lasted all of twelve hours until the afternoon edition of the *Grady Guardian* hit the newsstands. The lead story, bannered across the front page, started out like this:

"Sen. Rayfield Robinson will propose to the Alabama state legislature this session that the unfinished David Eisenhower Bridge be renamed after pecan magnate Benbow Hutchinson, who died in Grady earlier this week. Robinson told a press conference in Montgomery that Hutchinson 'exemplified the strength and character of the Alabama spirit. He did more for this great state than David Eisenhower or anyone related to him has ever done.'

"When asked by the *Guardian* how soon the huge, hazardous structure will be completed, Robinson answered, 'That's high on my list of priorities, but the money is scarce in Montgomery this year so I haven't realistically got my hopes too high.' He added that the chances of the legislature approving the name change were 'most excellent.' He expressed regret for the families of the twelve persons killed in traffic accidents at the big bridge last year.''

This bit of demagoguery angered many of the Trafford employees who strongly felt that (a) Benbow was nothing more than a medical moocher who didn't *deserve* to be memorialized, and (b) the persons driving off the span into the Alabama River couldn't care less if the bridge were named after Eisenhower, Hutchinson or Frank Lloyd Wright. They also were displeased with Robinson's concerned offer to put fluorescent warning signs along Highway 80 on the west side of the bridge, the *Selma* side of the bridge.

"I'll never vote for that bombastic asshole again," Shelly fumed.

"You won't have to," I reminded her. "You'll be in Tennessee next November."

We had quietly avoided the subject of our impending separation, probably because neither of us intended to change our minds. We toodled around the apartment, packing our clothes, hopping into bed, paying the last stack of bills, hopping into bed, scrubbing the cockroach-littered floors, hopping into bed . . . a fond but unspoken farewell. Our last big laugh together came late one night when the next-door neighbors, Broward and Jeanine Spurrier, began fighting over which one of them surreptitiously had guzzled their last bottle of Ripple.

On January 7th, Shelly sold her car to Melvin Dryden for five hundred dollars. That same afternoon I drove her to Trafford so she could say good-bye to her friends. We pulled into the E.R. parking lot where Buster's ambulance was backed up to the double doors. We could hear familiar sounds emanating from the back of the rescue wagon.

"Now that," Shelly remarked, "is nerve." She tapped on one of the curtained, narrow windows. The sounds stopped abruptly. "Buster?" she cooed.

"What is it?" His voice was muffled, plainly irritated. "What do you want?"

"It's me, Shelly, I just wanted to say good-bye."

From inside there came frantic whispers, followed by, "I'm kinda busy right now, Shelly. I'm practicing, eh, resuscitation. Good luck in law school."

"Good luck to you, too," Shelly said.

"Don't worry about me."

"I meant with your new job."

From the hospital we drove straight to the Montgomery airport, where Shelly was booked on a plane to Nashville, home of Vanderbilt University and the Johnny Cash Fan Club.

We held each other tightly before she boarded the plane. "You're going to be a great lawyer," I remarked. "You were right about Denise Carswell. You predicted Benbow would change his will."

"That had nothing to do with law," she said. "Anyway, you predicted he wouldn't last two months with her."

"Wrong. I predicted he wouldn't last two months, period."

"We still going to meet in the fall?"

"You bet. Let's see. Midway between California and Tennessee should put us smack dab in the middle of Nebraska at harvest time. We'll shuck each other's corn."

She laughed. "Good luck out West." We kissed and she turned to walk out on the runway where the passengers were lined up near the Piedmont DC-9. The wind enticingly tossed at Shelly's long golden hair and blew her pleated skirt up around her thighs. I winced at the sight. It was going to be a long, lonely trip to the West Coast.

"Good luck at Vandy!" I yelled. Shelly stopped at the top of the steps and waved. I doubted if she heard me over the roar of the jet engines. I watched the blue and white aircraft climb off the runway into the plaster gray winter skies. Lugubriously I trudged back down the concourse toward the busy lobby.

The P.A. system crackled. "Will the owner of a green 1968 Dodge Charger please report to the parking lot immediately? Your headlights are on."

Remembering the frail condition of my car's aged battery, I ran full speed through the airport, out the lobby doors and into the toll lot—just in time to see my car pull away. Two teenaged boys and a female companion gunned it out of the

200

crowded parking lot toward the interstate ramp. I considered pursuing them, but quickly realized the hazards of such heroics. "Shit," I said under my breath. "I hope they turn the headlights off."

The police were not much help until I told them I was a doctor, at which point a disinterested uniformed officer immediately called for a detective, who no sooner had arrived before he was deep into a description of his grandfather's prostate troubles. He did manage to put out a three-state alert for a dull, noisy car bearing Florida license tags. Discouraged, I suggested that the teenaged thieves were probably headed straight for Florida where neither the tags, the crazy teenagers nor the old car would draw notice. The police were mystified, too; I had parked the Charger next to a brand new Fiat. "Those kids," remarked the detective, "had lousy taste . . . no offense."

When I called Trafford I was surprised to find Sherman Flowers on duty. I described my predicament and he faithfully promised to drive to Montgomery the next morning, even if it required liberal amounts of amphetamines racing through his system to keep his eyelids open.

The next problem was a room. A search of my ragged wallet turned up four dollars in cash and a Shell credit card, neither of which would get me a suite at the Hilton. Summoning my persuasive skills from the vagabond summer, I was able to convince the supervisors of a nearby hospital of my good character and ended up with not only a bed for the night, but the name and phone number of a leggy nurse who eerily reminded me of Marie Duggan in prehousewifely days.

Before falling asleep, I phoned the bus station in Grady County to reserve a one-way ticket to San Jose, California, leaving in three days: Saturday, the tenth of January. I would be late, but *I would be there*. Halberstam would surely understand the delay; it's a long bus trip across the continent in wintertime. Hell, San Jose City Hospital might even spring for plane fare. I promised myself to call the next day, just on the chance that I could travel in grand style. Anything was better than the Hemorrhoid Express.

Sleep was long in coming and short in staying. I was interrupted twice for minor emergencies and ended up sharing the cot with a sweaty two-hundred-and-fifty-pound thoracic surgeon (who was enjoying the worst possible kinds of dreams).

Blessedly, Sherman located the hospital with little trouble the next morning. We wasted no time in finding Highway 80 again. Sherman had brought donuts and coffee so I ate and talked as we drove. "I can't believe those punks ripped off my car," I grumbled through a mouthful of cruller.

"The cops called about it this morning," Sherman related. "They found it already."

"You're kidding! Where?"

"Atlanta. The kids who were driving it knocked off a liquor store and got caught."

"Terrific. The Charger probably stalled outside. I suppose they've impounded it as evidence."

"No," said Sherman evasively, "not yet. They're still trying to fish it out of the quarry."

I started to choke.

"Don't worry, Otis. Mr. Anderson heard about the wreck and he immediately ordered the Atlanta cops to have the . . . remains . . . towed back to Grady. Melvin Dryden promised he'll give top priority to fixing up your car. He's already ordered a new engine from Birmingham."

I explained as calmly as possible to Sherman how I would die before relinquishing any personal possession to the stewardship of Melvin Dryden again. "If he wanted to fix the car, let him fix it at Anderson's expense. I don't want to see the damn thing again. All I want is the insurance money."

Sherman reached into the pocket of his corduroy coat. "Here's your bus ticket." He handed me the rectangular folder. "That'll be one hundred and eighty-nine dollars."

"I'll do you one better. Keep this week's paycheck."

Sherman was surprised. "That's real nice of you, Otis. Ordinarily I wouldn't think of accepting it, but the extra dough will come in handy. I'm thinking of buying a camper. Of course, I've been saying that for years."

"I thought you were thinking about buying the Hutchinson place."

"I was," said Sherman. "It's a toss-up between that, a camper, and investing in that new NFL franchise down in Tampa."

"Excuse me, Onassis. I don't mean to change the subject, but how come you were working last night? Isn't Thursday your night off?"

Sherman took a deep breath. "I didn't want to disturb you, Otis. I knew you had lots on your mind with Shelly leaving."

"What's the matter?"

"Hold on to your coffee," Sherman said, "I don't want you to spill that hot stuff on your groin."

"Will you tell me what happened?"

"It's Carl Hogue. He collapsed again yesterday afternoon. We've got him in ICU but it looks bad."

"Sherman, that's not funny. We don't *have* an ICU at Trafford Memorial."

"Dammit, Otis, you know what I mean. Room forty-seven. Benbow's old room with all the cardiac equipment."

"You're not kidding, are you?"

"No, I wish I were. It happened about six o'clock. One of the Oaks kids came in sick after drinking Clorox. Hogue was pumping the stomach when he just keeled over. Luckily, Gleason was there with a patient. He worked on Carl's heart but it took him forty seconds to get a pulse."

Sherman stared ahead at the road. A light fog was starting to settle dismally on the brown countryside. I gingerly dabbed at my pants where most of the hot coffee had ended up.

"He's only been back at work for a week," I said. "He seemed to be doing fine. His EKG's were good."

"It wasn't your fault," Sherman said softly.

"I don't know. Maybe I shouldn't have let him come back so soon. Maybe I should have kept him in bed another two weeks. I shouldn't have let him go back to work."

"And just how were you planning to stop him, Otis? Hogue has been looking forward to this week for a long time."

203

"Coming back to work?"

"No," said Sherman. "He's been waiting for the day you leave Trafford. He wants his kingdom back."

I AM SITTING IN THE APARTMENT NOW, MY EYES
skipping from fleck to fleck in the gold pattern of the Formica
countertop. I have been amusing myself in this odd way for
at least thirty minutes, probably more, and now I am noticing
a lone cockroach eyeing me from behind the salt shaker. He
is clutching a crumb of toast and pondering his odds of making it across the counter alive. He has doubtlessly seen me
in action against others of his ilk; he knows he must consider
his course of action with utmost care. His feelers wave like
small snakes on top of his shiny brown head. I pretend not
to notice.

He makes a dash across the counter. My hand shoots out
to block his path, but he darts beneath it deftly, like O.J.
Simpson eluding a linebacker. He scurries under a planter to
rest, and plan his next move, and maybe even nibble on the
crumb. I smile.

I am dead tired. No, make that *dog* tired. I don't much
like the word "dead." It applies to too many people I have
seen lately. It is a heavy, terse adjective. It weighs a ton.

I look at my wristwatch. Midnight. Now . . . ten seconds
into the eleventh of January. Midnight: I think of the hospital, all hospitals, where the woodwork of the community is
coming to life. I hear Lori Cameron screaming about black
widow spiders. Hyland Bashaw's missing penis. Thomas
Dixon with the scissors protruding from his rib cage. Gary
Murdock and his raccoon head. I think of the emergency
room at Trafford Memorial where Sherman must be pacify-

ing some hysterical medical misfit. If he is lucky, Kitty Lane will show up for her biweekly blood test.

In front of me, besides the crafty cockroach, there is a letter from Nashville. I am going to read it one more time.

"Dear Otis, Just a brief note to let you know I arrived safely. Even though it was only yesterday afternoon that you put me on the plane, I miss you already (and could kill myself for admitting it).

"Only three months until law school begins and already I am ulcerous with doubt and uncertainty. Thanks for all your support during the past six months. Both of us needed help; we worked well as a team.

"The job at McDonald's is a real peach. Financially, it will tide me over until April. Cosmetically, it could be the death of me; my whole body smells like a Big Mac.

"I hope this letter arrives before you leave for San Jose. Write soon. You're a good guy and a good doctor; I don't know which is more important but your patients will benefit from both. All my love, Shelly."

Well, at least she hasn't up and married a South African heart surgeon. I will write her tomorrow. No, maybe I'll do it now before I forget. Wrong again. I am enjoying staring at this countertop and thinking about the stew that is my future.

I did not sleep all night. I worked, then fretted, then gave up. At eight-thirty I walked through a wet fog down to the bus station and cashed in my ticket. I stuffed the one hundred eighty-nine bucks in the stiff pockets of my hospital pants and started walking up Juke's Ferry Road toward the Caldwell Funeral Home. It is a long way from the hospital, nearly five miles on foot, but it is really much, much closer.

"Hello," said a rigid, gray man in a black suit. "Can we be of assistance?" *We?* I looked behind him, but he was alone.

"I'm here to arrange for a funeral," I said carefully. "The family has asked me to take care of the details."

"Of course. I understand." The gray man's sallow forehead wrinkled up like an albino prune. "I'm *so* sorry."

"Sure, sure," I said wearily. "Now let's get down to business."

When I got back to Trafford Memorial it was eleven-thirty and I was starving, but first there was the matter of the young girl who rode her Christmas bicycle into the path of a truck. She was not dead, thank God, but she suffered a skull fracture that required close scrutiny. That done, I fled to the doctors' quarters for a pastrami sandwich. It was Buster Hogue's sandwich. Ever since he moved into his own apartment, he'd been making his own lunch: this was the worst sandwich I had ever tasted. But I ate it. If I didn't, no one would. Certainly not Buster. Not today.

At one, my parents called from Washington. Why aren't you on your way to California? What? Your car was stolen? My God, what is the world coming to?

My father generously offered to buy me a plane ticket to San Francisco and even the cab fare from San Francisco to San Jose. My mother was not satisfied and generously suggested my father buy me a new car. It took him five minutes to squirm out of that one. "What are your plans?" he asked. I told him the truth. He sighed very loud and very long. My mother stifled a whimper.

"I'll write you later," I said.

"Otis, did you see your sister's paper in the psychology journal?"

"Yes, Mother," I lied. "It was . . . brilliant."

Things were grim around the emergency room. Dan Dilborn was finding it difficult to study his Mad magazines between ambulance calls, especially difficult because the nurses continually berated his mindless irreverence. I decided it was as good a time as any for what Richard Nixon liked to call "decisive action."

Decisively, I reached up and grabbed off the custard-colored wall a faded sign that said: "The Doctor on duty today will not accept Medicaid in payment for his services." I crumpled it and tossed it into a garbage bag. Nurse Holt watched mordantly, her bony arms fastened to angular hips.

She began to cry. "Have a little decency! He hasn't even been gone twenty-four hours."

I did not answer, but directed my revisionist energies to another piece of artwork hanging near the double-doors. I have described it before; it read: "This is an emergency room, not an outpatient clinic. Emergencies are very serious medical problems for which treatment cannot wait. For example: gunshot wounds, poisoning, broken limbs, deep cuts and painful head injuries. The staff here will treat emergencies only! In plain language, an emergency is something terrible that has just arisen."

Staring at it, I remarked, "They certainly belabored the point."

Margaret Holt hovered behind me with half a Kleenex jammed up her nose in grief. "I suppose," she said stuffily, "you're going to rip that down, too."

"No," I replied. "That one stays. I want it repainted."

The remainder of the day was lazy and unproductive. Jeannie Montraine wandered the corridors in shock. Buster went home to be with his mother. William E. Anderson paced the hall like a sleepwalker feverishly replacing linen he had stolen during the previous four months. "We're in for trouble now," he kept saying to himself. "This is no place for pilfering." Billie Simmons kept spilling blood samples all over the lab; finally I was forced to frisk him and confiscate a small flask of Johnnie Walker Red.

I spent the last few hours breaking the news to his patients. "Dr. Hogue is dead," I said as kindly as possible. "Do you remember me? I'm Dr. Stone."

So now I sit here, staring at the countertop, fondling Shelly's letter and listening vaguely to Broward Spurrier's next-door imitation of Dolly Parton singing opera. Though it is late, I wait for the phone to ring. I have left a message with Dr. Halberstam's answering service. At ten forty-seven, West Coast time, he calls back.

"How are you?" he booms as if it were nine in the morning.

"Late," I answered dully.

"Well, there's more bad news."

He has not heard me. "I meant to call you sooner, Otis. I put a letter in the mail today."

"Oh?" Something is up.

"Let me try to explain. Dr. Jiminez has recently been doing some very, very interesting studies. Very unique. He has become wrapped up in these experiments and, eh, he's changed his mind about going home to Brazil. It's created a hell of a . . . situation for me."

"Oh?"

"They tell me Juan's got an excellent chance of getting the Nobel prize for this. The *Nobel Prize*!"

"Yes, I've heard of it."

"Well, then I'm sure you know what it would mean to a small hospital like ours."

"Fame, fortune, publicity. Tell me, Doctor, Jiminez' research wouldn't have anything to do with viral warts, would it?"

"Why, no!" Halberstam seems hurt. "I wouldn't edge you out of a job for *warts*! No, this is big league stuff. The Big C: cancer."

"And you want me to look elsewhere for a job?"

"Now I didn't say that. Just give me more time, at least until the results from Juan's research can be analyzed. Then we'll work something out, maybe. I promise."

"Oh?"

"We really want you working with us out here at San Jose City Hospital. That's the truth. If you can just hold on a couple of months . . . ," here Halberstam feigns jolliness, ". . . heck, you might even have your car back by then, right?"

I watch the cockroach dash from under the planter. He speeds to the edge of the counter, hesitates momentarily at the brink, then crawls with careful deliberation to the floor. I have to laugh out loud: by the time the speedy brown insect reaches safety under the Frigidaire, his precious crumb is gone. He has eaten it.

"I've got another car," I tell Dr. Halberstam, "and I've

got another job. Thanks, anyway.'' The car, I explain needlessly, is an old Ford Galaxy with a rear window missing. The job is here, at Trafford Memorial, where they tell me I am the new chief of medicine.

ABOUT THE AUTHOR

Neil Shulman, a physician in Atlanta, Georgia, draws upon his own experiences for his incredible tales of Dr. Stone. Dr. Shulman is also author of the humorous book *Finally . . . I'm a Doctor*.